No One Of Consequence
Vol. VII

By
Michael A. Burt

PUBLISHED BY:
Michael A. Burt

No One Of Consequence Vol.VII
Copyright © 2024 Michael A. Burt

License Notes
This book is licensed for your personal enjoyment only.
Thank you for respecting the hard work of this author.
This book is a work of fiction and any resemblance to
persons, living or dead, or places, events or locales is
purely coincidental. The characters are productions of
the author's imagination and used fictitiously.

Adult Reading Material

Table Of Contents

Lost and Found
Part 1 – Lost	4
Part 2 – Found	16
On Duty	30
Year of the Dragon	42
Time Lost	54
Moonlight Cabin	65
Long Hours	78
New Property	91
Strange and Unusual	109
Planting Seeds	121
Padded Cell Patron	135
Mimic	150
Under the Desert	164
First Freeze of the Year	176
Games of Children	191
At Sea	202
Storage Unit	215
Pandora's Antique Box: Appreciation	228
Night Watcher 7: The Talker	240
Rock Quarry Anomalies: Bad Weather	259

LOST AND FOUND

Part 1 - Lost

I fucking hate going to the supermarket. My wife used to do all the grocery shopping, back when we were still married. I'm not one of those male chauvinistic pigs that thinks only women are meant to do housework. Clarissa just had more time because she only worked part-time, and I pulled at least seventy-hour work weeks. She spent most of her time taking care of our little girl, which is what she wanted to do, and I supported that. Clarissa grew up a latchkey kid and was determined our little Celia wouldn't spend so much time alone.

I took a few days off of work when Celia was nine. Clarissa had gotten sick with the flu, and it was up to me to take care of everything. I didn't have a problem with it, but I was a bit out of my depth. Since she was having trouble keeping anything down, I went to the grocery store to get her crackers and soup. Of course, I took Celia with me. None of us had wanted her to get sick too. The day had started out so normally and I've replayed it thousands of times in my head. Nothing seemed off aside from Clarissa being sick.

Celia wanted to push the cart since she couldn't sit in the seat anymore and I was okay with that. I even let her lead the way as we checked off each item from the list. To my mind, it made sense because Celia went with her mother to the store all the time. Unlike me, she knew where everything was. There were only a dozen items on the list, and we'd just grabbed the fifth item when we went down the soup aisle. I'll never forget how fast it happened.

We were getting a small assortment of soups so Clarissa would have some options. Celia grabbed four cans of Chicken Noodle soup, and accidentally dropped one. She dumped the other three into the cart and reached down to grab the one she dropped. I marked soup off the list and when I looked up, Celia was gone. We were in the middle of the aisle, just the two of us, and when I looked up and down, she wasn't anywhere. I called out for her again and again, but she never responded. I ran all over the place yelling her name. An employee found me and within minutes, every single person in the store was looking for my little girl. Only, we never found her.

No one had seen her leave the store, and the police reviewed the security footage. Celia never popped up on camera after we left the front area of the store. Every nook and cranny was searched. Every vehicle in the parking lot, every box and container big enough for her to fit into. There was no trace of my daughter anywhere.

The police asked all the typical questions. No, there wasn't anyone that had a grudge against me that might've taken her to get back at me. There wasn't a malicious member of the family that snatched her for whatever reason. No, Celia wasn't prone to running away or causing mischief. She had been a happy, loved child and had no reason to want to run away. We never raised a hand to her, and the only punishments she ever received were minimal at best. Don't get the wrong idea, she wasn't spoiled or anything like that. Celia was a good kid, the best.

An amber alert was out long before I ever got

home, but nothing ever came of it. It's been five years since that cursed day, and not a day goes by where I don't blame myself. Clarissa has gone back and forth between blaming herself and blaming me. Most of the time she blames herself for trusting me to look after our daughter, so even when she takes on the blame, it's still directed towards me. Considering what happened, it's hard to fault her for that.

Our marriage was done and over with six months after Celia disappeared. It took another six months for the divorce to go through. Clarissa couldn't stand to be in the same house as all the memories she made with our missing daughter, so I got to keep the house. She took most of everything else, and for the most part, I couldn't care less. With Celia gone, not much matters anymore.

I don't work the same insane hours I used to. When I'm not staring blankly out the window or into space, I'm either at work or searching. After this long, there's no hope of finding her, but I go through the motions anyway. I've looked up all the known sex offenders in the area, scouted and stalked each and every one of them. I even stopped three abductions, two assaults and one murder while hunting those animals, but none of it brought me closer to finding out what happened to my little girl.

Every major holiday and Celia's birthday, I go camping since there's nothing left to celebrate. In my younger years I was quite the outdoorsman and loved spending time in the woods. I think it was because I worked so much, but Celia liked going camping too. Every chance we got, she'd beg me and her mother to go camping. Clarissa wasn't all that into it, but she had a hard time saying no to our daughter. Celia wanted to learn everything about the outdoors that I could teach her, and I taught her a lot. Hunting, fishing, fire building, how to make your own shelter, and so on. I didn't get to teach her everything, but she knew enough to survive on her own if it came down to it.

These days, my camping trips are mostly spent with me staring blankly over the water as I fish. I'm more concerned with the cooler of beer next to me than my line in the water. There was even one time a fish dragged my pole into the lake. I just watched it happen, not bothering to do a damn thing about it. By the time I'm sitting around a campfire at night, I've switched to hard liquor. Most of the time I don't even make it inside my tent, and just pass out drunk next to the fire. I'm sure my little girl would be ashamed of me if she could see me now.

Not only do I still live in the same house, but I shop at the same grocery store. I come back here every week and pick up the same assortment of groceries. Two boxes of Mac and cheese, a loaf of bread, a package of sandwich meat, a veggie tray with ranch dip, a half-gallon of milk, sliced provolone cheese, oyster crackers, and a small variety of soup. I didn't used to like tomato soup, and to be honest, I still don't, but it had been one of the soups Celia grabbed on that long ago day.

I don't normally deviate from this list, but today I feel different. I reach out and pick up four cans of the Chicken Noodle soup, just like Celia did. As I go to put them in the basket, one of the cans slips out of my grip and falls to the floor. The can bounces off my foot and rolls underneath the shelf. Had that happened when Celia dropped the can that day? I remember hearing it roll on the ground, but I hadn't seen which way it went.

Very little has changed in the store since then.

Lying face down on the floor, I look under the shelf. Along every section of the shelf is a grate that's supposed to prevent items from going more than a few inches underneath. I glance up and down the aisle to find all the grates are in place, save for this one section. It's dark under there, and I can't see the can, but it couldn't have gone very far. I heard it roll under, but I didn't hear anything after it disappeared into the shadow. The space itself is barely big enough for the can to go in.

Reaching my hand into the darkness under the shelf, I search for the wayward can and can't help but wonder. Did they ever find the can Celia was looking for when she vanished? For the life of me, I can't remember seeing a can on the ground that day. Is it possible I'm about to find two cans, one of them five years older? I don't know if I could handle that.

As I'm reaching under the shelf, I can feel the underside of the bottom, but for some reason, my hand isn't touching the floor. I reach lower for the floor but find nothing. There's only empty space underneath the shelf. Before my mind can comprehend that, something grabs hold of my hand with a seriously strong grip. I don't get the chance to react as I'm suddenly dragged into the darkness, the gap somehow large enough to swallow me up.

I fall an impossibly long way before slamming down onto the ground. The impact knocks the wind out of me, and it takes a minute for me to get it back. I can't tell where I am because there's barely any light down here. I turn to my side to try and get up and come face to face with the errant soup can. As I get to my feet, my entire body aching from the fall, it dawns on me.

Wherever the hell I am, this is probably where Celia was taken. Now if I can just figure out who or what pulled me down, then maybe I can find out what happened to my daughter.

Pulling out my cellphone, I try to call 911, but of course there's no service. If I'm underneath the supermarket there's no chance of getting a signal. Basements are notorious for having shit cell service, but that's assuming I'm in a basement. The search five years ago didn't include one, and I fell a really long way. Long enough that it's a miracle I didn't break something when I hit the floor. I'm choosing to ignore the fact that there hadn't been enough clearance between the bottom shelf and the floor for me to fit through. I'm here now, best deal with that before trying to explain something irrelevant.

Using the flashlight on my phone, I try to survey the immediate area. The ground is hard and uneven, covered in a thin layer of crap that I can't even begin to identify. Whatever it is, it's dark, damp, but for some reason, doesn't stick to me like mud. I manage to brush it off myself well enough, and it doesn't leave behind any residue. I've never encountered anything like it.

As I'm trying to get a lay of the land, I find the soup can I dropped. It landed about the same place I did and rolled a few feet away. The white label is in complete contrast with the ground and stands out like a sore thumb. What seems so odd is that it's standing up on end, but if it did that, how did the can roll away? I can clearly see a small trail in the grime on the floor, and as I question how that happened, I notice something. On the side of the can is some of that black crap, and it's in the shape of a hand.

Something slams into me from behind, and I'm

thrown to the ground. Narrowly missing the can, I roll onto my side and get to my knee. I lost my grip on my phone, and it's lying face down on the ground, the light pointing straight up. I'm not sure if that's better or worse, but I can see the thing that hit me. It's probably the same fucking thing that pulled me down here in the first place, and right now it's rearing up at me, giving me an unobstructed view of its body. God, I wish it hadn't.

Imagine a human sized caterpillar, but instead of having all the typical features of the bug, this thing was forged in hell out of human parts. The top six limbs are arms, and the dozen below are legs, all roughly the same length. The underside of this thing is covered in six-pack abs, but there's about four people's worth on the underbelly. The upper quadrant is rippling with muscles that would rival the action stars of the 80s. Topping it off, the hideous late night horror movie reject has two heads, but as it screams at me, I realize they're two parts of the same head.

Take two people's heads and turn them sideways with their jaws touching. Then remove the bottom jaws and fuse the throats together. Each upper lip of the two heads makes a half of the mouth, and that's what is staring at me. As for the skin tone, I can't be sure. The skin is covered in that grimy crap that's all over the floor, but the undersides of the outstretched hands and feet do appear to be albino white.

I've allowed my slack-jawed silence enough time to see all these details, though it'll take my mind a minute to really catch up to that. My feet at least have enough self-preservation, because the moment that thing starts coming at me, I start running in the other direction.

Unfortunately, I come to a wall and have to change directions. The light here is extremely minimal, and I'm sure as hell not going back for my phone. I keep finding walls, all the while that thing is hot on my trail. After finding a fifth wall, my eyes have adjusted to the dark enough that I can see a pitch-black space ahead and move right for it.

The opening is barely big enough for me to shove myself through, and the creature behind me has even more trouble. The rough stone is scraping against me as I continue to work my way through, and that thing behind me shrieks in frustration. I have just enough room to glance back, and see it scurry upwards. Here's hoping up doesn't lead the same place as this tight as hell tunnel.

Now that I'm not in imminent danger, I slow down. I was hurting myself more trying to manhandle my way through this tunnel to get away from that thing. I take my time now, managing not to bang myself up further. I've already got a lump on the top of my head from accidentally whacking it against a particularly low point in the ceiling.

Gradually the tunnel starts opening up, making my passage less claustrophobic. The light is getting a little brighter too, but I still can't identify the source of it. There's so much about this place that doesn't make sense.

I wander around for a while, having no clue where I am or where I'm going. I keep an eye out for any signs of life, but there doesn't appear to be anything. Then I come out another tunnel into a similar chamber as the one I first started in. As I get closer to the center of the room, I see something on the ground. At first it looks like I did a complete circle, but the item is larger than the soup can I dropped.

Bending down, I pick up the package and hold it close enough to my face that I can read the label. Only, the writing isn't in English. I'm no expert in languages, but these symbols look Asian and considering all the curves and loops in the characters, I'm guessing it's Korean. I know there are some Asian markets around town, but there's nothing like this in the grocery store I went in.

I look at the food package long enough to learn there's some kind of bread or pastry inside with a filling. I'm a little tempted to open the box, but before I can, my legs are kicked out from underneath me. Not only do I land hard on my back again, but the food container is plucked from my hands. I expect to see the human caterpillar thing, but that's not what took me down.

Between the limited lighting and the black stuff covering most of the body, I can't make out many details. What I can tell is that it's a young lady, maybe five and a half feet tall with long dark hair. Either that or her hair is covered in that black crap like everything else is. I can't identify the clothing she wears, only that she's covered. Whatever it is, it looks kind of thick, like leather.

She points a weapon at me, but it's not like anything I've seen before. It looks like a wooden club, but the end closest to me is covered in round, jagged metal. It's as if she used a can opener to completely remove the tops, somehow cut them in half, and secured them to this piece of wood. I've always known those tops were sharp, but to be used as blades? I guess that's one way to adapt.

She starts talking to me in harsh tones, but I

don't know what language she's using. I try to tell her this and not only does it work, but she changes to English too. Lucky for me, teaching English in her country is nearly mandatory. I've got a million questions for her, but she tells me to keep quiet. Something called the Manlar is on the hunt and is drawn to the sounds of talking. If I keep quiet, I am welcome to go with her to a relatively safe place, so I shut my trap. If getting to this safe place allows us to talk, I'm willing to hold my questions for later. If this girl is here, then maybe my Celia is too. For that possibility, I'd do anything.

She leads me through a long series of tunnels and chambers. This is the most elaborate underground passage system I've ever heard of, and I've been to a few. However, nothing about this place feels natural. At one point we take four lefts, but somehow we don't make a full circle. If there are directional markings of any kind, I can't identify them. This place seems to defy physics, and considering how I got here, that isn't all that surprising.

After coming through what seems like the twelfth chamber, I start to see things in the darkness that I wish I hadn't. There are piles of bones scattered around, along with food trash. It all seems to be junk food and cans, the kind of stuff that can easily be lost underneath a grocery store shelf. There's no way all this stuff came from one store. There are too many foreign languages, unless there's a grocery store at the UN and we somehow managed to get underneath it.

We finally come into a smaller chamber, but this one is nothing like all the others. This one is somewhat furnished with makeshift furniture, enough for a couple people to live in. Not exactly comfortable, but passable. I guess this is where she lives, and I don't wait long to start asking questions. How long has she been here? Where the hell are we? Is there anyone else here with her? What was that thing that pulled me down here?

It all came out in a rush, and I have to take a few deep breaths, which was a mistake. Not because there's something in the air that hits me hard, but the girl that brought me here does. She took advantage of me gulping in air to go in for a sneak attack. I land on my back for the third time, but don't stay that way for long. Before I can do anything in defense, she turns me over and ties my hands behind my back.

"Newcomers are a lot easier to capture than Manlars. You'll feed us for a few weeks, and your skin will make fine leather." Well, I guess I now know what her clothes are made out of. I guess people don't drop enough food under the shelves to sustain her. Though, she did say us, so there must be someone else here. Yeah, I'm kind of focusing on the wrong thing here, but finding out what happened to Celia is far more important than my own safety.

As she strings me up, I ask if she came across a nine-year-old about five years ago. "Sorry, old man. I haven't been here that long, but my sister was here before me. Maybe she knows. Unfortunately for you, I'm not waiting for her to get back before killing you. I haven't eaten in days." I try to tell her to eat one of those snack cakes she just got, but she won't listen. She claims it screws up her stomach to eat something heavy in sugar when she hasn't had anything else.

That's just fucking great. I finally find out what happened to Celia, but I'm going to get killed before I can get any real answers. No amount of pleading gets the young lady to stop. She picks up something that looks more like a kitchen knife, but still has those half can lids for a blade. She brings it up to my throat, but another voice shouts, "Wait!" Oh god, now what?

Part 2 - Found

I hear noise coming from a section of the labyrinth I'm all too familiar with, but when I get there, all I find is a can of soup. It's Chicken Noodle, which is the one soup I absolutely detest, but I pick it up anyway. One doesn't pass on a parcel of food no matter what it is, or how big the impact on your life it caused. Survival is more important than comfort down here.

I can clearly hear the muffled sounds of a Manlar moving around at the higher levels, but the noise is faint enough that I know it's not close. That humanoid caterpillar must've lost the prey it dragged down from the surface, otherwise it would still be eating. Aside from hunting one of us, it's the only reason one of those things comes to these chambers.

A feeding Manlar makes an easy target, and those things aren't very easy to kill under normal circumstances. They eat even less often than we do, and when they finally get ahold of some prey, their focus on it is complete. A freaking marching band could be playing behind them, and they wouldn't notice. It's like blood and flesh render them deaf, dumb, and blind while they're consuming it.

There are certain entry points I check on regularly, but I check on this one the most. Out of all the entries, this one has more lost food than any other location, and it usually comes in a can. Their cylindrical shape and tendency to roll makes them easy to lose under the shelf, and customers typically won't go fishing for one when they drop it. That's fine with me because cans are incredibly useful here. Without them we'd have no containers to collect water, and no weapons.

The can of soup makes four food items I've gathered today, which makes this a good day, and I decide to head home. Rayna was out trying to trap one of the younger Manlars, and I'd like to see how she did. The younger ones are easier to capture since they don't have as much experience as their elders. They aren't an overly familial species, choosing to hunt solo rather than in a group or pairs.

Sneaking around is easy if you know where to go. There are plenty of small tunnels at ground level the full-grown Manlars can't get through and it's one of the main reasons I'm still alive. I've also been here so long that my eyes are accustomed to the dim light, so I can spot them relatively quickly.

As I get closer to home, I pick up a new scent in the air. I recognize Rayna, but there's someone new with her. The scent smells vaguely of soap, which is sadly one of the things we never get down here. Perhaps she found the person that got dragged down here from that chamber I found the Chicken Noodle soup in. That means we're either going to have fresh meat tonight, or another mouth to feed. If the kid is a boy, it'll be fresh meat. The last male we let live tried to get abusive with us. It was the last thing he ever did.

I enter our home to find a man hanging from the ceiling. For some reason Rayna's explaining why she's passing up the chance to eat a snack cake over him because the sugar would screw up her empty stomach. I've heard her complain about it many times, not to mention dealing with her when she gives in and does it anyway. It screws with her head almost as much as it messes with her stomach, and her not firing on all cylinders is a volatile thing. The man tries to change her mind, not knowing his fate was sealed the moment she found him.

It's surprising that someone as old as him was dragged down here. The oldest person I've ever seen here was Rayna and she was fifteen when she was lost. That was only two years ago. As I watch the interaction, I detect something about the man that stands out to me. Rayna moves in with her favorite killing knife, and the man continues to plead. He says something about a daughter that was lost, and that definitely sparks something in my mind.

"Wait!" I yell at Rayna, and I can see by her reaction that she's not happy about me catching her. I know she's hungry, and so am I, but we've got food at the moment. We don't need to kill this guy yet. Canned food is alright, but nothing beats fresh meat. The sad thing is, Rayna had been a vegetarian before she was dragged down here.

I get my first good look at the man. He's looking at me like I'm his savior, but the truth is, he's still likely to be killed for food. The majority of our fresh meat comes from Manlars, and they don't just look like they're made out of human parts. They taste like it too. So technically, we're cannibals either way. Survival breaks a lot of barriers you didn't think could be broken.

My first kill had actually been a thing of mercy. I was scavenging for food when I heard screams. A young boy, younger than I'd been when I first came here, was being killed by a Womlar. It's the female version of the monstrous species, and often the more deadly. It had been a young Womlar, and I scared her off easily. I'd found a lighter a few weeks before and lit a cardboard food package on fire. Flames are very rare here, and the heat chased her off. As odd as it sounds, they don't seem to be afraid of light, just intense heat.

I found the boy lying on the ground, blood pouring out of a gash on his stomach. There was nothing I could do to save him, no matter how much he begged me. All I could do was end his suffering. I didn't have a knife or anything like that at the time, so I found a heavy rock that I could still lift. Back then, I wasn't all that strong, so when I brought the rock down on his head, it didn't kill him. He cried and wailed as I repeatedly struck him. It took half a dozen hits for the wailing to stop. By the time I was done, I realized the crying I still heard wasn't an echo in my ears, but the sound of my own wailing. I became truly broken that day.

Food items were hard to find, and I was growing increasingly hungry. After a while it became obvious what I had to do, and I returned to the body. I cried as I dug my teeth into the meat of his arm, but his face was unrecognizable, and it made it a little easier to eat. I threw up after the first time, but since it was the only thing around to eat, I forced myself to continue.

I'd tried hunting small game, but the only things alive down here besides me were the Manlars and Womlars as far as I could find. As for fishing, to this day I haven't been able to find a body of water. The only water we have access to comes through a few entry points, and it's always a small trickle. I wouldn't go so far as to say the water is clean, but it's wet and keeps us somewhat hydrated. So far, only two of the water points I've found are drinkable. I'm still trying to figure out how saltwater ends up dripping down from underneath a shelf.

I stand in front of the man and look up at him.

He asks me all kinds of questions, and even his voice is touching something in my mind. His name is Clarence, and he's looking for his daughter. She went missing five years ago and was nine when she was dragged down here. He's about to say more, but I interrupt him. "Five years, and you only now came down here? You must not have wanted to find her that badly." My voice is bitter, but the man claims he only just found out this place existed. I don't believe him. If he'd been there when she was taken, he should've seen what happened.

Rayna is growing impatient, but to sooth her, I pull out the can of soup and hand it to her. The look she gives me is very displeased as she takes the offered can. We open it and each take a drink of the broth before splitting the rest with another can. The man continues to talk, but we ignore him as best as we can. I really don't want to hear his lies. What kind of father loses his daughter and waits five years to come looking for her? If he was watching her as he claims, he would've seen her get dragged under the shelf. He either wasn't watching her, or he was relieved that she was taken. Either way, he's a bad parent.

After a few minutes of his questions going unanswered, his volume starts getting loud. Noise attracts unwanted attention and Rayna moves on him. Instead of taking her knife to his throat, she grabs a strap of cloth and goes to gag him. Clarence is crying at this point, begging for me to tell him anything about Celia.

I'm on my feet and standing in front of him, moving Rayna out of the way. "Did you say Celia?" I give Rayna an accusatory look, but she claims he never told her the daughter's name. I grow angry at the prospect and want to whack him with something like he was a pinata. Five fucking years and he only just now realized what happened to me. I call bullshit on him.

All that I've gone through over the last five years has turned me into a hard person. I'm only fourteen years old and I've become a murderer and cannibal out of necessity. That part of me wants to take out all my rage and frustration on the father that let me be taken away. Then something else rears up inside me. Something I thought died a long time ago. It's the little girl I used to be, the one that's still frightened and wants Daddy to wrap me up in his arms, to hold me and tell me everything is going to be okay. I haven't felt anything like that in a long time, and it comes on so strong that I start to cry.

With him still hanging from the ceiling, I wrap my arms around him and start bawling. "Oh god, Daddy." I become such a mess that I don't realize Rayna is letting him down until his arms are around me. He holds me tight, crying along with me, and the nightmare is chasing away. Daddy's here and everything is going to be okay again. He'll take care of everything, just like he used to.

Then I remember something, and it gets the tears to stop. He was there when I was taken, and he didn't stop it from happening. He didn't know what happened to me for five fucking years. Why do I suddenly think him being here is going to make a bit of difference? I actually think of letting Rayna kill him but force it away. I let him explain everything from his side of things, and though it's hard to believe, I realize something. Why would he lie? He doesn't look like the strong, confident man I remember. If anything, he looks like a shadow of his former self, a weaker version of what he once was. I guess losing your only child and a destroyed marriage will do that to a person.

Clarence tells me everything and he cries nearly the whole time. "Just a second," he says, "I took my eyes off of you for only a second, and you were just gone." I come to terms with everything quickly. Adaptability is one of the skills I've acquired in this hard life of mine, and I let my anger go. It wasn't his fault and he's promising me that he won't ever let anything bad happen to me again. What a nice thought, but an impossible promise to keep as long as we're here. It's like this place has reversed our roles. Here, I'm the knowledgeable parent and he's the naïve child.

Instead of catching him up on the last five years, Dad immediately starts asking questions about how the hell we're supposed to get out of here. Rayna berates him for asking something that stupid. "If we knew that, why the hell would we still be here?" Dad is clearly annoyed with her attitude but changes his line of questions. Clearly he's not accepting this hellhole as his final resting place, and now that he's found me, he won't rest until we all get out of here.

While Rayna and I enjoy our split can of soup, he asks a lot about the entry chamber he came through. I tell him what I can, but it isn't much. As far as I know, it's somewhere between thirty and forty feet from the ground to the ceiling. I don't know for sure because the light isn't bright enough to really see that far. Once, a few years ago, I got curious about that myself and threw a rock up as hard as I could. It hit something up there and took a few seconds to hit the ground.

His next set of questions is about building materials. We have some scraps of wood, such as the razor-edged clubs both Rayna and I have, but there's nothing larger than that. Besides, any scraps of wood we find are used to make fires. All the 'furniture' we have are merely piles of cloth and paper trash. Hell, our pillows are nothing more than plastic grocery bags stuffed with torn up newspaper.

Not hearing what he wants, he then starts asking about the Manlars. I have no idea how they can climb on walls and ceilings. The best I can figure is that they find hand and foot holds in the stone to grab onto, kind of like rock climbers. They're creatures of pure muscle so they can accomplish this easily enough while we can barely do it at all. Certainly not well enough to scale a wall and then cross the ceiling to the entries. I'm strong and limber, but not enough to do something like that. If I'm not, then Clarence sure as hell isn't.

I get frustrated when he starts asking about rope or any kind of binding tools. "Enough. We've tried everything we could think of to get out of here. We have searched the depths of this place and haven't found an end to it. The tunnels just go on and on forever. The only way out is the same way we got in, but there's no way to reach the entries." I storm off, leaving Rayna to deal with his never-ending line of questions. She's likely to kill him, but after all that, I don't know if I would stop her.

Half expecting to hear the telltale gurgle of someone choking on their blood, I'm surprised to hear Rayna's voice. She's actually talking with him, and it almost sounds like she's trying to be helpful. There's something in her tone that I haven't heard before. Maybe she's relieved to have someone around that might be able to take charge, to become responsible for us. Doing what you're told takes a lot of responsibility off yourself, and now that I think of it, she's listened to me pretty much the whole time she's been here. Occasionally she'll argue with me, but the last time she made a decision, that guy we let live tried to rape both of us.

Walking further away, I poke at a pile of bones with my club. I stopped dreaming about getting out of here years ago. My first partner in this place had been a girl two years older than me. She wasn't as skilled as me when it came to survival knowledge, but she was smart. She's the one that came up with the idea to use the sharp edges of can lids as cutting tools. It was her idea to stick them in pieces of wood for knives and to create something similar to a medieval mace.

Unfortunately, she didn't have the stomach for using such weapons and was snatched up by a Manlar. I watched from the shadows as that beast tore her limb from limb and fed on her insides. Then I snuck up on the fucker and bashed its weird head in. That was when I discovered something new about the damn monsters. You have to destroy both sides of the head, otherwise it can still function. Not nearly as well as it could before, but the nasty things have two brains and only need one to keep living.

As the memory of that flashes in my mind, I swear I can smell the stench of that beast, but I'd killed it a few weeks after it ate her. I'd found it sleeping in a midlevel tunnel and bashed the other half of its head in with my mace before it even woke up. I figure the memory of it is playing tricks on my nose but thinking like that is dangerous. I hear it a moment before it drops to the ground, and I have just enough time to bring the mace up when it reaches out to me.

I slice its hands open with a war cry as I hop backwards. The beast is big, larger than I'd normally engage with, but my rage is back. Dad being here is fucking with my emotions. I keep going back and forth between wanting him to be in charge to wishing he'd never come down here. The neglectful asshat had been safe up there, and before he showed up, I never let a Manlar this large get the drop on me.

The beast lunges at me, and I easily sidestep the grab, drawing the sharp edges of my weapon across its flank. It spins around, growling at me before it lunges again. As I keep putting distance between us, I dance around the piles of bones while it crashes through them. I do notice that none of the larger bones break despite the brute force behind the creature's movements.

Hiding behind a stalagmite protruding from the floor, I keep the pointy rock between me and the Manlar. It keeps trying to move around it, but I'm quick, and keep darting around. It gets frustrated and roars at me again, not noticing we aren't alone anymore. Something thin and tough wraps around its neck and yanks the beast backwards. The unexpected pull from the leather lasso causes the monster to fall, landing with a hard thud. I guess having Dad here is a good thing after all.

Without giving the creature the chance to recover, I leap upon it, bringing my mace down on its face. I strike again and again, grunting with the effort as a second mace mimic's my attacks. Rayna and I make quick work of the beast's head, crushing it on both sides in seconds.

I tell Rayna to start processing the kill while I go to build the fire. We only have so long to peel the skin off and start making leather. Unfortunately, the big ones like this are tough meat, but we get what we can from it. There are plenty of advantages to going after the young Manlars as opposed to the older ones. The foremost being, if we kill them while they're young, there's one less veteran killer to contend with.

Dad follows me as I start gathering what sticks we have, but as I told him before, none of them are useful for building. Rubbing two of the sticks together over some crumpled paper, I show him that the skills he taught me all those years ago have helped keep me alive. Once I have the fire going, he asks where the lasso came from. "I made it." Manlar leather is some of the strongest stuff I've ever seen, and certainly the strongest material we have access to.

Dad gets this strange look on his face. He starts looking around at the piles of bones and starts gathering the largest ones. There are plenty of those thick leg bones, and some of the arm bones are pretty big too. He takes the lasso and starts tying some of the bones together. After a few minutes, he's putting together something that begins to look like a ladder. He doesn't get very far before he runs out of rope. I see where he's going with this, and actually start getting excited, but then I remember how much rope we have. It isn't much, but I'm well practiced at making leather. The only problem is, it's going to take a lot more bodies to make enough for what he has in mind.

Over the next few weeks, dad gets to see more of the savagery I've developed. He watches as we hunt and slaughter five more Manlars, but he's not eating much. He can't bring himself to eat the meat we cook and has trouble watching as we devour the juicy morsels. "You get used to it after a while," but he's not interested. I've noticed his strength is getting used up quicker with the passing days.

We've managed to build a ladder that's nearly

twenty feet long, but Dad barely has any strength, and I've had enough of his stubbornness. I use what little seasoning we have to make a thigh muscle as tasty as I can. Rayna holds Dad down as I force the small pieces of meat into his throat, and hold his mouth closed until he swallows. After a few pieces, he noticeably perks up, realizing it doesn't taste as bad as he'd initially thought. At this point, he's too damn hungry to care about the cannibalistic aspects. It comes to him later, and he nearly throws up, but his body was too starved, and he digested it already.

It takes more than a month to get the necessary materials. We make the ladder thirty feet tall, then forty feet. It still isn't finding the damn ceiling, but we find it fifty-five feet up. How is it none of us broke bones when we were dragged down? Just one of the thousands of mysteries surrounding this place that has no chance of being solved. Like, how does this place exist in the first place? A question that has haunted me awake or asleep for five years.

I'm first up the ladder, and I find the entry. My eyes are blinded at the amount of light up here, and it takes a while for them to adjust. While they do, I feel around the hole and discover a problem. I can't squeeze through the space between the shelf and the floor. With my eyes finally adjusting to the light, I can see wheels passing by, and I start yelling for help. People on the surface are fucking dense, and I have to yell at them, "Please, I'm trapped under the shelf!"

I don't know what's going on up there, but I can hear what's happening on this side of the entry. Manlars are converging on this chamber thanks to all the noise I'm making. I start pressing up on the shelf, hitting at it to try and move the damn thing, but there's too much weight on it. There must be some heavy shit sitting on it, and I remember there're hundreds of soup cans right above my head. How is it that this damn market hasn't changed in more than five years?

Dad and Rayna yell up to me that the creatures are coming, and I need to get a move on. I can feel vibrations through the bones of the ladder and know they're both climbing up. We didn't design this thing to hold all three of us, and I doubt it'll hold for long. I can see lots of feet at the surface, and some knees. There are people frantically removing the cans from the shelf. The urgency in my voice is alarming them as I tell them to hurry.

Brilliant light floods my world as the entire shelf is yanked away from the entry. I hear gasps as the people up there see what's under the shelf and I scramble for the surface. Once I'm clear, I turn back and look down at Rayna. She's more than halfway up, and she puts on speed. Dad isn't far behind her, but the look on Rayna's face says it all. There's something coming for the hole, and the Manlar is going to drag me back through.

I look around but don't see anything that would work as a weapon. I couldn't climb the ladder with my mace. Before I can grab up the largest of the cans on the ground, hard flesh bursts through the opening, throwing me away from the hole. Screams erupt as people run for their lives, the giant monsters pouring through the hole like ants swarming out of an anthill. I lose count of how many come through before they stop.

I expect the bone ladder to be gone when the hard flesh clears, but it's still there. Rayna and Dad eventually climb out of the hole, both having as much trouble as I had with the light. It hadn't occurred to me that us getting out might've unleashed the Manlars onto the world.

I may not have kept count of how many came through, but I did notice one thing. It wasn't just Manlars pouring through the hole, but Womlars too. Unless they're dealt with quickly, those nightmares are going to start breeding on this side, and the world will have a new enemy to face.

ON DUTY

I've been a cop since the Clinton administration, and in all my time on the force, I have seen some seriously weird shit. The things that people do to each other can be so messed up, and on more than one occasion, I've wished I could just retire and be done with it. I'm talking about some of the worst things people can imagine, the kind of shit that'll turn your hair white. I guess that's why I went prematurely gray.

My wife says I'm too old to be carrying a gun and chasing bad guys for a living. I can't argue with her, and it's not just because it's always a lost cause to try. She's absolutely right, so last week, I turned in my papers. I'm finishing the month, and then it's nothing but comfy clothes and only carrying a gun when it's concealed. I've seen too much to ever leave home without a concealed piece. The risk just isn't worth it.

I'm not a detective, so I don't have open cases that will haunt me when I'm gone. No, the only thing that'll haunt me is my memories, and those aren't things you can ever completely get rid of. There are things you can do to push them out of your mind, but it's never a permanent thing. One way or another, they will always come back and usually at the most inappropriate time. Then again, is there ever an appropriate time for such things to surface? Maybe in a shrink's office.

Every cop is required to see the department shrink after they discharge their firearm, and I'm on a first name basis with that guy by now. I've pulled my gun and used it more times than I can remember, but with more than twenty years on the job, that's not uncommon. I don't even think I hold the record in my precinct, and to be honest, I'm perfectly fine with that.

My only solace is that I never shot someone that didn't have it coming. I'm not one of those cops that people are up in arms about because they shot a kid or someone that didn't do anything wrong. I always was and still am a good cop. A lot of the folks on the force are sad that I won't be around much longer.

One of the biggest clichés that cops are worried about is someone only weeks from retirement getting gunned down in the streets. Unfortunately, it happens more often than people are aware of. I know four people that were shot just days before turning in their badge. Thankfully, only one of those four actually died. Two of the others are fine and completely rehabilitated. The fourth is in a wheelchair for the rest of her life.

My reputation is stellar, and I've saved more butts in uniform than even I know. Everyone from the lowly desk clerks all the way to the Chief of Police knows my name. I've had a car to myself for many years, but the moment I turned in my papers, I suddenly found myself with a chaperone. Officer Curtis is a serious badass, and I know firsthand that she doesn't take shit from anyone. I should know, I was her training officer when she started eleven years ago.

The Chief himself assigned Curtis to shadow me just in case something happens. It doesn't stop there either. At any given time, there is at least one cruiser in close proximity to my car when we're on the streets. I've made a lot of friends, and they're all making sure I get to see retirement without making one last hospital visit.

I'm surprised and touched that everyone cares so much. I'm sure my wife Diane has something to do with it. She can be scary when she wants to be. Thankfully, she doesn't aim that scary at me. There was one time she aimed it at the old Chief, and it was the last thing that happened to him before he was fired. I'm not saying the two things are connected, but I'm not not saying it either.

Curtis and I are out on patrol, the last midnight shift I'm going to have before retirement. This is one thing I'm certainly not going to miss. From here on out, the only time I'll be up this late is because I want to be. Or Diane wants me to be. Or if I have trouble sleeping. Shit, never mind.

A call comes over the radio, there's a 211 three blocks from us, a suspected armed robbery in progress. Curtis is behind the wheel, and before she can say anything, I get on the radio and tell dispatch to show us responding. Whoever decided to rob that convenience store tonight done fucked up. Not only are we responding, but so are the two units that have been flanking me all night. They've been five blocks over to the North and South since we started the shift. On days there's only one unit nearby, but midnight shift upped it to two. Definitely makes a guy feel loved.

We roll up to the store just as two armed men run out the door. Before I can even get my seatbelt off, one of them has started shooting at our windshield. Curtis and I dismount at the same time, using the armored doors and bullet resistant glass as a shield. We exchange fire with the suspect as the second one flees. One of my bullets catches the gunman in the side, and Curtis tags him in the shoulder on the opposite side. He goes down hard enough that his gun skids away from him on the asphalt.

The cruiser on the North side of us comes out of

a cross street just in time for the second suspect to run into the front end. He was moving so fast that he couldn't stop himself in time, and actually lands on the hood. Must've been going all out because his forward momentum carries him over the hood and to the ground.

The cruiser on the South side comes up behind me and stops next to the suspect Curtis and I shot. The pair inside come out with weapons drawn, but the situation appears defused, so one moves in to cuff him while the other covers. That was surprisingly quick. I figured all hell was going to break loose, but it's nice to be wrong about these things.

Gunfire erupts from inside the store, and I hear glass breaking. The officer that was cuffing the wounded suspect, Officer Collins, takes a round in the chest and hits the deck. His partner, Officer Gentry, must have a clear line of sight of the armed suspect because he starts firing in retaliation. I can't see the shooter from where I am, and I take the opportunity to move.

I've worked these streets a very long time, and I happen to visit this convenience store regularly on patrol. Enough to know there's a backdoor in the alley, and that's where I'm headed now. I don't wait for Curtis to join me because whoever is inside is shedding lead like he's laying down suppressive fire and has the ammunition to do it.

By the time I make it down the block and to the mouth of the alley, the gunfire from in the store has stopped. If the suspect knows about the back door, he'll be popping out of it in a few moments. I'm in pretty good shape for someone my age, but it still takes me a minute to get down the alley. The space directly behind the store is a vacant lot that leads to the street. I'm within thirty yards when someone darts out the back door and goes straight for the lot.

I radio in my position and status as I continue the pursuit. As I round the corner and enter the vacant lot, I see the suspect is already at the street and headed west. It's hard to keep your mind on task when you're expending this much physical effort. The brain likes to get fuzzy around the edges with the blood pumping this much. What I can make out is the suspect's general shape, and the fact that he's carrying a duffle bag. To be honest, I can't be a hundred percent sure the suspect is a male or female, but at this point, it doesn't matter. I know the suspect is armed and has shown a willingness to use whatever firearm they possess.

A lot of people aren't meant for long distance running. Typically, a person will expend the majority of their stamina in the first five minutes. As long as you can maintain a visual, you stand a good chance of catching them. It also helps to have additional units move in to block them off, but you can't always count on that.

The suspect crosses the street and goes down another alley. With any luck, they won't know I'm right behind them, and they'll take the time to catch their breath. As I approach the alley, I slow my speed and come to a stop once I reach the corner. I call in my position over the radio again, then peek around the corner. There are dumpsters and loose trash strewn about the space, a typical sight for downtown I'm sad to say.

Unfortunately, the suspect is still mobile but must be running out of juice. Their speed has decreased, and they're trying doors in passing. So far, none of the doors are unlocked, and I start moving into the alley. Keeping to the shadows as best as I can, the suspect looks in my direction and catches my movement. I don't see the weapon coming up, but the shots let me know it has. Taking cover behind a dumpster, I peek over the top and see the suspect finally finds an open door.

There are five more gunshots before it stops, and I peek over again to see the suspect enter a building. I call it in, hoping at least Curtis is close behind, but not waiting. Quickly, I approach the doorway, peeking inside to see if the suspect is waiting. When I don't see anyone, I enter.

The space is dark with only dim streetlight coming in through the grime covered windows. It appears to be an abandoned warehouse or machine shop of some kind. In this area, it's unfortunately common. The economy in this section of the city has been going downhill over the last decade. It's no wonder there's so much crime here. Poverty ridden areas are a breeding ground for criminal activity.

I pick up on the sounds of movement from farther in the building, and I move in that direction. Turning on the flashlight on the rail of my pistol, I see old machinery all over the place, but no suspect. Having the light on gives away my position, but it beats trying to navigate the space in the dark.

As I keep moving, I hear more noises, but they're not coming from the same area I previously heard the suspect. This is more like the rattling of chains, which doesn't make any sense. I don't see any chains hanging from the ceiling, or anywhere else for that matter. I sweep my light from side to side, but there's no sign of where it's coming from. I swear I can hear it as if the source was right in front of me.

Softly, I begin to hear moaning, like there's someone lying in the dark injured. Did I manage to hit the suspect when I was exchanging gunfire with them before they darted in here? I start looking along the ground against walls, but there's no one here. Where the hell did the suspect go?

My light shines off something metal on the ground, and as I get closer, I see it's an empty pistol magazine. It's longer than an average mag, one of those ones that holds thirty rounds or so. I've seen them plenty of times, even own a few myself, but we're not allowed to carry them on duty. I only have them to take to the range, and mostly because I simply wanted a few. This would explain why the suspect was firing off rounds like they were nothing.

Floorboards creak above me as my light flashes on a staircase just past the discarded magazine. So, the suspect went up a flight, that's fine. I've been using the Stairmaster at the gym a lot lately. Ever since my knees have been giving me trouble going up to my bedroom, I've been doing my cardio on it to try and toughen up my knees. Thankfully, it's been working.

Taking the stairs slowly, I point my weapon up just in case the suspect is waiting for me. I don't think they're that close considering how far back the creaking boards were, but I'm not taking any chances. This whole 'weeks until retirement' thing has me on edge, but I've always been this cautious. For as many times as I've been in a live fire conflict, I've seen the inside of a hospital surprisingly little, and it's because I am so cautious. Getting shot because of running up stairs without checking them is a rookie mistake, and I didn't even make those when I was a rookie.

Making it to the second floor, I start hearing more noises, and I'm getting a bad feeling. It's the sounds of people whispering, but I can't make out what they're saying, which is eerie for a number of reasons. The first being that they're loud enough that whoever is doing it should be really close. The second, and much more alarming is that I don't see anyone.

There are old dress maker mannequins strewn about all over the place, some even still standing. I've seen something like this before, and it dawns on me where I am. This isn't the first suspect I've chased through this building, but last time I was here, it was still daylight. Even then I swore I heard something in the darkness that creeps in this building, and I hadn't been in here that long.

The suspect I was chasing back then had tried hiding, but within minutes, he came out of his spot screaming. I chased him as he swatted at things that weren't there, and it gave me the chance to tackle him to the ground. He didn't try to fight me as I cuffed him and led him outside. Later I asked him what he'd seen, but he wouldn't say. Eventually his lawyer convinced him to plead guilty to his crime, and last I heard, that guy was still in a mental ward for the criminally insane. I've avoided this building ever since, and that was five years ago.

Until now, I haven't had a reason to come back to this place, and I've been grateful for that. Sure, I've passed by while on patrol, and even in the light of day, this place gives me the creeps. A big part of me wants to turn around and get the hell out of here, but not without my suspect. I press on.

As I make my way further, my flashlight is sweeping back and forth more and more. There are lots of walls and worktables, those damn mannequins popping up at odd turns. I nearly shoot one as I come around a corner, and it gets me to ease up on the trigger. The last thing I need to do is give away my position more than my flashlight already does.

Creeping down the hall, I sweep my light from an open doorway on the left to another on the right. Seeing that door is closed, I aim back at the doorway on the left, but the door is closed now. I didn't hear someone close it, hadn't sensed any movement at all when I turned to the right. Checking that the hallway is still clear, I lean against the wall right next to the door.

With my back against the wall, I kick back at the door with my right heel. The door crashes open, and I expect the suspect to start shooting, but there's nothing. Pointing my weapon inside, I sweep the room and find it empty. There's nothing in here, but trash and a few chairs on their sides.

Entering the hallway again, I see something standing in the middle and can't help that I squeeze the trigger. My 9mm round hits the mannequin right in the chest, and it clatters to the floor. What the hell? I checked the hall before entering the room, and there was no mannequin standing there a few moments ago. There had been one on the floor, but again, I heard nothing while I was in the room. First the door and now this, what's next? I should just be grateful that it hadn't been Curtis or one of the other cops with us.

Continuing down the hall, I start seeing things move at the corners of my eye. They're just shadows, but they keep moving in ways that they shouldn't. The only source of light here is my flashlight, and I know that's not causing them to move like that.

Something slams into me from behind, and I

tumble to the floor. Rolling to my back, I point my weapon to where I'd just been standing and let fly a double tap. The bullets connect with a pipe on the ceiling and spark off the metal. My flashlight shows no one in the hallway, and I've had enough.

I get to my feet and double time it down the hall, occasionally firing at shadows. I'm awfully jumpy and running low on ammunition. I really wish they'd just demolish this building already. As I come out the other side of the hall, gunfire erupts from somewhere on this level and I hit the deck. Someone is screaming, and I pick my head up to see what I assume is the suspect. Quickly, I turn off the flashlight on my weapon and crawl behind an old desk.

While still on the ground, I poke my head around the desk and bring my weapon to bear. The wall to the right is lined with dirty windows, and I can see what's going on in the wide-open space. The suspect is flailing about, firing that weapon in all directions, but not at me. From what I can tell, my presence is unknown.

Something moves in the shadows at the gunman, hitting at him from various directions, but I can't tell what it is. It moves in for a strike, hits him, then is simply gone again. I can see well enough to train my weapon on the chest and as more gunfire erupts, I discharge my weapon. Two solid hits and the suspect staggers backward, right into a window.

Expecting him to fall through it, that shadow darts in again, grabbing the suspect before he falls through. I have trouble understanding what's happening, but my eyes take it in. The shadow pulls the suspect away from the window, but then slams his back into a large, jagged piece of glass. The gun clatters to the floor as the glass protrudes from his chest, blood covering the grimy peak.

I continue to lay there, watching as the shadow keeps doing things to the now dead bad guy. It reaches into the body, and starts pulling something out, but it's not guts and organs. Something dark comes out of the body, struggling in the shadow's grasp, and for a moment, I hear an inhuman wail. The shadow lifts the dark mass above it and seems to rip it open. There's a bright flash that nearly blinds me and the wail dies off into silence.

My eyes don't need to recover from the flash because it wasn't really a blast of light, not in the traditional sense at least. I'm stunned, not really comprehending what just happened, but too afraid to move. The shadow doesn't have a face or eyes that I can see, but somehow, I know the exact moment its focus turns to me.

Not wanting to be next, I jump to my feet and run like hell for the stairs. Those whispers come back to assault my ears, but my fear for that thing is stronger, and I practically fly down the stairs. I must be moving faster than I had when I was chasing the suspect because I find myself back outside in no time at all. Curtis is suddenly there, waving her hand in my face. I focus on her and can clearly see she looks worried.

I calm my uncontrolled breathing as she asks me what happened. All I can do at the moment is shake my head. Despite all the physical exertion, my skin is cold to the touch, and I shiver in the warm air. Curtis pats me on the back but exclaims shock when her hand comes away stained. It's not red because I haven't been wounded, but a thick black goop. I must've gotten it on me when the shadow hit me from behind in that hallway.

Once I've calmed down enough that my hands aren't shaking, I try giving my report to the Officer In Charge now that he's on scene, but I don't know what to say. I can't make sense of it in a way that doesn't sound crazy. Cops see weird shit all the time, but this would be a hard pill to swallow. Hell of a way to end my career.

YEAR OF THE DRAGON

Rolling Oaks mall hosts a Lunar New Year celebration every year, and since this is the Year of the Dragon, I wasn't going to miss it. I'm actually a Tiger, but like a lot of geeks, I used to have quite a fascination with dragons. I've gotten away from that a lot since I've grown up, especially since I seem to have a personality conflict with most dragons I know.

I wouldn't classify myself as a geek or nerd anymore, but some things never change. My fascination with Asian cultures has a lot to do with the food, and Chinese food is by far my favorite. I like sushi too, but most of the rolls I like are either fried or have tempura shrimp in them. Oh, and eel. For some reason I really like eel. I used to think sushi was disgusting because, you know, raw fish and all. It wasn't until I was in my mid twenties that someone got me to actually try it, and now I eat it when I can afford it. Sadly, that's not very often since sushi tends to be expensive.

Walking into the mall, I'm immediately immersed in the largest crowd I've been in since before the Covid pandemic. I haven't avoided crowds since then on purpose, but this is a bit much. I can't seem to find more than a few seconds where I'm not pressed up against a random stranger. Even though social distancing isn't much of a thing anymore, I would've thought this might violate the fire code for maximum capacity.

Managing to maneuver my way further in, I find why the crowd is so congested. There's a large space in the middle of the area cleared out for the dancers preforming the opening ceremony. I missed the bit outside where they set off a long string of black cat fireworks at the beginning of the ceremony. I've seen this a few times before, and I'd judge that I came in about halfway through the dance.

There are five colorful dragons dancing with three or four people inside each of the costumes. For the life of me, I can't remember exactly what the dance is for, but it always looks really cool. These people practice this ceremony year-round and are quite proficient. Their choreographed movements are in sync, timed down to the microsecond. You don't see a lot of that these days.

I find that as I get older, people's attention to detail and devotion to their craft have allowed for a much larger margin of error. It's like the majority of people don't care about perfection anymore. I guess that comes with a society that doles out participation trophies and grades on a curve. To me, it just breeds laziness. When I was still in school, I liked the curve because it meant my grades were better than I earned. It wasn't until I graduated that I realized how much that screwed me. I wasn't as smart as my grades suggested, and I struggled through college because of it.

Despite all that crap, I somehow managed to graduate with a masters, and have landed a decent job. Enough that I can afford to take a random day off and come down to the mall with a wad of cash to spend on things I don't really need. Granted, the last thing my place needs is a bunch of trinkets that just end up collecting dust on a shelf. I've got more than enough of that, and I hate cleaning.

About a year ago I hired a maid named Karina to come in once a week. Originally it had been to dust my cluttered shelves, and it took a month to get all of it.

She takes care of a lot, but I at least do my own laundry. I will admit that she does my grocery shopping, and occasionally cooks. That only happened because she boasted about being able to make the best Korean BBQ I could ever have. Needless to say, I pay her well.

Once the opening ceremony ends, and the dragons march off, the density of the crowd changes. It's still pretty tight with so many people, but I can breathe a little easier now. There are tables setup against every wall and storefront. This is one of those failing malls, so a lot of the shops are vacant. I think the only reason this place is still open is because of events like this. They have something going on almost every week.

The different vendors around the place have a wide variety of merchandise, spanning over many cultures. I'm actually hunting for something specific this year, and Year of the Dragon is the perfect time to find what I want. There are always vendors with those little red statues of the Zodiac animals, and I've been collecting them for years. For some reason, the dragons have been the hardest to find. Then again, I'm after something very specific.

The sizes available for these statues vary greatly, ranging from two inches tall to a full foot. I have a complete set of four-inch statues, but my favorite has always been the six-inch statues. For some reason, there is a level of detail in this size that is either lacking in the smaller ones or overshadowed on the larger ones.

Take the tiger for example. On the smaller statues you only get the obvious details like the tiger's shape and the fact that it has stripes. The six-inch statue gives you so much more, and the details in it's face are astounding. There's something about the size of the eyes that catches the light just right, and it makes it look like there's something there. A consciousness that is ever present and watching. I've spent a disturbing amount of time looking into that red statue's eyes.

I swear sometimes, the statue speaks to me in a way that only I can pick up on. Not with words, or even images, but with emotions that I can't even begin to truly understand. It's almost something primal. The foot tall statue has too much surface area in the eyes, and it loses the effect.

For the last several years I've been trying to complete my collection, but the damn six-inch statues either go quick, or they're hard to find. I've been working on this for four years now, and online shopping hasn't been any help because I run into the same problems there as I do at these things. What I'm looking for is either out of stock, ridiculously expensive, or no one carries it. For two years now, the dragon statue is the only one I've been missing.

I start with the closest vendor and make my way down one side. There are lots of interesting items, but not the six-inch dragon statue I'm looking for. Now that's not to say I don't buy anything. One vendor has a lot of different Ramen bowls. The designs on them are so cool that I end up getting a black one with a dragon design on it, and a matching pair of chopsticks.

Another vendor has a table full of those solar powered cat statues with the waving paw. They come in all sizes, and somehow, the guy has them all in sync with each other. To be honest, it looks a little eerie. Can you imagine how much work it takes to get nearly a hundred waving cats to wave at the same time? I can, and it's baffling. I wonder if there's some trick to it.

Every other table is covered in Anime merchandise, which isn't unusual. People into Anime and Asian dramas are drawn to these events, so it makes sense that vendors cater to them. I'd say one out of every five tables has anything remotely close to what I'm looking for, but no one has the six-inch dragon statue I'm specifically hunting. The closest one I've found so far is a five inch one, but it's not a red one like the majority of the others.

This statue is ceramic, and it's black with white and bronze looking cogwheels at the dragon's joints. It's a true first for me. I've never seen a steampunk dragon before. If it wasn't nearly a hundred bucks, I'd snatch it up.

When I get to the far edge of the mall's hallway, the crowd thins out enough that I can actually avoid touching anyone. There are a few vendors this way, but their tables are small. This is the furthest away from the main stage in the food court, so it makes sense that there isn't much over here. I don't have a lot of hope as I approach the tables, but if I find at least something small that I wouldn't mind having, I'll buy it. These guys went through the effort to come out, and they probably get the least amount of foot traffic in the whole mall. It doesn't seem fair to me.

The first table has the largest collection of chopsticks I have ever seen. There are designs here that I've never seen before, and I buy a couple sets. The second table has a lot of those paper lanterns and wall-hangings. I end up buying a calendar from him.

As for the last table, it has very little, but what there is, I must admit, is the best quality merchandise I've seen since coming inside. The figurines are small, but a lot of them are carved out of some of the creamiest jade I have ever seen. She has an entire set of Zodiac animals that're about two inches each. If I had the several hundred to spend on it, I'd be handing the money over in a heartbeat. As it is, I'm tempted to get the tiger.

I pick up the little tiger, running my fingers over the smoothness and admiring the craftsmanship. It is truly a magnificent piece, and I'm about to reach into my pocket for the money when I catch eyes with the woman. Her eyes are nearly a match for the jade in my hand, and I can't help but stare at her. We stay like that for a few minutes, and something seems to pass between us. Like when I stare into the tiger's eyes, whatever this is is indescribable. However, she seems to know something I don't, and she reaches under the table.

She places a white box on the table and says, "You can hold the tiger's gaze because that is who you are but use caution here. This is not your animal, and if you're not careful, it can consume you."

I don't know what to say to that, but it does make me hesitate. After a brief moment of confusion and a little bit of worry, I reach out to the box. Opening the top, I see something I never thought I'd actually find. It's the exact six-inch red dragon statue I've been looking for. My eyes roam all over it, taking in the intricate detail. When I get to the head, I look at the mouth, nose and horns, but not the eyes. I don't know if it's because of what she said or some primal instinct, but I avoid looking into the dragon's eyes. I feel chilled down to the bone.

Handing over two hundred dollars, I put the dragon back in the box as she places the jade tiger in a smaller box. Adding them to a bag I already have, I turn to leave, but the woman says one final thing to me. "Remember caution. The spirits are strongest in their year."

I don't bother visiting any of the other vendors. I don't even visit the food stalls or stay for any of the stage performances. To be honest, I don't know what freaked me out more. The woman, or the dragon statue. Finally finding the last statue for my collection was supposed to be exciting and happy, but it was anything but. Going through with the purchase had been automatic. Had I taken a moment to really think about how I was feeling, I probably would've passed.

When I get back to my place, I take out all of my new purchases and place them in various places among my already cluttered shelves. The calendar gets put on the fridge with a magnet and the paper lantern hangs from a hook on one of the shelf brackets. As for the new dragon statue, it gets placed in the empty space among the other six-inch statues. It is the only item that stays in the box it came in.

Over the next few days, I try to forget about the statue, but since half the time I work remotely from home, it's not easy to do. Pretty much every time I walk out of my home office, my eyes are drawn to the shelf with the six-inch statues. The contrasting white box stands out like a sore thumb, but somehow I don't think the dragon being out of the box would be much of an improvement. I still somehow manage to meet eyes with the tiger statue with a casual glance. Half the time I'm not even aware I've done it, but I know it would be different with the dragon.

Concentrating on work helps, but my mind keeps drifting to it. It's like an ear worm, or a really horrible scene from a horror movie that you just can't get out of your head. It gets to the point that I start going into the office on days that I'd normally work at home. Thursday is one such day, and I normally work from home because that's the day Karina comes over. She has a key and an alarm code, so I don't have to be there, but I like to be. Not because I don't trust her or anything like that. I like to chat with her when she's there.

I come home from work to find Karina puttering around in the kitchen. After all the jabs from my coworkers about my unusual presence at the office this week, coming home to the smells of delicious food is a lift to my spirits. I say hi to her as I drop my stuff in my home office, but when I come back out, I stop cold in my tracks.

My eyes are immediately drawn to the shelf with the six-inch statues, and I lock gazes with that set of piercing eyes. They catch the light just so, and they look so alive, I can't tell that they're immobile in the red statue. Something fires straight into my brain, a sensation of conflict that I've never experienced before. Images start flooding me, scenes of ancient battlefields and armies raging against each other. Swords and armor, blood and bone, rage that lights my blood on fire.

I feel the rough handle in my hands as I bring my sword up, facing off with an adversary in black and red armor. We stand perfectly still as the war carries on around us, waiting for even the tiniest hint of movement. My adversary moves first, and I move with him. My sword comes down for a powerful blow, but it's blocked with his sword. He moves for a strike, but I dodge to the side, bringing the point of my blade up from his side. It slips into a weak point in the armor, sinking into his torso, and I shove it in all the way. Blood is spit into my face, and I laugh.

Karina is in my face, trying to get my attention as the scene fades from my eyes. I've been zoned out for a few minutes, standing completely immobile and barely breathing. My skin is so pale that I look like I've seen a ghost. In a flat tone, I tell her, "I was just admiring my collection. I finally found the missing piece." Karina doesn't believe me. She found it odd that the dragon was still in its box, but now she begins to understand why.

"I'm fine," I say unconvincingly, and then shift our attention on the meal she's preparing. Just like that, I'm back to my old self and I see she relaxes. As we normally do when she's here, I watch her finish cooking before we sit down at the table together. I keep my back to my collection, and every once in a while, I catch her looking behind me. When she finds that I notice what she's doing, she smiles embarrassedly. The dragon isn't effecting her like it does me, but she seems to sense something. Part of me wants to ask, but I don't. I don't think the answer would help my troubled mind.

That night I dream of more battles and blood. I am a fierce warrior in ancient times, cutting a bloody path through the ages. At one point, I stop being a soldier. I find myself walking old cobblestone streets, keeping to the shadows as I hunt. Coming down an alley is a pair, a whore and her John. I am unseen as money exchanges hands, and the man begins doing things to her. I sneak up behind them, a razor in my hand, and I draw the blade across his throat. Blood splatters across the whore's face and she screams as I melt into the shadows and slink away. I wake in a sweaty panic.

You'd think sleep would be hard to achieve after that, but getting to sleep is never the problem. Even staying asleep is easy. Every night the dreams get more vivid and more disturbing. Sometimes I wake up and can swear I taste blood in my mouth. It's not from biting my tongue or cheek. It's the taste of my victims.

No matter how different the dreams are, one thing stays the same. I am a killer. I've fought in every major war the earth has known, from the time of the sword and axe, all the way to assault rifles and combat knives. In the more recent conflicts, I have stalked the enemy in jungles, deserts, and urban areas. I always stick to the shadows, and go in for intimate kills when I can, drawing my combat knife across throats as I look into their dying eyes.

The dreams are starting to effect my behavior. On Monday I went into the office and anytime someone interacted with me, I kept imagining killing them with an item on my desk. It wasn't even that they were annoying me. Someone said hi to me as I walked in, and all I wanted to do was throw my hot coffee in their face and stab them in the throat with a pen. Before lunch I'd put pretty much everything I wasn't actively using on my desk into one of the drawers. Especially after my manager came by to talk to me about new cover letters for reports. I didn't realize I was holding my scissors in my hand until he walked away.

I've started doing some research into the dragon zodiac, but nothing I come up with explains what's happening. The dragon is gracious, loving and conscious of their image. Something the woman said keeps coming back to me. I can hold the tiger's gaze because it's who I am. Could this be happening simply because the dragon isn't my zodiac? That doesn't hold much water though. None of the others have effected me like this. Then again, aside from the tiger, I wasn't as obsessed as I was with the dragon. I thought it had been because it was the only one missing from my collection, but maybe it had been more than that.

Wednesday night I dream of being the same killer I've been every night for a week, but the location changed to my office. I stalk the floor with an ax and machete, attacking each and every one of my coworkers. I slash at their bodies, lop off their limbs and decapitate them. It doesn't stop there either. I wear their parts like decorations, even going so far as to cut off my manager's face and wear it for a mask.

I wake, but not in a sweaty rush like I have been, nor am I in my bed. In fact, it doesn't appear that my eyes were even closed. My legs are crossed and I'm sitting on the ground in my living room, facing my shelves. The shelf with the six-inch statues are at eye level, and my eyes are locked with the dragon's. I remember lying down in bed, but I don't remember getting up. I'm still in my sleeping clothes.

Karina comes in to find me in that same position several hours later. I startle her so badly that she drops the bags of groceries, her hands going to her mouth to stifle a scream. For the first time, I wonder what I must look like, a zombie in blood-stained clothes sitting in a meditative state. The blood is my own, I know that, but where it came from I can't say. I have no open wounds, but my eyes are wet, and my vision is red around the edges. Have I been crying blood?

Karina tries to get my attention, to bring me out of this trance like she had last week. With lightning speed, I grab her by the throat and force her to my lap.

She stares up at me with pleading eyes as she struggles against me. It does no good. I have strength I never had before.

In a calm and collected voice, I tell her something that I shouldn't know, using a tongue I never possessed before. I speak to her in her native language and tell her the truth about the spirit of the dragon. It was once a ruthless ruler, gaining power through death. As the times changed, it's bloodlust continued, unquenchable through countless ages. Now the tiger spirit that had once been in this body is gone, and the dragon rises. She will be the first of many.

I tell her this as my hands slowly squeeze tighter, stealing the life from her. Those eyes gloss over as the light of life fades away, leaving behind a perfect porcelain doll. Karina will be the first doll in my new collection, and my reign of death begins with a bloodless death. There will be a lot of blood, but those I wish to collect will die like this. Perhaps one day I will collect the woman that sold me the statue that made this possible. She will become the crown jewel of my collection.

TIME LOST

I have always been bad about keeping time. My time management skills are abysmal, remembering things in the correct order is mighty difficult, and without looking at a clock, I couldn't even begin to guess what the time is. Most people wear a watch, but I can't. I've never been comfortable with one on my wrist and the last three I tried to endure ended up getting knocked off.

Okay, so I'm a bit of a klutz too. I occasionally bump into random things and walls, but putting a watch on my wrist seems to make it even worse. I easily trip over things that won't phase other people, lose my balance, and misplace random items all the time. I'd lose my freaking head if it wasn't attached. About the only thing I don't misplace is my wallet and money, but that's because I always keep them in my pocket. Things in my pocket tend to stay where they are.

My phone is an exception. Right along with my keys, I lose my phone more than anything. My theory is because I'm always messing around with it, then get distracted by something else and, without thinking, I put it down. Not back in my pocket, but on a table, counter or whatever. So, clumsy and absentminded. Talk about a winning combination.

When it comes to work, I'm always either really early to arrive, or late. It doesn't matter if I try to concentrate on being aware of the time, it always manages to get away from me. I've been written up about being late more times than anyone, yet somehow I still have a job. It probably helps that when I'm sitting at my desk working, I hyper focus. I'll manage to get through all my work with a few hours to spare because I don't take breaks. Hell, when I do, it usually ends up being a mad dash to the bathroom because the urge to pee has been building, but I wasn't aware of it. Strange how someone can ignore something like that.

Last week I accidentally left my phone in my desk at work, and didn't find it for three days. The calendar app on my phone is the only way I can keep track of all my scheduled events, and losing it made me nearly miss one that would've been disastrous. It's not that I forgot my birthday was coming up, but the alarm I set to remind me to be at Reggie's Restaurant would've gotten me there in time. I was only half an hour late, and the only reason I didn't miss it completely is because I have a landline at my apartment. How else am I supposed to find my phone when I misplace it?

A handful of friends as well as my family were sitting at a pair of tables when I got there. Among them was my cousin Ethan, who I was really surprised to see. We'd had a nasty falling out a few years ago over something that I still claim hadn't been my fault. He'd been staying with me for a few weeks because he was between places. On the night that he was supposed to propose to his fiancé, the ring he bought got misplaced. I swear up and down that I never touched the damn thing, but a $7000 ring doesn't just up and disappear.

Ethan and I tore the apartment apart looking for it, and he ended up being two hours late to dinner. It's not that we looked for that long, but he hit bad traffic on the way because of an accident. Someone was texting and driving, failing to notice the cargo truck blowing through a red light. There was a fatality and those always make traffic a nightmare. Cops have to completely shut down roads when that happens.

By the time he got there, Sharon had not only left the restaurant but broke up with him over a text message. He never got to explain himself because the accident that caused Ethan to be so horribly late was Sharon. Ethan blamed me for the whole thing, but I later heard he found the ring in his glovebox. Apparently, he left it there because the odds of it getting lost in my apartment were too high to risk. Still, we hadn't spoken in all that time.

Not only did Ethan come to my birthday dinner, but he got me a gift too. The small box was polished wood and looked rather old. Inside was a silver pocket watch with a chain and clip attached, an antique that was well kept. I couldn't believe it, saying that he'd spent way too much on it even though I didn't have a clue what it cost. Something like this could go for a thousand for all I know.

"Don't you worry about it," he said, "as long as you keep it in your pocket and clip it to your belt loop, there's no chance of you losing it. Just remember, you have to wind it the same time every day or you'll lose time." He was overly happy to be there and see me, as if the last few years had never happened. I found it odd but wasn't going to question it.

Ever since then I wind the watch at 11am, a time I'm guaranteed to be awake. I even set an alarm on my phone to remind me too. So far I've been successful, but today's workload at the office is pretty big. There's a lot of moving parts to a corporation as big as Pyramid and we've been struggling for the last few months. We lost our lead, who was responsible for doling out tasks and assignments. The position has been filled, but this new guy, Trevor, isn't nearly as good as the old one. I think our former lead died in a fire at their house or something like that.

As usual, I buckle down and hyper focus on my work. Data entry is pretty easy and straightforward, but it can be incredibly time consuming. I've got a mountain of papers to get through and unfortunately, the sources of these pages aren't using the same format. I keep having to hunt for the information I'm looking for and it's slowing things down.

It doesn't help that I keep getting text messages from Trevor asking me the dumbest questions. It ranges from basic stuff he should already know to stuff that he should be asking IT about. I get so annoyed that I start ignoring the damn messages and wish this was one of those times I'd misplace my phone.

After getting through an inch of the stack of papers on my desk, Trevor actually comes to my cubicle. He asks if I've been here the whole time, and I look at him with confusion. Where the hell else would I be? I know I've been ignoring his messages, but why would he think I've been anywhere else?

He notices the stack of completed papers and comments in a disappointed voice, "For someone who decided to work through lunch, I thought you'd be farther along."

What the hell is Trevor talking about? It's not even 11am yet. A quick glance at the clock on the wall shows it to not only be past 11am, but it's 1pm. How the hell did I lose more than two hours and not be aware of it? There's usually a feeling that comes over you when you lose time, making it obvious that that's what happened when you realize it. This isn't like that at all. It's like time jumped on me, not that I lost it. I, of course, don't share this with Trevor. He wouldn't understand and I don't feel like explaining facets of my life that he doesn't need to know about.

I'm a creature of simple tastes and habits. It's well known that I bring my lunch with me everyday instead of going out like most of my coworkers do. Trevor apparently came to my cubicle to invite me to lunch with the rest of the team around noon, but I just ignored him. He thought I was irritated with all the messages he sent me and shrugged it off. I know I can hyper focus when I'm working, but I usually come out of it when someone talks to me. I have absolutely no memory of Trevor stopping by before now. That's just bizarre.

When Trevor finally goes away, I take my sandwich, and the snack size can of chips out of my desk. While I work, I snack on them, trying to make up for the eerily lost time. On the upside, I manage to speed through and get caught up, only having half the pile left by the time 5pm comes around. As I get up to leave, I look around and notice that the other members of my team have more than half their stacks left. Even with more than two hours simply gone, I still got ahead of them.

Parking my car in my numbered spot, I walk up the three flights of stairs to my apartment. I made the conscious choice of living on the top floor so I don't have to hear upstairs neighbors making a racket above me. With that being said, I am pretty light of foot, and make sure not to make too much of a racket myself, though some people can never be satisfied. I am a klutz after all.

As I get to the second-floor landing, Miss Kingsbury, a seventy-one-year-old widow with nothing better to do than butt into everyone else's business, comes out of her apartment. I swear, she can either hear me coming or keeps an eye out her window for my arrival. I wouldn't mind it so much if she was asking me to do something like take a heavy bag of trash to the dumpster for her, which she used to do when I first moved in. Unfortunately, she lives directly below me and always has to berate me for stumbling around upstairs.

Last night, as I was heading off to bed, I tripped over my damn coffee table when I got up off the couch and landed on the floor with a hard thud. This also caused a lamp to fall over and crash on the floor, breaking the porcelain into a thousand pieces. She goes into her usual spiel about me being inconsiderate, and that my constant habit of banging around in my apartment is disturbing her birds. It always ends with me apologizing, but she ignores it in favor of swearing she's going to file a complaint against me. If she actually did it every time she threatened to, I'm sure I would've been kicked out of the complex by now.

I close the door of my apartment with her voice still calling up to me. After dumping my bag of fast food on the coffee table, I go to the fridge and take out a small bottle of apple juice. Reaching into a cabinet for a plastic cup, I grab the bottle of Carmel whiskey next to the fridge and pour in three fingers. Once that's back in its spot, I unscrew the cap on the juice and pour the whole bottle in, stirring it with a chopstick as I do. I've never been a fan of beer, so I make simple drinks like this whenever I want alcohol. I call it a Carmel Apple.

I take my drink to the coffee table and sit down to a quick dinner of burger and fries. It's not the healthiest thing in the world, but I'm too tired to do anything more complex. As I eat a handful of fries, my phone dings at me. Looking to it, I see all the missed messages from Trevor and an alarm that went unnoticed. Shit, I didn't wind my pocket watch like I was supposed to. I quickly pull it out and wind it up. As I do, it occurs to me that the time I completely lost was around the time I forgot to wind the watch. Strange.

The next day starts off as it always does, except for one thing. My pile of work increases before I even get started. Normally they wait for us to finish what's on our plate before dumping more on us. Either something big is going on in management, or Trevor is screwing with the natural order of things. I'm just glad there aren't insanely large data packets flooding the system and slowing things down. It's a giant pain in the ass when that happens.

I dive right in, only taking my eyes off the screen and papers to sip at my coffee. Even then I don't have to look away for long, if at all. Half the time I'm not even aware I'm doing it, which is why it comes to me as a surprise when I lift my mug only to find it empty. As much as I want to keep working, I didn't sleep well last night, and more caffeine is needed.

Going into the break room, my phone buzzes in my pocket as I pick up the coffee pot. I kill the alarm and fill my mug, going to the fridge for cream. Once I've got my coffee doctored to my liking, I reach into my pocket and pull out the pocket watch. Sadly, winding this thing one handed isn't a task I've managed yet, so I wait until I get back to my cubicle to wind it.

Setting my mug down and taking my seat, I wind the watch, slip it back into my pocket and get back to work. As I input data, I reach for the mug and take a sip. The moment it touches my tongue, I spit the coffee back out. What the hell? It's ice cold and tastes like it's been sitting out for hours. I just made this mug, so what gives?

Getting up to grab the box of tissues to clean off my computer screen, I notice something very wrong in the room. There's always a low murmur of activity in the office. Between idle chatter, the click and clack of keyboards and the copier spitting out papers, the office is never quiet during business hours. Now that I realize how quiet it is, I step into the tiny hallway among the cubicles and realize half of the lights are off. They only do that after everyone's gone home for the day and maintenance has come through to do clean up.

What the hell? How did it jump from 11am to… I look to the clock on the wall and see that it's 6:37pm. How did I lose that much time? It's not possible. Trevor didn't come talk to me at all that I'm aware of, nor did he message me like he normally does. That gets me to check my phone, and sure enough, there are several missed messages.

The first few are his regular dumb questions, but after that the messages are irritated. He complains that it's not professional for me to ignore him like this and that if I value my job, I should get back to him. There are several messages along this line, then an hour break between them and the last two. It occurred to him that I might've lost my phone. Well, I lost a lot more than my damn phone.

As I shut down my workstation, I try to make sense of this. Yesterday I lost time when I forgot to wind my pocket watch, but I did it today and still lost time. I go over it all in my head and it dawns on me. When I realized I forgot to wind the watch yesterday, I wound it up. Leaving work at 5pm, wading through traffic, stopping at the exceptionally long drive-through, then dealing with Miss Kingsbury, by the time I wound the watch it was a little after 6:30pm.

None of this is making sense, but Ethan's words come back to me. He said I need to wind the watch everyday at the same time and that I should keep it in my pocket. Maybe if I leave it in my desk this weird lost time shit will stop happening.

Removing the clip from my belt loop, I drop the watch into my middle desk drawer, lock it and move to the exit. As I do, a strange sensation bubbles in my stomach, like I'm moving very fast in a way that is completely alien to me. I reach out a hand to the stairwell door, and as soon as I touch it, the feeling is gone.

Before I can push the door open, someone calls my name from behind me. I turn to see the room is lit up like it's the middle of the workday and Trevor is standing there looking very confused. "Where the hell have you been? No one's seen you in days." I'm about to ask him what the hell he's talking about, but then that feeling bubbles in my stomach again. After a few moments it goes away and I find the room half lit again, completely empty.

If Trevor was right, I've somehow lost multiple days, but this is different than before. The other times it appeared that I was still in place, seen by anyone that happened by. There's no way that I've been standing at the stairwell door for multiple days, and no one saw me. Half the office uses the stairs because we have the world's slowest elevators and it's just easier to climb two floors than wait in the lobby. I think that sensation bubbling up in my stomach is me physically moving through time instead of just losing it.

I rush back to my desk, but halfway there, it

happens again. Unfortunately, the sensation comes and goes faster, and I only get a few minutes in the filled office. It's enough for me to glance at a calendar hanging in someone's cubicle, and if they've been keeping current with it, I've been gone for almost two weeks.

When I get back to my desk the office is back to half lit. All my stuff is still where I left it, which I find surprising. I was afraid my desk would've been cleared out after no showing for two weeks. The only thing missing is the usual stack of papers that have yet to be gone through. As quick as I can, I take my keys out of my pocket and fumble with the locked drawer.

That sensation starts to bubble in my stomach again, and I become frantic. I'm worried about how much more time I'm going to lose and if I don't get at the watch now, it might not be there when I get back. Slipping the key into the lock is harder than it should be, but I manage it, nearly snapping the damn thing in half. Reaching inside, I grasp the watch and pull it out quickly, but my frantic movements make me screw up.

The clip on the end of the chain catches on the lip of the drawer, and the watch slips out of my hand. I watch it in near slow motion as it descends to the floor and hear a crack of glass when it hits. Kneeling down, worry and dread mixing in my head, I reach down and pick it up. The soft ticking that I used to ignore is no longer there. The second hand is as still as the grave behind glass that is fractured all over. There's even a piece missing from the middle and a spring is poking out.

I feel completely and utterly screwed as I look at the broken antique, but then Trevor's surprised and confused voice breaks me out of my trance. He once again asks where I've been and I make up something about going on sabbatical, orders from my therapist. Looking at me skeptically, he understandably claims that HR never informed him about this. Since it's a load of shit to begin with, I mask my recovering reactions to being back in real time with irritation, blaming HR's incompetence. Honestly, if there's anyone in this building more absent minded than me it would be those clowns.

I'll have to reach out to my uncle for a backdated note to explain my absence, which he'll do with no questions asked. He was always the fun uncle, and it wouldn't be the first time he's written a note for me, though this is the first time since I graduated high school. Even though it's the middle of the day, I leave the office with promises that I'll be back tomorrow to sort all this out. With any luck, I'll still have a job.

Being gone for as long as I have been, I'm amazed to see that my car is still in the garage. Then again, I do park on the second to highest floor, and getting a tow from here is a giant pain in the ass. Even more surprising, my car starts up without an issue. I was sure I'd at least need a jump or something like that.

Driving home, I try to process what happened, but I've got a lot of unanswered questions. Most importantly, how the hell was it possible to begin with? I think the first step is going to be tracking down the store my cousin bought the watch from. The name had been carved into the box it came in, and at the time, I'd thought it funny that I was opening Pandora's Box. I guess Ethan is still holding a grudge against me for what he thinks I did, which I still maintain that I didn't. I believe he meant for me to get lost in time, but like all his big plans, things didn't turn out how he wanted.

MOONLIGHT CABIN

I have not had what anyone would call an easy life. Leaving home at the tender age of thirteen doesn't sound like the smartest move, but if I hadn't, I wouldn't be here today. My old man was more than just abusive, and my mother wasn't much better. She may never have raised a hand to me like he did, but she did other things. She had to make money somehow to fund her drug habit and she sure as hell couldn't be bothered to get a job. The regular nine to five of corporate life wasn't in their wheelhouse.

Between my father's rage and my mother's tendency to rent me out to any sexual deviant with money, my death wasn't far off if I didn't leave when I did. Being from the part of town I was, I'd known plenty of foster kids and heard a shit ton of horror stories. Most didn't have it as badly as I had with my so-called parents, but I was looking to better my situation, not trade one hell for another.

I lived on the streets for a long time, doing things for money that no one that young should ever have to do. When things in the city got too tough, or the red and blue flashing lights got too frequent, I relocated. Hitchhiking back then wasn't nearly as dangerous as it is these days, but I again found myself having to do things I'd rather forget about.

By the time I was sixteen, I'd made it clear across the country and was living in the woods. I took some of the hard-earned money I'd accumulated and bought myself a tent and sleeping bag. Living off the land wasn't easy and I was tired of doing horrible things to get by, so I made some changes. I was going to join one of those twenty-four-hour gyms so I'd have a place to shower, but there was a help-wanted sign in the window, and I amended my plans.

I've always been on the skinny side since my parents never cared enough to feed me much, but between living on the streets and in the woods, I had some decent lean muscle. The gym didn't pay much, but since I still lived in a tent and had a place to shower, I didn't need much more than food and maybe some new clothes. When I wasn't working, I tended to workout until it got close to dark. My campsite was deep in the woods, and hard to find in the dark, just what I wanted.

There were downsides to living in the woods. Anyone could happen upon you, it got really cold in the winter since I'd traveled further north than I was used to, and there was the occasional wild animal. I even got bitten by a freaking wolf once, but that was the worst of what happened. Compared to my childhood, I counted myself lucky. Between constantly having to gather and chopping firewood to keep warm, and all the working out I did at the gym, my scrawny, lean muscled frame filled out.

By the time I turned nineteen, I decided I wanted more than just a tent in the woods. I started looking for a small apartment, but the only one I could afford was a lot farther from work than I wanted. It would've taken me a couple hours to get to and from the gym, so I kept looking. In my wandering, sadly on the crappier side of town, I came across an establishment with a help wanted sign on their door. I went inside, having no idea what this place was, but as soon as I had the door open, I knew. The Moonlight Cabin was more than just a dive bar.

The bar was worn down, poorly stocked and I already knew the booze was watered down, but it wasn't the main attraction. There were two different circular platforms, and a main stage, tables and chairs scattered about the place. Along the opposite wall from the bar were booths with curtains and chairs. Being from a physically and sexually abusive home, I'd never cared to go to a strip club, but that's where I found myself.

I didn't bother looking at the stage to see the woman dancing because I was massively uncomfortable. Turning to walk right back outside, an older woman stopped me from her stool next to the door, behind the sorriest excuse for a counter I'd ever seen. She asked to see my ID, but I told her I wasn't interested in the show. I meant that to sound like I made a mistake in coming inside, which it was. How she took it changed my life forever.

She took one look at me and said I had the job, before telling me what the job was. I was thoroughly confused and looked to the stage to make sure there was a woman and not a man preforming. It was indeed a woman, and I breathed a sigh of relief. Strip clubs are always looking for new talent, so they don't hang help wanted signs outside for the dancers. The sign was for the position of bouncer, which she thought I was there to apply for.

Her name as Anita, and before I could tell her that I wasn't interested, she told me about the job. Not the duties and responsibilities, but the pay and benefits. It paid more than I was making at the gym, and if I worked both jobs, I'd not only be able to afford a small apartment, but I'd be able to get myself a crappy little used car.

My only vices were drinking and smoking, but I never got drunk, and I wasn't interested in drugs even a little. That crap reminded me too much of my mother and the last thing I ever wanted was to be reminded of them. My father always drank the cheapest, crappiest beer his meager means could afford. I prefer simple mixed drinks, usually a liquor mixed with soda, but have found a brand of beer I don't mind. The only thing my parents didn't do when I was around was smoke cigarettes.

Since I was still pinching pennies and didn't have much in the way of extra money, I smoked cheap cigarettes. I either used a book of matches that I got for free from certain gas stations, or I bummed a light from Anita or one of the dancers whenever I had a smoke. I wasn't allowed to drink while working, but Anita had no issues with me smoking.

In my first few months as the bouncer, the dancers kept their distance from me. Typically, I stayed near the door, but I'd periodically walk around, especially when one of our headliners was on stage. I never really paid attention to their performances because it was my responsibility to provide them with the safest work environment that I could. They didn't need me leering at them like all the horny losers that came in to throw money at them. Besides, with my background, sex wasn't something that was really ever on my mind. Anita actually thought I might be gay for the longest time.

Apparently, every bouncer she employed before me was always trying to sleep with the ladies and used their position as protector to coerce them. It explained why the ladies kept their distance from me, but I didn't mind. If it made them feel safer to keep away from me, then I was okay with it. People paying attention to me always made me feel uncomfortable. When I was a kid, the most peace I had in my parent's house was when they didn't notice me. That kind of thing is hard to break from.

My behavior compared to the men in my position before me started getting noticed by the ladies. They didn't entirely trust it, but they did actually start speaking to me. It didn't go unnoticed that my presence was equally apparent regardless of who was on stage. A lot of my predecessors only made themselves known when the headliners were performing, but I wasn't doing that. It didn't matter if it was the middle of a weekday, or during the busy times on the weekends, I was always there as a menacing shadow wandering the place in case a customer got out of hand.

About six months in, and I had my first serious confrontation. Before then it had been a drunk asshole getting a little handsy with one of the ladies. I tended to come up behind them, place my hands on their shoulders and squeezed really hard, asking if there was a problem. Up to then, it was all that I needed to do.

This regular we used to have, Joey, was a self-entitled prick, probably the worst I'd ever seen. He would slap the waitresses on the ass, get handsy with the dancers, and rough during lap dances. The first time I saw him slap Constance, one of our fulltime waitresses, I was going to go over and correct his behavior, but Anita stopped me. Joey spent a lot of money in this place and if I got on him, he'd take his cash elsewhere. I didn't like it, but Anita was the boss, so I did what she told me. That is until our main headliner came out.

Blake is way too beautiful and talented to be

dancing at the Moonlight Cabin. I don't mean that our other dancers aren't pretty or don't have their own talents, but Blake is and always has been on a whole different level. She's probably the one dancer that's actually caught my eye, on or off the stage, but I always did my best to treat her like the others. At five foot four, her jet-black hair reached down to her mid back, and she was sporting a midsize D-cup. She also had nicely thick thighs and a beautiful backside that got everyone's attention. The only thing covering any of her pale skin was a generous sprinkle of freckles, no tattoos or scars to speak of. I never thought of her in a sexual way, but I did find myself tempted to contemplate the possibility. A first for me.

Things always seem to get rowdier on the night of a full moon, and on this night, Joey decided he wanted more attention from Blake than a few dances. He was offering her a fat wad of cash to go back to his place and get horizontal. What the ladies do after they leave here is their business, but it is against house policy for the ladies to agree to something like this while here. Blake flat out refused Joey's offer, claiming it had nothing to do with that wad of cash being mostly singles. Joey didn't take too kindly to being denied.

I saw it coming, but I was too far away to prevent it from happening. I knew Anita wasn't at the front counter like she normally was, so she couldn't give me the go ahead or tell me to keep back, but at that point, it didn't matter. This was the first time one of the ladies was actually struck on my watch, and that was something I didn't take too kindly to.

Joey was reaching back to give Blake another hard slap to the face, but before he could, I had my hand around his throat and his feet were no longer on the ground. Up to that point, I didn't let on to exactly how strong I actually was, but everyone in the joint saw it in that instance. Bringing Joey closer to my face, I said, "We have a special room in the back for naughty boys like you."

Anita had shown me the backroom when I first started. It was pretty much a utility closet with a chair inside that had restraints on it. The chair was solid metal and bolted into the cement floor. The restraints were no joke either, consisting of two layers of thick leather that acted as padding against the steel chains hidden inside. You could strap a freaking bear into this chair, and it wouldn't get out.

Honestly, it hadn't been because Joey dared to hit Blake. I'd have done this regardless of which dancer he struck. Hell, I'd have done it if he hit Anita. The beating I gave him in that room was nearly as bad as I'd gotten on the regular from my father. In fact, I kept seeing my father's face while I pummeled Joey. It wasn't until Anita came bursting into the room that I stopped hitting the jackass. She told me that she'd deal with him, and I walked out to clean myself up.

Once I was clean of blood and sweat, I went to check on Blake, but the other dancers in the dressing room said she locked herself in their private bathroom. Anita had gone in there to talk to her and that's how she found out about where I'd taken Joey. I went back out to my perch next to the door and continued on with my shift, no one aware I was wearing a different black t-shirt. The other one was in the trash thanks to all the blood.

Eventually Anita came back out and said that Blake was doing okay. Joey looked like a mean guy, but apparently, he hits like a twelve-year-old girl. I think she told me this to get a laugh out of me, but I didn't so much as smirk. I wasn't in the mood for levity.

Anita went back to her stool, but I couldn't help noticing that she was acting a little differently. Normally she sat there with a bored expression on her face and propped up her head by resting her cheek in her hand. At that time, she sat up straighter and I kept catching her looking at me. It wasn't to give me a signal to get someone under control. After I lifted Joey off his feet, all the customers were on their best behavior. For some of them, I think they paid more attention to me than they did the dancers. This is exactly what I tried to avoid by hiding my true strength. I hate being noticed.

After that night, Joey was never seen at the Moonlight Cabin again. All the ladies started treating me differently too. During the off hours they often sought me out to chat, and most of them even found out about my job at the gym. Not sure how they found that out, but the majority of them joined the gym. At the time I'd moved up to personal trainer and they all wanted my attention for that. Well, to be perfectly honest about it, I think they wanted more than my attention.

It was weird that they all started paying more attention to me, but it didn't change things. I was more friendly with them, got to know them better, but I wasn't interested in a relationship, be it casual, sexual or serious. Even Blake was paying special attention to me, offering to give me a lap dance free of charge. I admit that her eyes were awfully captivating, but I never took her up on the offer. A month after the incident with Joey, I got quite a surprise.

When we close up for the night, I always walk

the ladies to their cars and make sure they get on their way without incident. Before my time, it wasn't uncommon for customers to linger around outside so they could get themselves something extra. That stopped happening when my intimidating form started gracing the cabin.

Blake was the last one out the door, which was odd all on its own. Normally she was one of the first ones to leave, but not that night. For some reason she took longer to get her stuff together, to the point where Anita left before she did, which never happened. I walked her outside, but the only car left in the lot was mine. Confused, I turned to her, and she held up a small black box. A gift for being a perfect gentleman and defender.

Inside was a shiny, one-of-a-kind lighter. Around the engraved standard shell of these metal lighters was a metal claw, made to look like a wolf's claw. I'd never seen anything like it and could only guess as to how much it cost. At first I refused the gift, saying it was too much, but Blake wouldn't hear of it. She kept telling me how much of a good guy I am, and that I treat her and the others better than anyone else ever has.

Maybe it was the sincerity in her eyes and the tone she used to convince me, but I accepted the lighter and offered to drive her home. It was my intent to simply drop her off, but as I drove the way she told me, I realized the way she directed me was way too familiar. When I parked my crappy car, I was in front of my own apartment building. First she found out about my other job, now she'd figured out where I lived. As far as stalkers go, I could've done a hell of a lot worse.

It took a little convincing, but I agreed to letting Blake in for a drink. She'd been trying everything over the last month to get to me, more so than the other ladies had, but that night she said something that hit me hard. Blake said she felt safe with me. I wasn't the kind of guy that would try to force myself on her, someone that didn't want anything more from her than to be her friend and to make sure she was safe.

She ended up staying the night, but all we did was sleep. That happened nearly every night for a couple weeks, but even though she was more than willing, Blake wouldn't push me. She wanted me to be as comfortable with her as she was with me. It was probably obvious that I came from an abusive background. Most of the people in this industry do.

Eventually, what won me over was one night, while we were sleeping, Blake was having a nightmare, the kind where you're physically fighting against something that isn't there. I held her in my arms to try to calm her, and she was asleep the whole time. As soon as my arms were around her, she calmed, as if my physical presence was the thing that chased back the monsters living in her head. We were an official couple after that.

It's been a couple years since then, and not much has changed. Blake and I live together now, and though all the dancers still act like they've got a crush on me, I'm monogamous with Blake. She may do her dance, give lap dances and turn on every guy in the joint, but she's only got eyes for me. Things between us are pretty serious.

Last month, on the night of the full moon, a bunch of rowdy frat boy type douchebags graced the club with fat wads of cash. They were loud, drinking a lot, but spending a lot of money, more than I thought college dipshits should've had. When Blake came out to do her thing, those guys lost their damn minds. Yeah, they made it rain, but for some reason, it made one of the pricks think it gave him special privileges. He got up on stage with her and started putting his hands all over her. This had happened once since we got together, and Blake had handled the situation well until I calmly got the guy off stage. For some reason on this night, I wasn't handling the situation too well.

I dragged that little shit off stage and took him to the backroom. His friends didn't try to fight me after I gave them my hard stare and stayed where they were. I tuned the asshole up really well, but before I'd had my fill, Anita came into the backroom. She told me she would handle it from there, and though I wanted to stay, I relented. Good thing too, because another one of the frat boys was getting fresh with Candice.

It wasn't happening on stage, but at the end of the bar near the door to the back area. I got him in a headlock, covered his mouth and discretely dragged him out of sight. It was so quick and quiet that only Candice noticed what had happened, and that's only because she was facing me when I did it. When I opened the door to the backroom to teach this guy a lesson, I froze in place. There was blood everywhere, and for the first time, something other than freckles sprinkled across that pale skin.

Blake stood there with the guy I'd already roughed up restrained in the chair. She wasn't as I knew her to be, but slightly off. Her ears were longer on the top, coming to points. Her mouth had gotten wider and were filled with predatory sharp teeth. That same mouth that I had kissed thousands of times was covered in blood and chunks of flesh were in her teeth. Even her hands had become dangerous claws.

Her voice was deeper when she spoke. I'd interrupted her dinner break, but it looked like I brought her some dessert. Without saying a word, I tossed the guy I had in a headlock into the room, closed the door and walked away.

So many things didn't make sense to me at that moment, so I did the only thing I could think of. I went out to my stool, asked Candice if she would be kind enough to get me a whiskey and soda, and lit a smoke. Anita came out from the backroom almost a full hour later. She kept her eyes averted, not daring to meet my gaze. I wasn't angry or afraid. Mostly confused.

It had never occurred to me before that Blake and Anita were never in the same room together. They always left at different times, and I never saw Anita outside of work. Forgetting for the moment that they look absolutely nothing alike, how is it possible that they're the same person? Not that an answer to that explains what I'd just seen in the backroom, but it does explain why all the major troublemakers were never seen again.

By this point, I was head over heels in love with Blake. Due to my time on the streets, I know there are things in this world that can't be explained. Hell, the only reason I managed to convince myself the wolf that attacked me years ago hadn't been a werewolf was because I didn't change when the full moon came the next month. As far as the dead guys in the back, I'm no angel. I've killed people before, but I never ate them. Even starving hadn't made me resort to cannibalism, though I doubted that would be the term for Blakes case. When she finally dared to look up at me, I told her we needed to talk when we got home. It felt very strange saying that to Anita, but I knew better now.

It turned out that there wasn't even a name for what Blake is. She's a kind of shape shifter that can choose her form, but there's one that she can't always control. It's the flesh hungry one I saw in the backroom. The closest thing she can figure it to be is a kind of fairy, and not the kind from fairy tales.

This is more like the Fey which tend to be more like monsters than Pixies and Sprites. The only way she can keep the flesh hungry form sustained is by eating a person once a month. The whole full moon thing is just a convenient way for her to keep track of when she needs to feed. Her Blake form is her original form, and Anita is just something she created to run the cabin.

As I said, by this point I was already in love with Blake, in it to the end. My only question for her was, if she bit me, would I become like her? Tonight is the full moon, and her flesh hungry form is going to feed. We'll see if I'm joining in on the feast, or just catering it.

LONG HOURS

Being on the bottom rung really sucks, but everyone has to start somewhere. If my dad had been some rich donor to the university, I wouldn't be some lowly research assistant. Then again, if I came from a rich family, I might be doing something completely different with my life. Odds are I'd end up being one of those rich assholes I always see when I'm working in the dining hall between classes. The me of this reality would probably think the me of that reality is a douchebag, but money has a way of doing that to people and those without it resent them for having it. You can thank my philosophy class for that little tangent.

My college experience hasn't been the nonstop party everyone in high school thought it would be. Any time I'm not in class or studying, I'm working in the dining hall or assisting Professor Meyers with her latest obsession. With any other professor it would be called a project, but not with Meyers. Not by a long shot.

Professor Meyers gets so obsessed with her work that it damn near consumes her world. That's okay when you're single, have no family, and research is your job. She's usually left to her own devices as long as she continues to teach her classes, but there are times when she neglects even that. Her teaching assistant does most of the work anyway, so that at least is covered.

As her research assistant, I get to be apart of what is most important to her. Don't get the wrong idea, this comes with a lot of drawbacks. I don't actually help her with her research like my job title suggests. I'm more responsible for maintaining her while she's working. This also means she likes to monopolize my time. There's nothing she can do about the time I spend in class and at work, but anything outside that belongs to her. Those are her words, not mine.

I have a desk in her workspace that I get to sit at when she isn't demanding something of me. It's the place where I get to work on my classwork most of the time, and also where I get most of my sleep. Sundays usually end up being the only day I have for myself, but even that's a fifty-fifty shot. At least I'm paid hourly, but it's only minimum wage, and overtime is demanded, but I don't get time and a half for it. What a fucking jip.

You'd think this kind of monopolization of my time would indicate that I never get laid, but that couldn't be farther from the truth. When I said I maintain Professor Meyers while she's working, I mean that in a lot of ways. To her, sex is a biological necessity like eating, drinking, and sleeping, just not one that needs to be satisfied quite as often. It doesn't matter to her who she gets it from, only that she gets off.

The woman is a relentless slave driver, but it's not like I can tell her no. If I get on her bad side, she could ruin everything for me. The only way I can afford to come to this university is on a scholarship, and even then, I need the dining hall job to help on top of the pittance I get paid from her. I'm still digging myself into a serious financial hole, but once I graduate, I should be able to get a good job. If I can manage that, then all the shit I'm going through will be worth it. At least, that's what I'm telling myself. Here's hoping it's not a pipe dream.

The professor's latest obsession is an ancient book that she's been trying to translate. As far as I can tell, she has no idea what the contents of the brown leather tome are, but she's insistent that it's important. I haven't been allowed to handle the book myself, but I've seen inside it enough when I bring her food or drink. If it wasn't for me, she'd have starved to death a long time ago. She gets that wrapped up in her work.

The odd writing is like nothing I've ever seen, and as a studying linguist, I'm at least a little familiar with nearly every current language in use. I haven't dabbled in many of the dead languages, but I've seen samples of some written. I can honestly say I've never come across something with so many curves and sharp angles before. If you unfocus your eyes while looking at the text, it almost looks like a combination of Cyrillic and Korean.

The tome contains more than just text the professor hasn't figured out how to read. There are drawings scattered amongst the pages. Some of them are crude while others are rather detailed. What I find the most fascinating is how well kept the ink on paper is. Usually something this old is faded and impossible to discern. These pages, though impossible to read, look as if they were created yesterday.

When I got my first glimpse inside the tome, I asked Professor Meyers if she was sure the book was actually as ancient as she'd been led to believe. Oh damn, had that been a mistake. She'd been there when the relic was first discovered during a dig in some country I'd never heard of. Of course she had the book tested, and sure enough, it was several hundred years old.

Over the last three months, she's been studying

the drawings, having gotten nowhere with the text itself. Recently, she'd been focused on one image in particular. Professor Meyers claimed there was something about it that kept nagging at her, but she couldn't figure out why. I didn't have to sneak a look at this picture like I did for most of what I'd seen in the book.

In order to better study the image, Professor Meyers took several photos of the page. She even used a lot of scientific tricks to uncover anything hidden, but nothing was as far as she found. These images have been blown up and plastered to the walls of the workspace for the last week. I've started seeing the damn thing in my dreams.

A man with some kind of ceremonial goat's head mask stands to the left of an alter, an oddly shaped tablet in his hands. On the altar is the body of a slender girl, naked and chained. A second man stands on the other side of the alter, a large weapon in his hands. I never could decide if the weapon was some kind of blade, or blunter than a sharp edge, but it's a weapon I've never seen.

It's clear that this image is depicting some kind of human sacrifice, but that's all I can get from it. Professor Meyers has been obsessing over the image hard, even going so far as to keep her eyes glued to it while demanding I pleasure her. Sex with her can be pretty cold, but shortly after I started, she got crazy into it. Probably the most intense sex we've had, but the fact that she was always looking at the image was disturbing.

Afterwards, while we both were enjoying a post-coital cigarette, my eyes were drawn to the tablet held by the goat headed man. It was a very discernable shape, almost wavy at the top and jagged at the bottom. It was clear that there were etchings on it, but they were nothing more than indistinguishable lines. Before that moment, it didn't occur to me that it was a stone tablet. I'd seen something just like that before. I made the mistake of telling Professor Meyers that.

Two semesters ago I was taking an intro to dead languages course. Before I dropped the class because I decided to focus on current languages, I ended up at a lecture given by a visiting professor. He spoke of several tongues that have long since been dead, and different avenues for the written word. One of the examples was etching into stone tablets, and he had photos of various stone tablets that had miraculously survived the harshness of time. He even claimed to have one such tablet in his possession at his university, and it's the one that looks like the one in the picture. I know this because there were several different pictures of it in his slideshow.

After a series of phone calls and a lot of pleading mixed with less than vague threats, Professor Meyers failed in getting the other professor to loan her the stone tablet. According to the easily irritable man on the other side of the phone, the tablet is a priceless artifact that he won't trust another living soul with. He claimed it is under the highest security and it takes going through a mountain of red tape just to gain access to it.

Professor Meyers wasn't convinced by the man's avalanche of bullshit. This sort of thing is common in the academic community. Scholars and researchers are extremely protective of their sources, resources, and notes. They always fear someone will come along and make off with their work to make a breakthrough of their own. He wouldn't even send over a picture of the tablet just so she could see the etchings.

There isn't a lot you can do in this situation. The best Professor Meyers could do is get the university president to reach out to their president and try to broker a deal. The downside of that is it takes a long time to negotiate something like that and it often costs someone a lot of money one way or another. Considering no one really knows what Professor Meyers is up to, there's no way our president is going to even attempt it. Since I don't know what all this is about either and I'm in on her work, there's nothing I can do to help the situation. Or at least I thought.

In my youth, I was less than a law biding citizen. I got myself into some crazy situations and obtained certain skills that I try really hard not to utilize. Criminal activity, no matter how small, can ruin any chance at getting the kind of jobs I want. I've kept my nose clean since I was eighteen, until now. Professor Meyers knew nothing of my past, but she threatened to ruin my future if I didn't find a way to get her that tablet. I never should've opened my fucking mouth.

Now here I am, driving back from the other university, a stolen artifact and box full of notes in my trunk. The other professor's claim of high security had been a crock of shit. A child with a paperclip and a pair of scissors could've picked those locks. The man's workspace wasn't even that big, the size of a standard office. I did think it was odd that there was a box of gloves sitting next to the tablet, but I was already wearing gloves, just not rubber ones. He didn't even have the artifact in a protective case or anything like that. It was just sitting out in the open and I spotted it as soon as I got in the door. For someone paranoid that someone would come along and steal his work, he didn't do much to protect his assets.

The pitch-black road stretches on and on in front of me. I haven't seen another car for at least an hour. It's still technically Saturday night, but I have two more states to drive through. A look at the clock tells me I've been awake for more than twenty-four hours. The cold dregs of my fifth cup of truck stop coffee isn't going to do it, so I reach into the plastic bag for one of the half dozen energy drinks I purchased.

The only upside to this whole insane excursion is that Professor Meyers game me a few hundred dollars for travel expenses. It's part of a discretionary fund she has access to, and I don't even need to give her receipts. Of course, I take advantage of that. Every fuel stop I've had to make, I purchase at minimum one twenty dollar scratch off. So far, I've managed to double the money she gave me. This is going into my emergency fund as soon as I can get to the bank.

My eyes start drooping again, and that's my cue to pull out another cigarette. Loud music and caffeine can only do so much. As I put the cig in my mouth, I reach down for the lighter and there's a sudden boom. My car becomes hard to control, and I slow down to a stop on the side of the road. Well, I'm fucking awake now.

Knowing this isn't anything good, I go ahead and light the cigarette before getting out of the car. I get the feeling I'm going to really want one when I see what happened. Taking in that first drag, I once again find myself regretting all the decisions I've made that have led me to this place. Hindsight sucks.

The back right tire blew out on me, but it

doesn't look like I hit something. The tires are a bit old and worn down, so that explains why the sidewall gave out. At least it was only the one tire, but I do need to figure out how I'm going to budget getting new tires. Sadly, this isn't the first time this has happened to me, but my experience has made me better prepared than times before.

Last time I had a tire go out on me, I had one of those donut spare tires in the trunk, and I barely got the car to the shop before that piece of crap went out. While I was there, I decided to upgrade my spare to a full-on regular tire. They say you're not supposed to go more than fifty miles with a donut, either in distance or speed. I wanted something that wouldn't hinder me at all if I needed to use it.

Popping the trunk, I have to pull out the stuff I stole. The stone tablet sits at the top of the open box, and I have to admit, I do find myself having trouble not looking at it. That's why I put it in the trunk instead of the passenger seat like I'd originally intended. I also take out the large tool bag that holds my roadside assistance kit before removing the floor piece. Getting the spare tire and tools out is easy, but jacking the car up and removing the lug nuts takes some effort.

By the time I get the spare on and stow away the ruined tire, I'm covered in sweat and grime. Since this isn't my first rodeo, I take out a few shop towels from the roadside bag, and a bottle of water to wet them down. Originally I had a package of baby wipes in the bag, but the last time I tried to use them, they were completely dried out. With my current set up, it's not an issue. I clean off my hands first, getting as much of the black crap off me as I can. Next I scrub my face and neck, not sure if I had any of the grime on me there, but it feels nice anyway.

Gathering up my trash, I notice one of the wet shop towels dropped into the open box. I remove the dirty towel and notice a wet spot on the stone tablet. I don't know if water will damage something so old like this, so I pick up the stone and dap at the spot with a clean towel. The stone is oddly cold despite the unseasonably warm weather.

After returning the stone to the box, and all my stuff to the trunk, I return to the driver seat. Getting back on the road, I immediately feel tired all over again. With several hours still ahead of me, I debate stopping somewhere to get some rest. Unfortunately, I haven't seen any motels or rest stops in the last several hours, and there are no signs indicating that any are coming up.

Pulling off to the side of the road and taking a nap seems like a really bad idea, especially with stolen goods in the trunk. I just need to press on and get this over with. Maybe once the professor has this stuff in her possession I can finally get a decent break. Doubtful, but if I pass out at my desk from exhaustion, there won't be anything she can do to wake me up.

I pop open another energy drink and barely get a sip when something darts across the road in front of me. Slamming on the breaks and cranking the wheel to the side, I drop the can as I try to avoid hitting whatever the hell that is. I only caught a glimpse of it, not enough to know if it was a dog or what, but the coloring of it had been white. I think that's the only reason I was able to see it.

After quickly picking up the spilled drink, amazed only a little splashed onto the floor, I look around. There are no signs of the thing that ran out in front of me, which is good. I didn't hear a thump or anything like that, so I believe I avoided hitting it. As I place the energy drink in my cup holder, I see that my hands are shaking. I can feel my heart jackhammering in my chest. I'm wide awake again, but these wakeup calls really need to stop.

Everything in the car has been thrown around, and I suddenly worry that the stone tablet may have been damaged. Quickly, I get out of the car and open the trunk. The box is on its side, a mess of papers are scattered all over the place. I find the tablet hiding under a notebook, and thankfully, the stone is still intact. Exhaling a sigh of relief, I gather up the papers and put everything back in the box, closing it this time. I don't leave the tablet on top either but stashed in the middle in case something like that happens again.

Just when I have the box closed up, I hear the sound of something hard stepping on the road, and whirl around. Standing in the middle of the street is a white goat with large horns on top of its head. Had this been the thing that darted in front of me? If it was, why did it come back?

Closing the trunk lid, I turn to the goat and try to shoo it away, but it continues to stand there. I really don't know what to make of this, so I get in my car and get it back on the road. As I point myself in the right direction, I look over to the goat, but it's not there anymore. I guess it ran off.

Continuing on my drive, I continue to drink overly caffeinated drinks, smoke cigarettes and listen to loud music. I'm doing everything I can think of to keep myself awake and alert. I even start singing with the music and I've got to say, my voice is as sweet as salt.

I still haven't seen another car on the road, but I

just passed over the state line. At least getting through this state is going to be quicker. As I jam out to something loud and heavy, I feel my car shift slightly. It's not caused by a change in the road but feels more like when a person shifts heavily in the backseat.

Looking in my rearview mirror, I catch sight of something out my back window. I see four vertical white lines, an inch or two thick. I'm really confused, but understanding gets a lot harder when the lines start disappearing one by one. First the second one from the left, then the one on the far right. Next is the far left and then the last one. What the hell is going on?

I slowly bring the car to a stop again on the deserted highway. Turning this way and that, I look out every window for any signs of life, but there's nothing out there. Opening the door, I get out slowly, trying to look in all directions at once. There's absolutely nothing in the road or at the edge of the woods on either side of the highway.

Going back to the trunk, I don't see any indentations on the metal, no new scratches, or any evidence that something had been on it. Feeling severely creeped out, I open the trunk and pull out the tire iron. As far as weapons go it's a poor choice, but the only one I have.

Closing the lid, my heart leaps into my throat at the sound of an animal crying out. Spinning around, I bring the tire iron up in order to strike at something behind me, only there's nothing there. Hadn't that been a goat bleating I just heard?

Turning to get back in the car, I'm startled as I lock eyes with the most demonic eyes I have ever seen. Goats have always weirded me out because their eyes are so freaky and until now, I've successfully avoided them. Standing on top the roof of my car is the same white goat that was in the middle of the road one state back, which is impossible. There's no way that thing got on my car and managed to stay on while I was driving eighty without me noticing until now.

Once again, I try to shoo away the dumb animal, but it continues to stare at me. I'm starting to get the feeling that it's looking at me like I'm an idiot. Those judgmental eyes are starting to get on my nerves, and my nerves are already fried after the extremely long day I've had. Raising the tire iron, I swing at the goat.

The goat remains perfectly still, but before the tire iron makes contact, something shoves me back with a lot of force. My back lands on the asphalt hard, and I get the wind knocked out of me. I try to get to my feet, but I can't. The goat continues to stare at me, and something occurs to me. Those aren't typical goat horns, but they do look awfully familiar.

I think back to the image Professor Meyers had plastered all over the workspace, of the sacrifice. The guy holding the stone tablet had been wearing a goat head mask, and the horns on that thing look exactly like the horns on this goat. This isn't a coincidence.

Without warning, the goat leaps off my car and lands on my chest. I expect to feel a painful blow that will break my ribs, but there's nothing. The goat is standing on top of me, but I don't feel the weight of it at all. It lowers its head to mine, pointing its snout further down my body so it can look me in the eyes. Then, without warning, it rams its head into my forehead. I feel that one.

The goat rams into me several times, the pain becomes more excruciating with each blow. I don't know how many times it takes for me to feel something break in my head, but that's when it stops hitting me. Blinking doesn't help the double or triple vision I'm experiencing, but I can tell the goat is moving again. Is it going to hit me one more time, finishing me off?

My vision goes dark as the goat lowers its head, but it doesn't ram into me this time. In fact, it suddenly disappears, and my vision is back to normal. I no longer feel any pain or fatigue. Getting to my feet, I realize I feel better than ever, but there's an obvious change in my mind.

Back in the driver's seat, I go the speed limit all the way back to the university. I now understand what happened. The brown tome Professor Meyers is obsessed with wants to be translated and used. In order to accomplish this, the sacrifice depicted in that first drawing needs to be preformed. It will unlock the knowledge needed to read the text.

Professor Meyers wanted to be the goat so she could be the one to wield the tome, but I touched the tablet with my bare skin, becoming the first person linked to it in several hundred years. That's why there'd been a box of rubber gloves next to the tablet. The other professor somehow knew about the linking and that's why he was so protective of it. He was trying to prevent this very thing from happening.

When I get back, I'll need to make something clear to Professor Meyers. I'm the one in the driver's seat now, not her. If she wants to be apart of what's going to happen, then she will have to accept the role of executioner. Otherwise, she will become the sacrifice, and I know she won't want that.

NEW PROPERTY

My GPS completely cuts out when my cell signal dies as I drive through the old rusty gate. It had been a bitch to get open since no one has been out here in ages. I know shit roles down hill and being at the bottom sucks, but this is a whole new level of suck.

I started at the real estate agency three months ago, and so far, I regret this career choice. Granted, it wasn't my first choice, but how often do first choices actually work out? Never in my experience.

Since day one I've been given every shit job there is to do for the agency. I've run errands, rushed across town to get documents signed, and even stayed at houses to the late hours of the evening getting them ready for open houses. I couldn't even begin to guess how many pieces of furniture and props I've carted around the city to dress up a home for viewers. This project is nothing like anything I've done before.

My understanding is that some rich guy up north recently kicked the bucket, and his entire estate is being divided up among the surviving relatives. The estate is massive with several landholdings all over the country. This one is the furthest south, and no one in the family even knew it existed. Makes sense considering no one's lived here in more than fifty years. The agency I work for has been contracted to evaluate the property and assign it a dollar value. The first step in doing that is to get eyes on it.

Everyone else at the agency has been busy with various listings, so the boss man gave me a camera of excellent quality, a company credit card for expenses, and a physical map. I was warned that cell service was spotty at best, but being given an actual map told me it was going to be worse than that. I never should've let him find out I grew up in the rural outskirts. He'd otherwise have probably given this task to someone more experienced.

The map has a square marked on it, consisting of about seven hundred and fifty acres according to the estate lawyer. The old records indicate there is a house on the property somewhere, but there's nothing specified about its exact location. For all anyone knows, all I'm going to find is the disheveled remains of what used to be there.

There's probably one other reason I was chosen to come out here. Unlike all of my coworkers, I own a Jeep, and it's the only vehicle among all of those at the office that stands a chance of traversing this property. There isn't a single truck or 4x4 aside from mine, which says a lot about my coworkers. I even have a wench on my front bumper in case I get stuck, which used to happen every once in a while when I still lived at home. The wench hasn't gotten much use since I moved into the city and I'm perfectly fine with that.

The grass is nearly as tall as the hood of my Jeep and there isn't even a hint of what might've been a road. There are bushes scattered around, clusters of trees here and there and a few standalones in the immediate area. The trees get considerably denser after several hundred yards. Part of me wants to skirt the fence line for as long as I can to get a sense of the property, but if I do that, I'm afraid I'll be out here all damn day before I find anything.

I continue forward at a painfully slow pace. I'm hesitant to go more than five miles an hour. The grass is so tall and dense that I can't possibly see if there's an obstacle on the ground in front of me. If anything happens to my Jeep, my boss is going to pay for the damages one way or another. I'll sue him if I have to. I love my Jeep. It's my most prized possession.

It takes nearly five minutes for me to get to the denser trees. As I approach, I see two large trees standing wide enough apart for two vehicles to sit comfortably between them. In my youth, I used to do work for some wealthy landowners that were close by my family's ranch. A few of those places had massive houses set away from their front gate and used strategically placed trees to create a driveway. The more expensive the house, the more likely that driveway was paved, but I still saw it with at least one dirt road.

It's not until I'm directly between the two trees that I see what I was hoping to find. The lack of maintenance makes it hard to make out, but I can kind of see what they originally did. I'm probably the only person at the office that could understand it. The others would just see trees, but the spacing tells all. If it wasn't for the trees growing new limbs lower to the ground, I'd have a straight line of sight.

Starting about ten feet up, there's an arching pattern to the thicker tree limbs. Whoever designed the driveway turned the trees on either side of the road into a canopy, creating a covered driveway. Unfortunately, since it's been uninhabited for half a century, nature has blocked the way again. Unless my desire to be right is making me see something that's not there, the house should be down that way.

Sadly, there's no way in hell my Jeep is going to make it through that. Hell, I'd have trouble getting through that on anything with wheels. The only way I could do it is on foot, and there's no telling how long it would be before I got to the end. I decide to skirt the trees to see if there's an opening that'll get me directly to the house.

The grass gets shorter the closer I am to the trees, and I can go a little faster, but the dense trees continue on for quite a ways. So much so that I find the property line fence without finding a way into the trees. Turning around, I follow my own tracks back to where I started and continue on that way. There's a curve in the tree line to the right, and I follow it a ways. I have to slam on the breaks at one point, but it doesn't stop me from hitting something.

The hit was hard enough to make the front end of the Jeep jump up, but I stopped in time from going completely over whatever I hit. Slowly, I back up but find the drop back to the ground isn't that far. Reaching into the back seat, I grab the pump action shotgun I brought with me. Rattlesnakes are a serious concern this time of year, and I'll be damned if I get bit out here. And yes, I made sure to buy a few boxes of shells with the company card. You send me out to the middle of nowhere on company time, you're going to buy me ammo for whatever gun I deem necessary to bring.

I stay in my tire impressions, keeping the gun pointed at the ground. It turns out what I hit was a tree that fell over god knows how long ago. The trunk of it is pretty rotted through, enough that my tires crunched through about half of its thickness. Seeing that there's no visible damage to my tires, I slowly proceed over the down tree.

Regrettably, this was a waste of time. There were a couple spots where I managed to get my Jeep into the trees, but I ended up having to back out. Maybe if I had a dirt bike I could've gotten through. Or better yet, a four-wheeler. If I don't finish the assessment today, which is likely, I'll see about getting mine from my parent's place.

Getting back to my starting location, I weigh my options. I could go ahead and run over to my parents' place to get my four-wheeler today, but that would take too long and coming back wouldn't be worth it. I have to do something that won't get me yelled at back at the office, so I'm going to have to proceed on foot.

Now that I know there's no way to get further onto the property without the use of a four-wheeler, my boss isn't going to be able to send out anyone but me. Not unless he's willing to rent offroad vehicles, and I know he won't when I have access to one. I sure as hell am not going to allow someone to ride my four-wheeler. It's my favorite thing in the world after my Jeep and I've had countless hours riding around on it.

Parking my Jeep between those two trees, I grab my backpack and begin the arduous journey through the trees. Fifty years is a long time for the landscape to reclaim what man designed, and it's not easy to get through. I'm just glad there isn't a lot of underbrush. If there was, I'd never get through this.

These kinds of driveways could be short, or they could be up to a hundred yards. It honestly depends on how far the people who put it in place wanted the house to be from the front gate. After twenty minutes, I still haven't made it far enough to see a house. Carrying around a full-size shotgun is making my passage a little difficult, but I was raised to be better safe than sorry. There's a number of dangerous snakes that attack from the trees as much as there are on the ground.

Ducking under low branches, climbing over

fallen limbs, there's barely any space that isn't occupied by some sort of obstacle. Within a few minutes I confirm my earlier suspicion. Under the dead leaves and dirt, I can feel something hard in the ground. Brushing the surface aside, I find hard stones underneath it all. They're old and covered by at least half an inch of earth, but they're flat and laid out in a uniformed pattern. This was an old, expensive driveway.

The heat is oppressive, and the air is humid, a horrible combination for anyone that spends more of their time inside than out. I kind of wish my boss had sent one of the others with me just so I could see how badly they'd fair out here. My ranch style background prepared me for this kind of thing, but even I'm covered in sweat.

Propped up against a dead tree leaning against a larger, still living one, I break out a bottle of water from my pack. Downing half the contents in one go, I look around. The density of these woods is very intense. I can't see my Jeep from here at all with as thick as it is. I suddenly feel cut off and isolated. For a moment, I was starting to enjoy this. Being out of the office is nice when you get to take a leisurely jaunt through the trees, but this stopped being that a while ago.

As I continue on, my mind starts to wander so I'm not thinking about how isolated I am. With as dense as all this is, is it even worth it for me to trek to the house? It would take weeks and considerable cost to clear out this driveway, and that's just to get to a house that may or may not be there. If it is still standing, I can't imagine how much it would cost to bring the place up to code. It would be easier to demolish what's there and rebuild, but does anyone even want to do that?

None of my speculation changes what I'm doing out here. Before even a single decision can be made, the land has to be assessed and evaluated. I remind myself once again that I'm simply here to confirm whether there is a structure out here, and what else exists on the land. Seeing the end of this unusable driveway is my goal for the day. Once I'm done here I can go back to the office, show my boss the pictures, make my suggestions and go from there.

Seriously, this is one long ass driveway. Whoever designed this place really didn't want anyone to be here that didn't belong. It kind of reminds me of my parents. You can't see much of their property from the road because of all the trees and vegetation along the fence. It provides a lot of privacy but makes it a pain in the ass to inspect and maintain the fences. I should know, it used to be one of my primary responsibilities and one of the things I regularly did on my four-wheeler.

After what seems like forever, I finally start seeing a break through the dense trees. There's a clearing coming up, and I start picking up the pace. The urge to be out of this claustrophobic density grips me like a vice, and I start moving faster than is safe. My leg catches on something I don't see, and I go tumbling. I lose my grip on the shotgun, and it goes off, thundering in the silence.

I lay on the ground, looking up into a bright cloudy sky. I've finally made it out of the woods. It's just lucky that I didn't accidentally shoot myself. That happened to an uncle of mine once, but he'd been drinking on a hunting trip.

Rolling over, I finally see the reason I'm here.

From the ground it looms high over me, as tall as the trees. For a two-story structure, it's huge. It was white once upon a time, with columns covering the entire outside that look like they came from ancient Greece. Dirt covers everything, vines wrapped around the columns and creeping up the walls. Nature has tried to reclaim this too, but it looks sturdy. I can't believe it. Not only is it still standing, but it's withstanding the test of time. I've never seen anything like it.

It's an old plantation house. I've never seen one in real life. There's a wraparound porch on both floors that looks like it might go all the way around. Every window I can see, and there's a lot of them, look to be completely intact. Granted they're caked in dirt so I can't be sure.

Getting to my feet, I find my shotgun propped up against the side of a tree. Thankfully the barrel is pointing straight up, and a branch above it took the brunt of the buckshot. Now I'm glad I came out here by myself. Having someone witness my blunder would not only have been embarrassing, but potentially dangerous.

Racking in a new shell, I put the safety on and hang the weapon on my shoulder by the sling. I dig the expensive camera from the office out of my backpack and start snapping pictures. There was a pool going on at the office whether there'd be anything left of the structure out here, but since I'm the newbie, I wasn't allowed to get in on it.

Even standing, this place looks massive. Just from the outside it looks like each floor of this place is fifteen feet tall. I can't even begin to guess what the square footage of the house is, but it looks like the front is about a hundred yards wide. I can only imagine how many rooms are inside.

The grass around the house isn't nearly as tall as it was at the beginning of the property, but it's more than what a lawnmower could handle. I walk around the entire structure, taking a ton of pictures. The trees don't come within fifty yards of the house, and there are no bushes. Each side of the house has a set of double doors save for one, but none are as large as the front. This place must've been amazing in its prime. A true symbol of decadence for the time.

Rounding back to the front, I walk up to the porch and stand before the double doors. Reaching for the dirt encrusted knob, I give it a twist and push. Of course, it doesn't budge, and I didn't expect it to. Hoping I won't have to break a window to get in, I shove against the door with my shoulder. The door creaks open on old, rusty hinges.

The inside is bathed in complete darkness. My skin crawls as I imagine all the creepy crawlies that could be inside. I immediately wish I'd brought a shotgun with a flashlight on it and purchased some rock salt rounds instead of buckshot. Yeah, I watch too much TV, but the inside has a major creep factor going on. It's easy to imagine a place like this crawling with ghosts.

Turning on the flash, I take a couple pictures of the entryway, and the brief flashes only make it creepier. Digging into my backpack again, I pull out the flashlight that normally lives in my Jeep. Turning it on, I sweep it across the floor, noting an unbroken layer of dust and no insects of any kind. That's a relief at least. If there were animals living in here, I'd see their tracks in the dust.

I slowly start investigating the inside, taking

enough pictures that I start to get a headache from the flashes. The air is musty and stale, but thankfully I can't smell the distinct musk of animals. Somehow this place seems to be well preserved, despite the dust.

The walls are bare of any decoration, but there are light fixtures on every wall that look like old sconces. The bulbs in them are just as old as everything else. Not expecting them to work, I flip every light switch I come across. Sure enough, they don't work, which is kind of sad. I'd really like to see the chandeliers in this place lit up. I take a few pictures of each one knowing those things are expensive as hell.

The entryway is spacious and holds duel sweeping staircases that lead to opposite sides of the upstairs but is joined by a balcony running along the backside of the room. There are at least two hallways up there leading to what I assume are bedrooms. Even though the stairs look stable, I decide to start with the downstairs first.

I find what I assume is a dining room, but that's only because it has the largest table I have ever seen in it. You can easily fit five people on each side, making it designed for a dozen. There aren't any chairs, but I suppose the only reason the table is still here is because it would've been a bitch to transport. I wonder why these people abandoned the property.

Progressing farther into the room, I find a counter on the back wall with a large indoor window, but the shutters are closed. Next to it is a swinging door, and to my surprise, it actually swings open easily. In the center of the room is a large island and two of the walls are lined with kitchen counters. There are three doors in this room aside from the one I just came through. One leads to the outside, the only side of the house that didn't have double doors.

The door directly next to the longest counter seems to be locked. Logic tells me that this is probably a pantry, but my curiosity has me wanting to open it. If I remember correctly how far the side door had been from the back wall, there's a considerable space beyond this door. It may not be that important for my assessment, but I want to know what's on the other side of this door.

For a brief moment, I consider unslinging my shotgun and blasting the door open, but I don't. I somehow think my boss or maybe the property owner will get upset about me busting up a door, even if it ultimately gets torn down in the end. Seriously, I can't imagine someone spending the money to restore this place. At the same time, I can't imagine tearing down such a well-preserved plantation house as this. It would be a shame.

Placing all my stuff on the counter, I lay the flashlight in a way so the light is directly on the door. With both hands on the knob, I twist the round orb and shove with my shoulder. The wood makes a series of creaks as I try to force it open, but it doesn't want to give it up. I throw my shoulder into it once, twice, even a third time. Normally I'd give up at this point, but my determination seems abnormally charged by this mystery.

Giving the door one more hard shove, something finally gives, and I fall into the space beyond. I land hard on the floor, kicking up a cloud of dust. Taking a sharp breath in, something floods my mouth and throat, causing me to cough up a storm. Oh god, the taste of it reminds me of mildewed grass trapped under piles of cut grass after a rainy week. It's so bad that I gag and throw up.

My head is pounding, and I feel like my lungs have been violated. This is worse than the only time I tried to smoke a cigarette in high school. I threw up then too, but even that wasn't this bad. Ugh, it feels like something slithered its way inside me and won't leave no matter how hard I cough. Yeah, I should've left this damn door alone. Why had my curiosity been so strong for this anyway?

After a few minutes, I finally stop trying to hack up a lung. I eventually pick up the flashlight and look into the pitch-black room. As I suspected, it's nothing more than a pantry. Granted, it's big enough to make my room at my parent's place seem small. The shelves are bare but could easily hold enough food to feed an army for a month, if not longer.

Aside from the puddle I created, there's something more than dust on the ground. I honestly can't tell what it is, but parts of the crystalline substance catch the light. My mind again goes to that spooky TV show I used to watch because I'd swear it looks like the floor is covered in salt. Then again, this is an old pantry, and they likely kept bags of salt in here. Who hasn't spilled something on the floor? Feeling like crap and very disappointed, I pick up my stuff and continue my search.

Going through the last door, I find myself back out in the hall. It leads to the back of the sweeping staircases and goes farther back into the house. Some of the doors won't open and I find some small rooms that I can only speculate what they'd been used for. There's no furniture or anything in any of them, so it's hard to tell.

At the back of the house, I come to another

door, but this one is different from all the others. Instead of swinging in or out, they appear to slide open, disappearing into the walls. Gripping the handle on one side, I try to slide it open, but the damn thing won't budge. You can't really put your shoulder into this one, so I try the other side. It doesn't move either.

This is probably the fourth or fifth door that hasn't wanted to open in this section of the house, but this one disappoints me. I'm willing to bet there's something really interesting on the other side of this one. Though, after what happened with the pantry, I haven't wanted to force any other doors too hard.

Checking the camera's memory, I see that I've only taken up a fraction of the memory card's space even though I've taken nearly two hundred pictures. I loop around to the other side of the house and find another extremely large room. The wood floor in here seems extremely well preserved and once I brush some of the dust out of the way with my shoe, I find the floor still has a bit of a shine to it. I think this was a ballroom.

Back in the entry way, I move to the right staircase. Giving the first few steps a test, I press hard on the stairs, listening for any creaks or groans. It makes some noise, but not anything that makes me think it's going to collapse with me on it. I want more than anything to grab onto the railing as I climb, but the amount of dust keeps me from doing so. Still, I take each step very slowly, all the way to the top.

Halfway up the stairs, I feel a scratch at the back of my throat and start coughing again. Again, that taste comes back to me, but it's worse this time. I don't outright throw up again, but I do end up spitting a lot of phlegm out. I'm probably going to have to go to the doctors after this. Maybe they can do something to clear this shit out of my lungs. It's making me feel weird, like my head is filling with fuzz. Still, I continue on.

The landing at the top creaks a little under my feet, but again, not so loud as to make me think the floor is going to give out on me. It amazes me that there's been no evidence of water leaks from the roof or even around any of the windows. They really knew how to build a house in the old days. It makes me wish modern builders were held up to the same standard. However, if they were, houses would probably be a hell of a lot more expensive, and they're plenty expensive as it is. Even my crappy apartment costs more than I'd like to pay for the piss poor quality.

The rooms up here are as bare as the ones below, but they're much bigger. Each one has a walk-in closet that could easily hold a king-size bed in it. I'd love to have a closet like this even though I don't own enough clothes to fill it. There must be a dozen large bedrooms up here, and I haven't even come across the master bedroom yet. Unless there isn't one and they're all the same. That doesn't seem right.

I once again find myself at the back right corner of the house, standing in front of yet another unusual door. It's only a single door, but this one seems to slide into the wall too. I find this very odd but go ahead and grip the handle. I put a lot of strength into my pull to slide it open. A little too much. The door slides open rather easily, and I jam my hand between the wall and the handle. Damn that hurts.

I shake my hand out trying to dispel the pain radiating from it. Flexing the digits, I find that they all move. I'll have a bruise, but thankfully nothing is broken. That would make getting back out of here a lot harder considering the state of the driveway.

Shining the light into the room, I'm overwhelmed with confusion as I try to understand what I'm seeing. There's a railing inside the room, maybe three feet from the wall, but on the other side of it is open space. There's no floor beyond the rail. My overactive imagination immediately tells me that this room holds the mouth of a bottomless pit, but I shut that down quickly. I'm too old to think something that asinine.

Stepping inside, I see this room is similar to the entryway, an open space between the ground floor and roof. Sweeping the light around the vast room, I notice the walls don't look right either. It takes turning to the walls on either side of the door I came through to understand. The walls are nothing more than elaborately carved wood panels and shelves. Shelves and shelves as far as the eye can see.

On the other side of the room, clear across the open space is a tightly wound spiral staircase. It's made of metal and looks like it would clank while someone walks down it. In fact, thinking that makes me remember a scene from a Harrison Ford movie. It was the one where he was an archeologist looking for his father. He climbed a similar staircase and found that giant X on the floor. This is a freaking library.

Looking down to the ground floor, I can see an old chair with a small table next to it. As far as I can tell, all the shelves are empty, but that small table looks like it might have something on it. Slowly, I make my way around the walkway, taking several pictures. Even though there's plenty of space for it, this room doesn't have a chandelier.

Once I get to the spiral staircase, I give it a hard rattle. The metal does make some noise, but like the rest of the house, it seems stable. This time I do grip the railing despite the dust, and slowly descend. My nerves are as rattled as the steps are, and I find myself coughing again, but I make it down to the floor without incident.

Snapping more pictures, I move to the chair and give it a test too. I'm surprised to find it in such good condition, and even dare to have a seat. It creaks as much as the stairs at the front of the house did, and like them, the chair holds steady. I find this very surprising, and in a good way. I could use a rest.

On the side table is an old book. I don't mean just because it's been sitting here for fifty-some-odd years. No, it was old before the house and property were abandoned. Like everything else in the house, the brown leather book looks like it could easily fall apart but is surprisingly well preserved. The heavy book is solid in my hands, covered in dust, but doesn't crumble.

With the flashlight in one hand and the book in my lap, I open it. I expect the old leather to creak like everything else in the house does, but it is silent as it opens. It opens toward the back and what is inside surprises me. The pages are completely blank. I flip toward the front, and it becomes clear what this is. The handwritten words reveal a journal.

As much as I want to start at the beginning, I find the last entries instead. This might actually give me some insight as to why the property was abandoned. My blood grows cold as I read the cursive handwriting.

I don't know what else to do. My wife seems to be possessed by some kind of entity. One of the maids, Chloé, is a practitioner of Voodoo, or some such thing. I often have trouble understanding her with the accent she has, but she seems to have a better comprehension of what's happening than I do.

Several weeks ago, my Sandra went on a walk in the woods north of our lands. She often takes such walks, but normally sticks to the lands to the east and west. I don't know why she ventured to the north, and I may never know. The family that lives that way is not friendly to any of us and has refused any social invitation that has been presented to them.

When Sandra came back, she complained of a headache, and difficulty breathing. I had a doctor come to the house, and he said she was suffering from some kind of allergic reaction. He prescribed her some medication, but it ultimately did nothing. In the days that followed, she got sicker. Her complaints of the horrible taste in her mouth like mildew started to decrease, but only because she became more violent.

Sandra began lashing out. She would have violent outbursts, such viciousness that she was never capable of before. The staff were the first to experience this, but it quickly escalated. Soon she started leaving her room to target the children. For some reason I was left for last. By that time, I managed to arrange for the children to stay with my brother in the north. My neck still throbs from where she bit me.

Things got so bad that we had to lock Sandra in the kitchen pantry. Chloé claims this is no allergic reaction, but an invasion of sorts. She knows of things that live in the wilderness that are rare and turn people into monsters. The last I saw of my Sandra, her skin had started to take on a scaly texture and putrid tone. I'm not a man of faith, but I'm starting to believe Chloé's claims. I want my Sandra back, so I'm willing to do anything to accomplish this.

Chloé has made a potion or spell. Some kind of

concoction in a leather pouch that she claims will force out the evil inside Sandra, but there's a catch. Once the evil has been expelled, we must flee this place. Chloé can lock it away in safety for a time, but eventually the evil will be able to reach out beyond her protections and compel someone to free it. If that happens, we will have to go through this all over again. I have already made arrangements for us to join my brother in the north.

Tonight, we attempt to free Sandra from the evil that is inside her. For the first time in my life, I pray.

I cough again as I read those last words. There's nothing more in the journal. My mouth is flooded with the taste of mildew again, and I curse. Slamming the book closed, my head grows hot with anger, and I throw it across the room. It doesn't hit one of the bookshelves, but one of the windows. The silence in the air is replaced with the shattering of old glass and natural light floods the abandoned library.

Shit. I don't know anyone that practices Voodoo, and I'm pretty sure my medical coverage doesn't include possession.

STRANGE AND UNUSUAL

When we were kids, our parents told us we could be anything so why not shoot for the stars? Back then we were wide eyed and full of wonder, so of course we believed them. Why wouldn't we? They were our parents, and they wanted the best for us.

That was also during a much better time in the world, or at least it seems that way when I look back on it. These days it's all about working a job you hate in order to provide for a family that doesn't appreciate the soul sucking shit show you have to go through on a daily basis. That same family who does nothing but complain that you're never there and that work is consuming your life. When you are the sole provider for a family of five, what do they expect? I needed to put in the hours to pay for all the things they want and can't live without.

Well, that's not the case anymore. They all left me for greener pastures, and I suddenly found myself coming home to an empty house after twelve hours at the office on a Saturday. The divorce papers weren't far behind, but alimony wasn't going to be an issue. My ex got married nearly as soon as the divorce went through. I don't know if the affair really started before they all left or after. Not like it matters all that much.

Honestly, I thought I was handling things pretty well, until the cops showed up one night at my front door. Multiple neighbors called in noise and domestic violence complaints. The cops were surprised to find me alone, but the house was in severe disarray.

The doctors kept referring to it as a nervous breakdown. They claimed the loss of my family was shattering my world and I wasn't coping with things in a healthy manner. I really don't know what happened. All I know is that I sat down to a TV dinner, burned my tongue on the cobbler that apparently was still hot as molten lava, and then there was nothing. I came back to myself out of breath as the police pounded on the door. The moral of the story is, don't go for the dessert before you eat dinner.

Spending court mandated time in the hospital wasn't as bad as I always imagined it would be. Sure, there were some seriously deranged nut jobs in there, and they truly belonged, but not me. I was as laid back and straight laced as it gets. According to my therapist, I wasn't dealing with my problems, I was ignoring them. That's what caused the blackouts. Before that first appointment, I hadn't known I'd had more than one.

The doctor informed me that there'd been an incident at my office earlier that day. My boss came into my corner office and dumped a giant project in my lap. It was crunch time and the three people that had started it had completely screwed everything up. He was tasking me with fixing all the mistakes, revamping the entire face of it, and having it ready to go in two days. There wasn't a single facet of the messed-up project I could use to work with, so it all needed to be done from scratch.

A project of that magnitude takes a minimum of a week and requires the work of two or more additional people. Not only was this a big ask, but rather typical. I can't count how many times this same thing happened to me in the ten plus years I'd been with the firm. Well, it turns out that it was also the last time.

The doctor didn't give me the full details, but

there was a bit of an altercation. My boss made it out of there with a few bumps and bruises, but the office itself was trashed. If nothing else, that explained the busted-up knuckles and cuts on my hands. I remember getting home and cleaning the wounds, but not how I got them.

I spent a few months in the hospital with near daily counseling sessions. On days I didn't have one on ones there were group sessions. My god, those were a freaking nightmare. So many times I wanted to get up and walk away, but I stayed in my seat and stared off into space. I couldn't bring myself to give a shit about someone's out of control eating disorder, or the nymphomaniac with unresolved mommy issues. Then there was the guy with severe OCD. That guy drove me nuts.

I knew spending time in the hospital was going to break me if I had to be there longer than was necessary. I took my meds, shared my feelings halfheartedly, made 'major strides' during my one on ones, and suppressed all my anger. I became a model patient just so I could get out of there.

Going back to my life wasn't an option simply because I didn't have one to go back to. My job was gone, my family left me and wanted nothing to do with me. The only thing I had was my aunt and uncle, but they were out of the country. I did reach out to them and caught them up on everything that had happened in the last four months. They said something that nearly mirrored what my therapist said. I need to get away for a while and recharge. Get back to me and decide what I want to do with the rest of my life.

My rampage through the house didn't really leave me with much in the way of material possessions. I packed up what little there was, made arrangements with my lawyer, and put the house on the market. There was one good thing about neglecting my family and working ridiculous hours. The house was paid off a couple years ago. Once it sold, I'd have plenty in the bank to start over somewhere else.

My aunt and uncle have a place in the mountains. It's a nice two-story cabin that they used to use for weekend getaways in the middle of nowhere. I've been there a few times, and it is really isolated. As long as I bring enough food to last me for my entire stay, I won't have to see another person unless I really want to. After spending a couple months in the hospital constantly surrounded by other mental patients and medical staff that didn't want to be there either, less people is definitely better.

I've never been much of a cook and can only make a few things that require actual cooking without risking food poisoning. I get enough basic food items like bread, sandwich meat, cheese, chips, and frozen meals to last me a few weeks. I also get things like hotdogs, steaks, burger patties, and microwave side dishes.

The outdoors wasn't really my thing growing up. I didn't like camping, direct sunlight or the bugs that always find you outside. As I got older, I started to appreciate the solitude of the forest, but not enough to buy a tent. The few times I came out to their cabin were great, but I didn't do it very often. Maybe if I had, my family wouldn't have abandoned me, and I wouldn't have blown up my life. Though, looking back on it now, it's probably a good thing they left when they did. I hate to think what might've happened if I'd blacked out while they were home.

Driving through the forest, I marvel at the tall

trees. There is snow in patches on the ground and in the high limbs, but the road is easily passable in my second hand 4x4. Along with selling the house, I got rid of that stupid luxury SUV I hated driving for something more suited to my current circumstances. I'd gotten the damn thing more for the family than for myself, though I don't know why. We always piled in my ex's car when we went anywhere.

As my 4x4 glides over the wet road and I climb higher and higher, I can feel the isolation seeping in. The worries and cares of the rest of the world are melting away as quickly as the snow is. Granted, this high up in the mountains, the snow can come back quite easily. It rarely gets warmer than seventy up here, but I'm okay with that. There's plenty of firewood, and I don't need much in the way of electricity. I'm not going to spend all my time up here on the computer or watching TV. Hell, I don't even have a computer at the moment. It got trashed in my last blackout.

It doesn't take much longer for the road to start leveling out, and just like that, I'm at the cabin. I park right in front of the porch, but instead of heading for the front door, I round the side of the house. There's a toolshed over there, and I find the keys exactly where I was told they'd be. Next to the shed's door is a series of softball size rocks. The keys are in a baggy underneath the middle one.

Before bringing anything inside, I inspect the cabin, which is freezing cold. The first order of business is to turn the power and water pump on. Those switches are located in the mud room at the back door. Once that's done and I can turn on the lights, I check to make sure all the windows are intact, and no animals have managed to get in. From what I was told, a few years ago there was a bit of a raccoon problem, and a repeat occurrence isn't out of the question. I probably should've asked for more information on that.

As I'm searching, I swear I hear noises, like kids laughing or something like that, but there's nothing. I search every room, but there's no broken windows, no holes in the wall, or any evidence that something has been inside. I declare that there's nothing out of the ordinary with the cabin, so I start bringing my groceries and belongings in. It's going to take a while for the fridge and freezer to get cold, so I keep the cold stuff in the cooler. I'd love to crack open a beer, but I decided to forgo such things. Alcohol and medication don't go together, so I avoid booze completely.

Grabbing a pair of leather gloves, I go outside and find the firewood shed, which is different from the tool shed. Since my aunt and uncle rarely come out here, they had a small shed built specifically for storing firewood. The doors aren't locked, so I pop it open and start bringing in as much as I can carry. There's even a couple buckets with smaller pieces of wood. My fire building skills are limited, but I know you're supposed to use the small stuff to catch the larger pieces.

It takes me a couple tries, but I manage to get a fire going in the fireplace. Again, I swear I hear voices talking in whispered or distant tones, but there's no one around. I even check outside for the third time to make sure there isn't another car here. There isn't even an old stereo or anything in the cabin that could be the source of the noise. I just write it off as my imagination.

Back when things were still good, we brought the kids up here once, but it ended up being a short visit. Daniel was chasing his little sister around and tripped on a rock. He'd smacked his head against a tree root and got a two-inch gash on his forehead. We hadn't been here more than fifteen minutes and had to get to the nearest emergency room. That was nine years ago.

In the minute before Daniel's accident, the kids had seemed so happy. I'd thought maybe this could've been a thing we could do as a family every once in a while, but we never went back. In my time of self-reflection, many times I wondered if things might have turned out differently if Daniel hadn't cut his head open so badly.

I shut down that thought quickly as I go back outside for another load of wood. The stockpile in the shed is only about half full. Perhaps during my time up here, I can grab some tools and find a nearby fallen tree to cut up. It would give me something to do and replenish some of the wood I'm going to end up using while I'm here. The fireplace is the only way to heat up the cabin.

As I return to the front door with another armload of logs, I see movement through the front window. I'm quick up the steps and look in, but what I see has me dropping the logs at my feet. There's two high school age kids sitting in front of the fire, laughing and joking with their parents who sit on a couch nearby. For a moment, I think my aunt and uncle double booked the cabin, letting someone else stay here while I'm here, but that's not the case. I know that because the parents sitting on the couch is me and my ex.

I stand there for a flabbergasted moment, not understanding what I'm seeing. The other me glances up just in time to see me dart for the door, but when I yank it open, the living room is empty. What the hell? I go back to the window, but all I see is what was there before, no people. My heart rate starts climbing and questions start spouting from my mouth. There's no one around to hear me ask them, but it doesn't stop them from coming.

Closing my eyes, I take a deep breath and reach into my pocket. I've been keeping the pill bottle in my pocket since I was discharged from the hospital, but I haven't needed to take one outside my normal twice a day before now. Without water, I pop one of the little white pills into my mouth and dry swallow. Thankfully I've become an old hand at this lately, so the pill doesn't get stuck in my throat like it used to.

Once the pill is in my empty stomach and my heart rate starts coming back down, I pick the fallen wood back up. I make it a point not to look at the window again, but just get the wood inside. This is just my imagination acting up, something my therapist said might happen from time to time. It's likely that similar things happened in the moments before my blackouts, but I really don't know. I'd had three of them at the hospital, but I never remembered what triggered me.

Getting the wood onto the pile next to the fire, I go into the kitchen to make myself something to eat. The fridge and freezer have finally gotten cool enough for me to store my food in it, and I start to transfer things from the cooler. As I do, I notice two slips of paper stuck to the fridge with magnets. One is a list of emergency numbers, one of which being animal control, for the raccoons I surmise. Oddly, the animal control number has been crossed out.

The other slip has one name and number on it. Instead of saying in case of emergency, it says in case of strange and unusual activity. What the hell does that mean?

Ignoring it, I cook up a steak over the fire with a cast iron skillet and nuke a side of macaroni and cheese. I keep having to add logs onto the fire, more than I thought I would. It figures though, the tub for holding wood is big enough that I'd need to bring in four armloads. By the time I've eaten my dinner and cleaned off the dishes, it's still light enough out. I put a few more logs on the fire to keep it going and decide to walk around the outside of the cabin for a while. If the fire wasn't going I'd venture farther away. With my luck, I'd burn the cabin down if I'm gone for too long.

The immediate area is still surrounded with some of the tallest trees I have ever seen. Just past the woodshed is a little path that only goes about fifty yards away, and it stops at a couple of benches. They're made of large logs and face a magnificent view of the valley below. I take it in for as long as I dare to be this far from the fire. Truly magnificent. The kind of natural beauty that words can't describe. I could sit out here for hours just looking at it. This is a spot to recharge the soul for sure.

I stay outside for a while before I decide to head back inside. Picking up my first armload of wood, I have to finagle my way into opening the front door, which isn't easy. After dumping the first load into the tub, I drop a couple more logs onto the fire, which was starting to get a little low.

By the time I'm retrieving the third load, it's gotten significantly dark out, and the sky starts talking. Great big bellows of thunder belt out from the dark clouds and heavy gusts of wind nearly knock me down. The temperature is dropping quickly too, and I hurry to the front door. If a storm is going to drop a crap ton of snow on me, I'm going to need more wood than what the tub can hold.

I made sure not to close the door all the way when I came out this last time, and I nudge it open with my foot. The wind has other ideas about how gentle I tried to open the door, and it crashes open. Just as it does, the back door slams open and a figure stands in the doorway with an armful of wood, just like me. In fact, aside from having more color to their skin and looking generally healthier than me, the person at the backdoor is me.

Our eyes lock and we mirror each other's confusion, but the other me reacts quicker. They drop the wood, all save for one thick log, and the other me raises it up to use as a weapon. "Who are you? What are you doing here? Why do you look like me?" The voice is the exact same as mine as these questions are fired off. I am truly at a loss here.

There's a seriously deranged look on the other me's face, and I know I'm in trouble. I have the urge to get something more substantial in my hands than an armful of wood. Next to the fireplace is a poker and a few other tools, and I'm about to make a move for it, but the other me speaks again. "I'm yelling at the other me, don't you see?" My eyes never leave me, but clearly the other is talking to someone else in the room, not that there's anyone else here.

"Go into the back bedroom and get the rifle under the bed." Okay, clearly this is escalating, and I really need a weapon. I take one step toward the fireplace, which happens to be in the same direction as the bedrooms. The other me shouts, "Hey," and hurls the log at me. Not only does the log hit me in the forehead and knock me on my ass, but I hear glass shattering a moment later.

As I lie on the ground, I hear multiple sets of boots running from the living room to the bedrooms. When I look up, the other me is gone. Getting to my feet, my head throbbing from where the log hit me, I glance at the window and see it's completely intact. I'm really confused, but I ignore it in favor of getting the fireplace poker. With the cold iron in my hands, I press my back against the wall near the hallway and wait.

A minute later, I see the barrel of an old Winchester rifle slowly peak out from the hall. I let whoever it is come a little closer before swinging the fireplace poker. The hard metal connects with the other me's head, and the gun goes flying. It lands hard on the ground and goes off, the bullet tearing through the meat of my arm just below the shoulder.

Looking to the me lying unconscious on the floor, I expect to see a bloody gash on their forehead, but all I see is an angry red mark. I could've sworn I saw blood a moment ago, but there's none. Now that the threat is down for the moment, I inspect the wound on my shoulder. Only, there is no wound. This doesn't make any sense. I felt the bullet hit me.

Going for the pill bottle in my pocket, I take another one quickly. My therapist said to take one of these anytime I feel my mind's grip on reality slipping, and I'd say this qualifies. Talk about strange and unusual.

That rings something in my memory. The number next to the list of emergency numbers on the fridge. I bound across the room for the landline next to the fridge and quickly dial the number. It doesn't even fully ring once before a tired voice comes on the line. Instead of a greeting of any kind, the guy on the other side asks, "How many raccoons are there?"

The question is so unexpected that I actually look around. Of course, there are none, and I tell him so. "Shit, okay. I was told this might happen. Are you the one with the family, or the one without?" I couldn't be any more confused than I am at this moment, but I tell him the truth. "Okay. I'll probably be having this same conversation before too long, assuming you two idgets don't kill each other first." I'm about to start asking questions, but he cuts me off. "This'll go faster if you just let me talk." I shut up.

"There are places in this world where the veil between realities is thin, like your aunt and uncle's cabin. If you happen to be in one of these places at the same time as another you, the two of you will be able to interact with each other. It's not advised because people tend to try and kill the other them before they realize what's going on. I advise you get the hell out of there."

Unfortunately, with the storm overhead that's not going to happen. Through the open back door, it looks like four inches of snow has already fallen. "Then I suggest you calmly sit down with yourself and figure out a diplomatic solution. Otherwise, the other family is going to lose you too."

Yeah, talk about strange and unusual. Though, I can't help but wonder, what does this have to do with raccoons?

PLANTING SEEDS

I've always been different from other people. When I was younger I could see things that no one else could, things people couldn't begin to understand. It was frightening to my parents, and they didn't know what to make of it.

The kids at school already knew there was something off about me. I wasn't much for conversation or playing, and the few times I would join in on whatever they were doing, it never went well. It was like we didn't think the same way or something along those lines. They'd occasionally ask what was up with me and all I could do was shrug. To them, the most logical way of doing anything was to go from point A to point B. Me, I saw a dozen other points in between that no one else ever did. Growing up in a small town was hard enough, and the rumors that I regularly went to a shrink didn't help matters.

In elementary school I sometimes talked about the things I saw, but the only ones that believed me were the kids my age. For a time, it was enough. Then I made the mistake of describing the figures and creatures I saw. It scared the others so badly that they stopped talking to me altogether. They wouldn't even look at me, claiming I gave them nightmares.

My therapist, Dr. Elder, tried to catalog the apparitions I claimed to see. In one session I described thirteen different figures, no two alike, and there were plenty more. Each thing was dark and sickly, covered in some kind of mucus or sludge. Some of them had wavy appendages like tentacles, while others sported wings. They varied in size, shape and consistency, and none stuck around very long. It's like they came to observe me for a brief time and then simply left.

During our fourth session, Dr. Elder gave me paper and crayons. She asked me if I could try to draw the creatures, but since I was so young, the images I created were obviously not that good. I did well enough to give a general idea, but it didn't do any of them justice. She thought they were all small until I started adding in a stick figure of myself. It was my first experience with scaling, and she finally began to understand the size of these things. The largest of them at the time were the size of a small house.

Dr. Elder was fascinated that I could come up with so many variations, claiming someone my age shouldn't be able to do that. She believed it all stemmed from some kind of early trauma, probably sustained before I could remember anything. One of those early experiences that has a deep effect but goes beyond repressed. She suggested it happened before I could even form memories.

My parents didn't keep it a secret from me that I was adopted. Unfortunately, they had no insight as to what my past was like. I'd been left on a church doorstep one night before I was even a year old. The mystery of my birth and biological parents are forever gone, but my adoptive parents loved me and wanted the best for me.

By the time I was in the fifth grade, I had grown tired of answering Dr. Elder's questions. I was also tired of being looked at as a freak by my classmates and I really hated that I didn't have any friends. I knew the only way to change that was to stop talking about them. I told Dr. Elder that the things I saw were simply gone. Now granted, when I told her this, there was one standing right behind her, but I managed not to let on to that fact.

This particular apparition was one I'd seen many times before, the only one that kept coming back. It was a big creature with tree trunk legs, wavy arms and long black hair with a beard that moved on its own, like it was made of small snakes. I used to think of it as a guardian because, like all the others, it didn't seem to want to do me harm. On rare occasions it would even help me.

I remember one incident on the playground in particular in the third grade. There was this fourth grader, Scott Gerald, who liked to pick on me a lot. Sometimes he'd get physical and beat me up, but most of the time it was just name calling. This one time was an incident where things got physical, and he tried to take it too far.

Scott chased me around the playground, all the way to the top of the jungle gym. We were at the highest point, the top of the slide and Scott was going to push me off. I don't mean he was going to push me down the slide. He wanted to push me off the side of the jungle gym. Looking back on it, it seemed like an insane drop but was probably at most ten feet. That was still a high enough distance to do some damage to my small body.

My guardian was right behind Scott, and I could sense that he was really angry at the punk kid. Kind of like an older brother when someone is picking on their younger sibling right in front of them. Just as Scott was reaching out to shove me, I saw those wavy arms of his strike out and hit the boy in the back. Scott ended up going down the slide headfirst at a tremendous speed and busted his nose on the way down. He also pissed his pants and all the kids that had been watching laughed at him. It was the last time he ever messed with me.

No matter how hard Dr. Elder prodded, I wouldn't tell her that I still saw them. It wasn't hard to tell the difference between what only I saw and what was physically there. It goes beyond just the fact that the creatures aren't human. They were darker than what is in the real world, as if shrouded in shadow. This also made it easier for me to ignore them.

It's not like they ever startled me or anything like that. Not once did they ever frighten me, not even the first time I saw one. I could almost sense when they were around, and I actively made it a point to not look in their direction if I could help it. Eventually, their visits started decreasing, but it took years for that to happen. By the time I was in the eighth grade, only my guardian still showed up, and it wasn't that often.

I'd made exceptional strides in becoming a more normal kid at school. My classmates stopped looking at me like I was a freak and anytime someone asked about the things I used to see, I'd just claim it had been a child's overactive imagination. I would never again admit to seeing those things out loud. In my mind I couldn't deny them, but that was okay.

I never grew out of the habit of drawing the creatures and things. The inaccuracy of those early drawings bugged me as my talents got better. I felt a need to capture them as best as I could, and it didn't matter to me that there were literally hundreds of them. Each one got multiple attempts, and the best got stashed in my portfolio. For some reason it was very important to me that the paper be rather thin. It didn't matter if the ink of my pen bled through to the other side. I didn't use the back of the pages anyway.

My mom found my sketch book of my drafts one day and got worried. I assured her I wasn't still seeing them and it wasn't devolving into an obsession, though that last part could be argued. I was simply creating art and was even thinking about creating a comic book or graphic novel. This wasn't true, but it did get her to stop worrying so much. Not completely since the things I drew were horrific and always had been. It's not like I drew them in the throws of violence or anything of the sort. They were monsters, plain and simple. My pen was just really good at capturing their menace. Dad compared them to someone named David Cronenberg, but I didn't know who that was at the time.

The first day of my freshman year was alarming, and for more than just the usual reasons. Being at a new school was jarring all on its own and I didn't know my way around well enough. I was looking for my homeroom when I started to hear something. It was music, but not like the stuff kids were listening to through headphones. This was very different, yet oddly familiar.

The melody was slightly melancholy while being majestic and reverent, almost like a religious song. There were no words to the song, or at least none that my human ears could perceive. For a moment, it made me flash back to a long time ago, before I was left on the church doorsteps. Back to a time I shouldn't have been able to remember.

People were standing around me in dark robes, singing some kind of prayer over me. I could smell something in the air, something metallic like copper. Each person who looked down on me held a clenched fist above my infant body, and at least one drop of something fell onto me. The memory was so vivid that it felt like I was living it all over again, but for the first time.

I came out of the vision and caught sight of my guardian standing outside a classroom. I walked right up to him and was going to ask why he was there, but then I caught sight of the room number. He was standing outside my homeroom. All day long he kept helping me find my way around, but I didn't have another vision. At least, not that day.

The next day my guardian returned, but it wasn't to show me to my art class. No, this time he was already in the room when I entered, and he was standing behind an empty chair. This classroom was in the science wing, so instead of those individual desks with the little basket under the chair, they had those black top tables big enough for two students.

The second chair was already occupied by a girl, but when I looked at her, I wasn't standing at the classroom door anymore. I was in a dark place, some kind of large warehouse or something. The building was at least three stories tall and the only light that came in from the outside was from small windows along the top. In the center of the space was a monolith that nearly touched the ceiling.

The monolith wasn't a large black rectangle like in that 2001 movie I'd seen when I was younger. This was much larger with a wide base that was easily ten feet wide, and it rose up to a fine point. It looked like the large part of a crab's claw but stretched out and slightly twisted. There were precisely carved symbols all over the smooth surface and though I recognized them, I didn't know what they meant. I hadn't realized it before that moment, but each of my finished drawings had one of those symbols somewhere in them.

The vision lasted only a few seconds, and I immediately took the seat without asking if it was alright. The girl had been talking to someone at the next table and didn't even notice me until class started. The truth is, I'd known her for years. Not so much that I knew her, but I was aware of her. We never had a class together, but we'd been at the same school since elementary.

As the teacher was going over the syllabus for the school year, something really strange happened. My guardian took the seat I was already in, with me sitting in it. To my eyes, it was like I was in his body, and I could see his wavy arms overlapping mine. Suddenly, I wasn't in control of my own body.

I opened up my sketchbook to a blank page and started drawing something new. This wasn't like anything I'd drawn before. I always started with my main subject and filled in the background after the image was complete. The subject of this drawing was the background, or rather, it was a landscape, and it was coming together very quickly. Faster than I'd ever drawn anything before.

The point of view was from the bank of a lake surrounded by forest. There were no buildings, boats or any manmade objects in sight, as if the place was completely untouched by outside influences. Though the lake held more than water, there was an island in it. It was large enough to hold a dense cluster of trees, so much so that the entire island looked dark and mysterious, as if something was hiding there.

The girl next to me noticed what I was drawing and asked about it. The words started flooding out of my mouth quietly. I told her it was a nature preserve nearby that no one is allowed to go in, but I'd snuck in there a few times over the summer. It was a peaceful place to get away from prying, judgmental eyes. A sort of oasis in a world filled with people where you could truly be alone. The water in the lake was so clear that you could see schools of large fish swimming just below the surface.

Like the drawing, these words weren't mine, but my guardian's. I'd never been to this place he was describing. As he was talking to Erica, I felt like a seed of an idea was planted in her mind, one I wouldn't understand for years to come. I was back in control of myself shortly after that and tried not to dwell on the strange event too much. It wasn't easy since being possessed was a first for me, but it eventually faded.

As school progressed, art class introduced me to new mediums to work with. My teacher thought I was a great artist, if but a little dark, but painting definitely wasn't my thing. What did turn out to be where I shined was sculpting. I knew it wasn't the best idea, but for an assignment with clay, I created a miniature of my guardian.

While working the clay, I used a sharp instrument to form the details of his webbed feet. The instrument slipped and I sliced open my finger. Not deep or anything that a Band-Aid couldn't deal with. Instead of stopping, I continued with my work, getting blood all over the clay. No one seemed to notice.

As I progressed, I felt something happen. My blood was infusing with the clay, becoming part of the whole. This was no longer a sculptured likeness of my guardian but becoming an effigy.

Once all the clay projects in the class were fired up and cooked in the kiln, the teacher graded them and gave them back to us. I noticed that mine was darker than the others, and I knew why, though I did not share. I was a little surprised that I only got a B on it, but the teacher had wanted me to create something different than what he called my 'eldritch style.' I had no idea what that meant, but for some unknown reason, the word seemed fitting.

High school taught me something that I hadn't really been aware of before. People are obsessed with labels and placing others into categories. I wasn't a jock, geek, academic, skater, or punk. I was an artist and that is where my focus stayed. By junior year I had nearly seven hundred drawings in my portfolio, each with their own special symbol. My guardian was usually around while I worked on these drawings in my room, and I knew the symbols were coming from him. I started to think of them as signatures, like artists do to paintings and such, but instead of signing my name, I signed theirs.

There was this one Saturday that still stands out in my mind. It was the last time I would ever see my guardian again. I heard a loud thump when he appeared. I'd been drawing a creature similar to him, but much larger with bat like wings. It was the only time I'd ever seen him angry at me, so I stopped working on the drawing and threw the paper away. He really didn't like me working on that image.

I noticed he was swinging one arm ever so slightly. When it was coming forward it would suddenly stop, as if hitting some barrier I couldn't see. Every time he did this I'd hear that echoing thump again. It was as if he was trapped in some kind of chamber.

That song I heard outside my homeroom

freshman year came to me again, stronger this time. It wasn't just the music though. My guardian actually spoke to me. He said, "I have to go away for a while, but know I will always be with you." It was always rare for him to be able to physically touch anything, but he reached his other tentacle out and picked up the effigy. He placed it in my hands and began fading away. "Keep to your work, my Gardener."

After that, I fell into a hard depression. I alienated myself from the friends I made and embraced the whole brooding artist persona that everyone thought I already had. If someone got in my way, I'd lash out at them hard, even getting physical a time or two. My drastic change in demeanor was almost as bad as what happened with Emma after her sister went missing.

Senior year was a blur of halfhearted schoolwork and deep emersion into my art. It continued on into college, but I rarely got physical anymore. I began to ignore everyone, just like I had the creatures I used to see when I was little. My parents were worried because I was deathly pale, didn't eat much and had taken to smoking. By the time my freshman year of college was over, I weighed less than a hundred and fifty pounds.

My art began to evolve from just bio-pics of the creatures. I began to draw elaborate scenes of violence, of people becoming monsters and doing unspeakable things. There was even one that depicted an entire town of evolving people taking to the sea, leaving dry land behind. These drawings came from dreams I was having, but I could only remember snippets.

Things were happening in the world, and I was actually starting to tune into it. People have been getting meaner than they used to be, and a lot more irritable. Here I thought it was just me, but it's more than that I think. Crime is on the rise all over, and people keep going missing. I even overheard a news anchor comment that psychiatric hospitals were overflowing with patients, as if insanity was spreading like a disease. There was even a riot at a cookie factory that resulted in several deaths. Could it be that I just didn't notice all this going on and the world had always been this crazy?

A few months back I was jumped by two guys while walking back to my dorm. One of them held a knife to my throat and asked the strangest question. "Have you embraced the madness?" For a moment, I could feel the effigy of my guardian sitting on my desk three blocks away. I felt connected to it in a way I hadn't since I created it.

Something flashed in my eyes as I stared those two down, and I began to laugh. Not like there was something funny about this, but like I knew something they didn't. It was the kind of laugh a sinister villain directs at his victims before he brutally murders them. I could feel this was coming from the effigy, and my guardian was lending some of himself to aid me.

They let me go and apologized, all the while calling me, "Sir." Strangest damn thing that has happened to me since I got to college. Well, before today.

I got a letter in the mail from some real estate group I'd never heard of. I figured it was some kind of advertisement and nearly threw it away, but something caught my eye. Next to the return address is a company logo, like a tall, thin pyramid, but twisted in the middle. It was a simplified version of the thing I saw before sitting next to Erica in my freshman art class.

Immediately I open the envelope, and sure enough, it's not an advertisement. There isn't much to the letter, just some instructions and a bus ticket inside. Why the hell would I want to pack a bag and ditch school just because someone sent me a freaking bus ticket? Then I see it at the bottom of the letter. In place of a signature is one of those odd symbols I've drawn a hundred times. It's not just any old symbol, but the one designated for my guardian. I pack a bag immediately.

The bus drops me off in the middle of nowhere, and I get lucky enough that a rideshare driver is in the area. He takes me to a farm about thirty miles away. I can see a lot of people working in the fields, not one of them looks older than thirty. As I approach the gate, I see two guys standing just on the other side, almost like guards. They look familiar, and it only takes me a minute to realize they're the two who jumped me not long ago.

Without saying a word, they open the gate for me and usher me in. Together, they escort me across a dirt road leading to a very large barn or warehouse. It looks old, like it was built more than thirty years ago. As we pass the people in the fields, everyone stops what they're doing and looks at me. I've never been in the spotlight before, but it doesn't seem to unnerve me like I expect.

The guy that held the knife to my throat rushes forward as we get close to the building, and he pulls back a heavy door. Now that I'm this close to it, I can tell exactly what it had been once upon a time. It was a slaughterhouse for pigs. My escorts stay at the door and let me go in alone.

Walking inside, I get the sense that I've been here before. The room is easily three stories tall and the only light coming in is from small windows near the ceiling. The only thing missing is the large red monolith.

As if reading my thoughts, a deep, rumbling voice like waves crashing against rocks calls to me from the darkness, "It's only missing because you haven't built it yet." A large man in an expensive suit comes into the light, but I'm not fooled. I can see the image of what he really is superimposed over this human façade. I always wondered what he would look like in the flesh, and it appears I'm still wondering. I don't know how he's doing it, but he's wearing some kind of meat suit. Perhaps he can change his outer appearance, but to me, I still see who he truly is.

I ask if he has a real name or if I should continue to refer to him as my guardian. "Everyone refers to me as Master, but you alone may call me Guardian." I find myself feeling honored. Many times I'd wondered how I would feel if he came back into my life. For the longest time, I was angry about being abandoned, but I'm not angry now. If anything, I am relieved that we are together again. Excited almost since we're both physically here, mostly. This human meat suit doesn't feel like him.

"Years ago, you planted the seed of my release. Now I need you to do it again. May I see the book?" I take off my backpack and pull out the brown leather book. My portfolio got too big for the folder I used to keep my completed bio-pictures in. When I started drawing the images of violence, I felt like I was done with the bio-pics and turned it into an actual book. It wasn't hard to turn it into a leather-bound tome. This way none of them would fall out. What was difficult was putting them in the right order. I rearranged them several times before I felt like I'd gotten it right.

He thumbs through the thin pages of my book. There are exactly 1,134 individual drawings, each of a different creature. "My followers are here to provide for your every want and desire. Do not hesitate to ask something of them, nothing is out of bounds. They will get you whatever materials you need to create the monolith. Clay, kiln, blood, whatever. This is what you were born to do."

I flash back on the first time I heard his song and those people standing over my infant body. It had been a ritual where they anointed me with their blood. Part of me always knew that.

He wants me to create more than eleven hundred effigies like the one I made of him. That's going to take a long time. "We have enemies trying to stop us, but you will be safe here." He gives me back the tome and places those thick hands on my shoulders, but I feel the tentacles more than the fingers. "You are my best kept secret. Everyone here will die to protect you." It feels great to have my guardian back.

All my life, the things I could see, my drive to draw them in excruciating detail, everything has been building to this. I never knew where it was going, but now that I'm here, I get it.

There is a door that can not be seen by the naked eye. It does not exist in a physical sense that we can understand, but it's accessible everywhere in the universe. The monolith is both lock and key. Once it is built and the proper combination is infused, the door will be opened. The question is, what will be released?

"You haven't figured it out yet?" My guardian asks me. "The ancients you've spent your whole life drawing. We're going to bring them into this world."

PADDED CELL PATRON

Most people don't know this, but there's a freelance version of pretty much every job and profession out there. Sometimes they have a different name than the regular version. Take Detective and Private Investigator for instance. My freelance work isn't anything as exciting as that. I'm a freelance organizer.

Yeah, that sounds weird and made up, but I can assure you it's a real thing. The biggest difficulty is getting hired, but that's another story. People far and wide can be pretty bad at organizing and for a number of reasons. Either it's too complicated for them, they're too lazy or they just have too much on their plate to deal with it. That's where someone like me comes in.

This whole career path started off at a tax office of all things. I was a tax preparer for a local company. During the slow times I didn't just sit at my desk twiddling my thumbs like my coworkers. Mostly out of boredom, I put myself in front of the rows of filing cabinets and started going through every single one of them.

It used to be that when a client came in to do their current year's taxes, we pulled their previous year's file. The problem was, when you have everyone in the office putting stuff in and taking stuff out of the file cabinets, things get misplaced or lost. Some people are too lazy to put them in the right order. I got tired of not being able to find the files I needed, so I decided to organize them.

For that previous year's returns, there were around ten thousand files. I spent all my downtime during the tax season working on organizing those files. When the season ended and all the preparers were let go, the boss decided to hold onto me for an additional month to organize the files for the season we just completed. It turned out that I didn't need that much time to get through it, so I started on the returns from two years prior. The boss was impressed, but not enough to keep me on full-time.

While I was hard at work fixing everyone's filing mistakes, word got around to the other small tax offices about my filing abilities. When the month was up, I was getting phone calls from the other local tax offices to fix their files. It became contract work so they didn't have to give me any benefits, but I did start negotiating better terms and rates.

It was when I was working on my fourth contract that things changed for me. The boss's wife had an online business selling products that she made by hand, and her workspace and inventory was a mess. On behalf of his wife, he asked if I could do anything to help her. It wasn't reorganizing files, but it wasn't that unsimilar either. It took about three weeks to get her business organized and it improved pretty much everything for her. Products stopped getting misplaced and lost, orders were being fulfilled in a timelier manner, and her reviews started getting better. She had me go back every three months to give her workspace an overhaul just so it didn't get that bad again.

My work for her business got me even more contracts with other small companies. Eventually my reputation was spreading to bigger companies until I was contracted with a major business. Due to legal reasons, I can't say which one, but I did make mid five figures for three months of work. The next thing I know, I'm getting contacted by a lot of high dollar clients and doing the kind of work that required me to sign confidentiality and non-disclosure agreements. For a brief period, I even did some work in a DEA evidence locker.

I tell you all this because it brings us to my last contract and the reason why I'm locked up in here. My last employer wasn't one I ever thought would reach out to me and it's only partly because I'm a non-believer. I don't share a lot of the church's ideals, but I guess they decided to look passed that because of my discretion. You wouldn't believe the things I've seen while sorting, cataloging and organizing the lives of some really rich and powerful people.

A representative of the church reached out to me about two months ago and requested a meeting. We met in a private location, somewhere no one would overhear us, or even see us for that matter. It was probably the strangest meeting I've ever had, and I had one client that actually used spy-like codes. That had been a little annoying, but it paid well enough that I didn't complain.

A long-standing church in the northeast had suffered a major tragedy. The priest assigned there was a well-known scholar of early Catholic history in America, and he was found dead. I was told the circumstances of his death were of no concern to me, but nothing could be further from the truth.

Father Pat had a lot of items in his possession, bordering on hoarder level. The church was so isolated that very few people attended service there. No one at the home office knew just how bad the hoarding had gotten. Resources within the church were tight at the time and they didn't have an in-house clerk available and wouldn't for at least a month.

In order to find the church, I was driven there by another priest. Father Jacob was assigned to another church closer to town but had been to the other one a few times. He'd been the one to identify Father Pat's body at the morgue but hadn't stepped foot in the church itself for nearly three months. The two had a standing dinner meeting once a month in town, but Father Pat kept calling to cancel.

Father Jacob picked me up in a well used 4x4, which was needed to get to the isolated church. We traveled through dense trees on a dirt road that looked more accustomed to wagon wheels than modern rubber ones. We were also climbing in elevation, and I began to wonder why a church was established out here to begin with. After forty-five minutes, I finally broke down and asked that very question.

We'd been rather silent since I was picked up, but I could tell Father Jacob was uncomfortable with it. He took my question and filled the air with chatter, going on and on. The church was once the main hub of a town in the early days. The town itself only stood for maybe twenty years before there was a major event that either evacuated the population or killed them. It was a great mystery that no one solved, but Father Pat had been determined to. He didn't mind that hardly anyone came to service there. It gave him time to work on his research.

He kept going on, but I stopped listening the moment the trees broke, and we came into a clearing. There was maybe three-square acres of cleared land with grass that was waist high and moved like ocean waves with the wind. In the middle of that ocean stood a stone behemoth, dark and tall, withstanding the test of time. It gave me the creeps. The complete cloud coverage and the setting sun didn't help matters. Neither did the lack of any lights.

I couldn't see it from where we were, but on the other side of the church was a cliff edge. Father Jacob said the drop was more than a hundred feet to the coast below. If there had been more of a congregation, they would've put up a fence to prevent anyone from falling off. As it was, it would've been an unnecessary expense.

We got out, loaded the handcart with our stack of cardboard boxes and a few rolls of bubble wrap, then headed for the large wooden double doors. Father Jacob used one of those really old keys to unlock the heavy doors. I expected to hear the old metal creaking when they opened, but the only noise I heard was the whooshing of wind as the doors flew open. They banged hard against the walls and dead leaves strewn in through the opening across the floor.

I admit that I jumped when it happened, but Father Jacob told me that always happened. Apparently, it was always windy around the church, which became obvious when he took up a broom that was leaning against the wall. Maybe if Father Pat had taken some time to maintain the landscape he wouldn't have had to sweep leaves out all the time.

Once the entryway was cleared, Father Jacob returned the broom to its place and flipped on the lights. If the stone structure was intimidating from the outside, I'd need to come up with a whole different word for the inside. We weren't in a lobby like I'd originally thought, but the chapel itself. The ceiling was so tall you'd need a man-lift to reach the top. Everywhere I looked there was dark wood, heavy cloth and polished metal. The lighting wasn't standard white like modern bulbs, but yellow, as if imitating candlelight. The wheels of the cart squeaked in the silence, and it made me uneasy.

The only times I'd been in a church of any kind had been for weddings and funerals, and none of those had looked like this. It definitely came from a much older time, when intimidation was more of a key factor for the church's control on their people. I personally always thought that was counter productive, but it worked for them for some weird reason.

Despite the lack of a congregation, there were still rows and rows of wooden pews that looked as old as the rest of the place. The wood had a shine to it that surprised me. I figured Father Pat's lack of landscape maintenance would translate to inside, but that wasn't the case. The place was immaculately pristine, as if waiting from inspection from the Pope himself. Even though there were lights everywhere and the entire place was lit up, it still seemed dark to me.

Father Jacob led me to a door in the back corner, next to a pair of booths with doors, one of which was slightly open. I really thought it was out of place, but he informed me it was the confessional. It was then that he realized I wasn't a man of faith, and I could see he wanted to question why I was chosen for this job, but he didn't. The military isn't the only organization that has its people following orders without question.

We entered a room at the back of the church. The rest of the place was just as dark and regal as the chapel itself, but without the high ceilings. There was a second story to that section of the church, the living quarters. My business wasn't there, but in this large storage space. The walls were lined with bookcases, but there was a lot more than just books, though there were plenty of those. This would be my workspace for the foreseeable future.

I'd slept plenty on the plane, so I had more than enough energy to get started right away. There was a large wooden table big enough for eight people to sit at in the center of the room, and it was cluttered with objects. Everything in the room was covered in a fine layer of dust, like it hadn't been touched in ages. Well, everything save for a cluster of objects. I decided to start there.

Pulling out my laptop, I opened a new spreadsheet as Father Jacob started setting up boxes. Picking up the first object, I ran my fingers over it and found the carved wood to be smooth as glass. It was a figurine of some kind, made of ebony, and unnaturally shiny. The only thing it had in common with a person was the fact that it was a biped. There weren't any arms, and if it had a head, there wasn't a neck to separate it from the torso. The shape of it was strange too. Kind of like a summer squash with legs.

The only discernable mark on the whole thing was a symbol carved into one side. It was a triangle with the point downward, and a line descending from it by the same length of the triangle itself. I'm well versed in common languages, but this didn't look like anything I was familiar with. On the spreadsheet under a heading titled 'Box 1', I inserted a description of 'ebony carved figurine with symbol.'

Next was an unusual cross-like object, but it had two extra pieces under the traditional horizontal piece, each one slightly smaller than the one above it. The wood was mahogany, also glass smooth, and had a symbol engraved on one side. This one was similar to the other, but the overall triangle was much larger with six smaller triangles in two rows on the top. This one was labeled 'cross-like object with carved symbol.' I was getting the impression that carved symbol was going to be a descriptive factor for a lot of these odd trinkets.

As I inspected each item and cataloged it into the spreadsheet with a description, Father Jacob took the items and wrapped them in bubble wrap before placing them in the first box. As he was wrapping the weird cross, he happened to glance at the symbol and remarked upon it. He said the carving was Babylonian and represented the number seven. I decided to alter the descriptions and asked him to look at any symbols I came across.

By the time Box 1 was filled, we'd gone through the cluster of trinkets without dust. Each one had a Babylonian number carved into them, but there wasn't a complete set. The numbers jumped around all over the place, ranging between one and fifty-three. After that we set to work on the rest of the table.

Most of the items covering the table were easier to identify and catalog. There was an antique chalice made of polished silver, a rusted double edge dagger with a jewel encrusted handle, and an iron cross that had seen better days, just to name a few. Some of these things were museum quality while others weren't worth the materials they were made out of. Things didn't start getting interesting until day four, when we cleared the table and started working on the first bookshelf.

We'd already filled eleven boxes, but I thought the next batch would go a lot quicker. Books are a lot easier to catalog because they have titles. For the purposes of that job, it wasn't my responsibility to organize them or put them in any specific order. The only reason I even needed to crack them open was to look for a title because none of them had visible titles along the spine. I inserted it into the spreadsheet, slapped a sticky note onto it with a catalog number, and handed it to Father Jacob to place inside the box. Things were going smoothly, though half the books were in languages I didn't recognize. Thankfully, Father Jacob was knowledgeable of a number of older languages and helped with translations. What we couldn't identify, I did my best and moved on.

    The books themselves varied in size, thickness and color. Most were leather bound and old, others were slightly more modern, but none were younger than seventy years. Even the bibles that littered the shelves were antiques. Plumes of dust blew off in small clouds as I closed the covers, and after a while, we needed to air the room out. Father Jacob had been dusting off everything I handed him, and it had created a lingering cloud that filled the room.

    Our work schedule stayed as it was when we first started, so halfway through the day, we broke for dinner. The kitchen was well stocked, and we made something quick and easy. Neither one of us wanted to spend more time there than we needed to. It wasn't just me that got the creeps from that church. Granted, Father Jacob might've been creeped out more by sleeping in Father Pat's old room. I'd won the coin toss and got the spare room. It didn't make much sense for us to drive all the way back into town, especially since it started raining on and off since day two.

    I pulled down one large book made of brown leather, and it stood out to me more than any other. This one wasn't covered in a layer of dust and there wasn't any hiding in the pages either. When I opened it the language was impossible for me to read, but I happened to glance at the bottom and saw one of those Babylonian numbers. The title page was missing and the only reason I knew that was because there was fragments of a missing page sticking out from the binding when I opened it.

I labeled it as 'damaged Babylonian brown leather tome,' stuck a numbered sticky note to it and handed it to Father Jacob. He quickly noticed the lack of dust but didn't put it in the box like he had all the others. Instead, he opened the book and looked to be reading the ancient words. I kept working until a little while later when my stomach decided to rumble right along with the storm. Something about dinner wasn't agreeing with me, and I had to excuse myself. I told Father Jacob to take a break because I got the sense that I was going to be a while, and I was.

When I eventually came back, it was on wobbly legs because they'd fallen asleep. For a minute there, I'd thought I was dying of dysentery, but it eventually passed. I'd been gone for more than half an hour.

Reentering the storage room, I found Father Jacob was gone. I didn't think much of it and got right back to work. After another hour he still hadn't returned, so I started dusting off the pile of cataloged books and putting them in the box. As I did, I realized one was missing, and it was the brown tome Father Jacob had been reading. I placed a sticky note onto the box, indicating it was the one the missing book belonged to. I went to bed shortly after that.

I woke up really late the next day, having gone to the bathroom twice more throughout the night.

Believing I'd finally expelled whatever had screwed up my stomach so badly, I went into the kitchen for coffee and to make something light to eat. There was no evidence that Father Jacob had been in there since dinner, which was evident by the cold pot of coffee. He'd had a fresh pot ready to go every day I'd woken up, and though I'd slept in, I hadn't slept that damn late.

Looking out the window, I saw two things. His car was still outside, and the rain was coming down hard. I'm talking thunder rumbling and lightning flashing. Cell service had been spotty at best when we first arrived, so I wasn't able to get an updated weather forecast. I got to work making coffee and toast.

Father Jacob hadn't been in his room, nor was he anywhere upstairs. I was just about to head to the storage room when something caught my eye. It was in the living room, and the only reason I'd noticed was because a lamp had been left on in there. We hadn't spent any time there in the near week we'd been at the church.

There were papers scattered over a coffee table in front of the couch. Some of them were modern lined paper with mad scribblings all over. I read some of the erratic writing, but none of it made sense. It kept talking about a code of some kind, but there were no details that I could find. Shrugging my shoulders, I turned to leave when I tripped on something on the floor.

The brown book that Father Jacob had taken was left open on the rug. I bent down to pick it up, and I noticed more page fragments at the binding where it was open. He'd torn a page out, and I took another look at the papers on the coffee table. There were dozens of old pages amidst the modern lined paper, and several had sticky notes on them. The writing on them was a similar erratic script, but it was obviously discernable from the lined paper. More mentions of a code, but these notes had numbers on them. Arrows pointed to passages on the papers, but I had no idea what it all meant. More to the point, I wasn't paid to know or find out.

I gathered up all the old pages and the book from the floor. Going down to the storage room, I planned on placing it all in the box and decided it was someone else's problem. When I got down there, I finally found Father Jacob.

He was standing over the far end of the table, Box 1 tossed across the room and bubble wrap flung everywhere. The items from inside lay on the table on top of pages from the tome. Each one was an engraving, a detailed picture of the items that stood on top of them like paper weights. Father Jacob was jittery like a tweaking addict and muttering words I couldn't understand.

As if he sensed me, his face shot up and eyes with bloody tears looked at me in derangement. His words came out fast and furious, that strange tongue sounding vaguely demonic. The items on the table began to shake and I could suddenly smell something like rotten eggs. Then, I shit you not, Father Jacob started to levitate. It wasn't a trick or anything like that, and I took off running. The scream that he shrieked out still sends a shiver down my spine when I think of it.

I didn't have anywhere to go, but I was determined to put distance between us. My feet took me to the front doors, and I could hear Jacob pursuing me, so I flung them open and went into the storm. The whole thing unnerved the shit out of me so badly that I couldn't remember where the road had been. I just ran and the only light was an occasional lightning flash. All I could see was waist high grass as the rain pummeled my face. I'd never been in such a bad storm.

The wind was kicking my ass all over the place and assaulted my ears. Or at least, that's what I thought was causing the noise. Jacob came at me from the darkness with a large knife and the sudden appearance of him caused my feet to falter. I slid on the ground and kept going for a few feet before the ground was suddenly gone. Too late I'd remembered the cliff edge so close to the church and I was going over the edge.

I twisted around and grabbed onto the edge before plummeting to my death. As I dangled there, I kicked around for something to gain purchase on with my feet and found a large enough protrusion to plant my feet on. Lightning flashed as I tried to hoist myself up and there was Jacob coming at me at full speed. He dove for me, and I ducked down, leaving only the tips of my fingers on the ledge.

Jacob screamed curses at me as he sailed over my head and into the blackness behind me. I didn't bother looking because I wouldn't have been able to see anything anyway. It took some doing, and I nearly slipped and fell to my death a couple times, but I pulled myself up.

Thankfully Jacob had left the doors open and I used the light to guide my way back to the church. There was a landline in the storage room, and I used it to call 911. As I was on the phone with the operator, I looked over at the objects on the table. There were captions underneath the engravings on the pages, and the longer I looked at them, the more I understood what they were saying.

I turned my back on them and told the operator

that there'd been an accident, and that Father Jacob had gone over the cliff. She said they'd get someone out there as soon as they could, but with as bad as the storm was getting, it was going to take a while. As I hung up the phone, I heard something behind me and immediately whirled around. Up until that point, I figured that Jacob had been a little mentally unstable and being isolated in that place had caused some kind of psychotic break. This was far from the case.

The objects on the engravings started to dance across the table into a pile like how I found them days ago. At the same time, the engravings slithered across the table and the brown book that I'd brought back down opened. I watched as each engraving reentered the book and magically mended themselves back into the binding. Within moments, the book was back to its original glory. I suddenly felt unhinged, like my grip on reality was becoming loose.

So that's it, that's why I'm here. I tell you all this because the police found me ranting and raving about powerful forces, about objects and relics in the church making people go insane. No one had a clue that I'd thrown the trinkets over the cliff, but it's only a matter of time before someone finds them and the book. I tried to burn the damn tome to ashes, but it was completely resistant to fire, so it went over the cliff too. It gets worse than that.

My powerful clients are afraid that my fractured psyche will cause all their little secrets that I know to come tumbling out. The only way I can survive is to become a permanent resident of this institution and only tell you, my deranged looking mirror cellmate, the truth. If we're both lucky, no one will ever learn that we're not actually crazy, but just hiding. I just hope they don't take this mirror away from me. I don't want to be alone, even if seeing you makes my mind fracture slightly.

MIMIC

This is going to sound really weird, but the pandemic was a godsend for me. I know it's wrong to think something so horrible could be a good thing, but it accomplished something I'd been trying to get done for years. No, it's not kill a shit ton of people on a global scale, but something much less significant, and centralized to me. What kind of monster do you think I am?

I have been socially awkward since as far back as I can remember. It probably started in middle school when I asked Stacy Decker to be my girlfriend. She publicly humiliated me so badly for it that I became the number one school pariah. That followed me all the way to high school and then some. Thanks to that, I never got comfortable around other people, and I did everything I could to keep myself away from my peers and strangers.

College was a little better, but only because I was able to take online courses. In four years, I only stepped foot on campus twelve times. I didn't even go to graduation and just had them mail me my diploma. It didn't matter that I had a perfect average. There was no way I was going to go to a ceremony with that many people present.

To be completely honest, it's a miracle I got a job at all even with all my qualifications. Understandably, I don't interview well, and every single person I sat in front of could easily see I was uncomfortable. I got turned down fifteen times until someone decided to take a chance on me. It was partly out of desperation on their part, but I managed to negotiate an office for myself in the deal. I was able to close my door, draw the blinds and work in complete isolation while still being at the office.

Not once did I venture out to the break room for a coffee or lunch break. The most anyone saw me was those few occasions when I couldn't hold it any longer and made a mad dash for the restroom. My office was as self contained as I could make it. There was a small fridge I had brought in at my own expense, and I even got my own coffeemaker. It was one of those fancy ones that takes the individual cups. It didn't make much sense to get a traditional coffeemaker. I monitored my liquids intake so I wouldn't have to go to the bathroom more than necessary.

My social anxiety was so bad that I wouldn't take the elevator. I tried it the first two weeks I was there, but even going up three floors was a nightmare for me. I was probably the only person that saw the stairwell more than just during routine fire drills. Oh god had those been hell for me, but thankfully they were limited to twice a year. After three years there I finally got a heads-up from my boss about them, and I used vacation days to avoid them. She said it was technically a violation of their regulations, but because I did such a good job for the company, it was overlooked.

Social distancing changed everything, and my request to do my job remotely, which would've been easily accomplished from day one, was finally approved. Granted, they had to do it for everyone to keep the company going, but I wasn't complaining. No, that didn't come until they started bringing people back in after the crisis slowed down, but I fought to stay remote.

It hasn't been easy, but I've managed to keep my boss from forcing me to come back into the office. Between my claims of developing a germ phobia and my online therapist diagnosing me with agoraphobia, they can't really force me to come back in. Now, if my work output starts going down or isn't of satisfactory quality then I could be in trouble, but I'm still doing stellar work. She even had someone analyze my output and since I started working remotely, my productivity has increased by 37.6%. Bringing me back in would only decrease that and that's not in the company's interest.

Thanks to the internet and damn near every worthwhile consumer-based business being online, I literally have no reason to leave my apartment. You'd think I'd have to at the very least take my trash out, but my complex actually has a concierge service that brings me my mail, packages and deliveries as well as takes my garbage. It's not like they come into my apartment to do this. I simply leave my trashcan outside my door with the bag tied off, and someone comes to pick it up.

Next to my front door is a small table, and I even had the maintenance crew bolt it to the floor, so it doesn't go wandering. This is specifically for any and all deliveries I have coming to me. From groceries and take out, all the way to mail and packages, it all gets left on that table. I haven't had to go to the store for anything since the lockdown. I even subscribe to one of those meal box services that teaches me how to make chef level meals.

The only time I have to deal with actual people is when something needs attending in my apartment that I can't do myself. The maintenance crew consists of four very nice people who are paid well enough to accommodate the residents and their personal foibles. Also, when they have to come inside, I tip them depending on how little interaction I have with them. Typically, I'll lock myself in my home office while they're here after I've shown them whatever problem I've been having.

The first few times this happened when I first moved in, I started to suspect the crew were stealing from me. I ordered and set up discrete security cameras in every room, two for the larger ones, just so I could keep an eye on them. The most daunting ones I installed had actually been outside my front door, but I don't mean the doorbell camera. I actually installed two cameras on either side of my hallway so I could see if anyone was coming or going. As far as I know, no one knows about them.

After having my morning coffee, I dress for the day. I don't just go into my home office in my pajamas like a lot of people did during the lockdown. I dress in a button up shirt and slacks, and it's not just because I have to do a video call with my boss every morning. One of the issues with everyone working remotely was that they were too comfortable, and it slowed down their productivity. They were surrounded by distractions and creature comforts of home. I don't have that issue.

My home office is set up rather similarly to the office I had at work, minus the mini fridge and coffee maker. I do take coffee breaks now and eat lunch in my kitchen, but I don't abuse the privilege like my coworkers did. I've even given my boss a virtual tour of my workspace and do so at least once a month. It's always at random and at my boss's request to make sure I'm not doing what so many others did. Anything to make sure I don't have to go back into the office, I'm willing to do it.

As I sit at my workstation and make my daily video call, a ping on my wall panel alerts me to someone's presence outside my front door. The panel is the size of a regular digital tablet, and I can see the video feed from my chair. Someone in a blue vest is placing a few boxes on the small table outside. I recently made some purchases online, and if I remember correctly, there should be four boxes.

Speaking to my boss in video chat is a lot easier for me than it was when we did this in person. By not physically being in the same room as another person, I feel less anxious, and can compose myself in a professional manner. It helps me open up to my therapist a lot more too. Dr. Finn likes to think of it as an improvement.

The call lasts about half an hour, the usual length. I have my action item points mapped out for my workload today. The first item is getting a fresh cup of coffee. Normally I'd wait a little longer for this, but I want to get my packages inside before someone decides to make off with them. It's only happened twice since I moved in here, and I don't like to chance it. It helps that I live on the top floor. Thieves don't like to climb that many stairs from what the crime stats suggest.

As the coffee maker does it's thing, I open the door and grab up my boxes. There's actually five of them, not four like I initially thought, which I find odd. I give the labels a quick glance and sure enough, they're all addressed to me. Leaving them on the island counter, I doctor my coffee and return to my office. It's not like there's anything I'm overly eager to get at in my packages. It's mostly clothes and a new pillow.

As soon as I get back to my workstation, I dive right into my assigned tasks. Having an action items list makes getting through my workload so easy. It can take anywhere from twenty minutes to two hours to check off an item, depending on what it is. It's all relatively easy and pretty boring, but I enjoy the work. Today's list has just over a dozen items, and I blow through more than half of it by lunchtime.

As my meal is heating in the microwave, I decide to open my boxes. The plain colored t-shirts and pants get tossed into the washer, and my new pillow with the new pillowcase gets put into my bedroom. I break down the four boxes and put them in my recycle bin as the microwave dings at me.

Sitting at the table, I click on the TV and pull up one of my streaming services. Even though I work from home, I'm still required to take the hour for lunch, so I queue up one of my shows. Sometimes, when the workload is heavier than usual, I work during lunch. If I don't knock out all my action items in a day, I have to deal with them first thing the following day, and that can easily snowball.

By the time I've finished my show, I have my dishes in the dishwasher and have moved my new clothes from the washer to the dryer. Once the dryer is done, I'll take a quick break to pull them out in order to keep them from wrinkling. I may never leave home, but I hate it when my clothes are wrinkled.

On my way back to work, I grab a soda from the fridge. As I turn, my eyes are drawn to the island. Something seems off about the blank granite countertop, but I can't figure out what. Running my hand over the smooth surface, I confirm what my eyes see. There's nothing on it, so why does it look wrong?

I stand there for a few moments, my mind not comprehending what my eyes seem to be picking up on. Noise coming from down the hall startles me. It's the sound of a video chat request, which is really odd. Only one person calls me like that, and I can't remember the last time my boss called me in the middle of the day. This can't be good.

Shrugging off the weird feeling about the countertop, I move down the hall and pick up my phone to answer the call. Of course, it's my boss and she doesn't look that good. In our chat this morning I noticed she looked a bit frazzled, but I wasn't going to say anything. Now that I think of it, she's been looking a bit warn down more and more over the last two weeks. As soon as she starts talking, I groan knowing exactly what this is about.

Company policy mandates that every employee needs to use their vacation time. I've always thought that made sense, but for those that actually leave their home, not someone like me. Since I have nowhere to go, I don't feel the need to take time off. This is a fight I have with her every year, but it usually comes toward the end of the year. I sort of figured this was going to come early, especially since I managed to skip doing it last year.

It turns out I kind of shot myself in the foot. Skipping my vacation last year means I have to take my two weeks off starting at five today, but I'll have to do it again before the end of the year too. Vacation is nothing more than a reminder that there's more to this world than my apartment. The problem is, I have no desire to go out there, which is something my therapist is trying to break me from.

He once asked me, "If your apartment was on

fire, would you flee to safety, or would you allow yourself to burn to death because you feared going outside?" I'd told him that I would go outside, but I didn't say it convincingly. Not even a little bit. The most I've done since the lockdown is go out on my balcony and it does help that I'm four floors up. That and I can't see the balcony next to mine because of a wall that separates them.

When five o'clock hits, I sign off on my workstation and power it down. Unbuttoning the three top buttons of my shirt, I go into the kitchen, pull a beer from the fridge and toss the cap into the recycle bin. After taking a long pull, I pull back the curtain covering the balcony door and open it. The air is significantly warmer than inside with a noticeable humidity level. Why the hell do people go out in this? It's so much nicer inside.

Telling myself that I won't have to interact with another person, I step outside. The clouds blanket the sky, threatening rain, but not a drop has fallen yet. I can hear the sounds of people below, children at the pool. I'd wanted a unit on the other side of the complex, toward the back and away from the amenities area, but there wasn't one available at the time. The closer I get to the rail, the more of that area below comes into view.

It takes about a minute, but I finally make it to the half wall. I'm grateful that it isn't just a metal railing like a lot of balconies have. The most time I've spent out here at one time was five minutes, and I only managed that because I sat on the floor where no one could see me. It was a remarkable improvement from the first time I ventured out here. Someone was out on their balcony across the way, saw me and waved. It was so unexpected and freaked me out enough that I didn't go back out there for a month.

Dr. Finn has been encouraging me to do this at the end of every workday, but that's too much for me. The most consistent I've been about it is every Friday for the last two months. Seriously, fresh air is overrated.

I lean against the half wall with my back to the world and finish my beer. By the time the bottle is empty I am drenched in sweat, and little of that is because of the humidity. I am so anxious that my heart is practically in my throat. Still, I slowly walk back inside instead of hurrying like I'd like to do. It's times like this that make me wonder why I bother. There isn't anything that will make me want to go back out into the world. I have no desire for companionship and am not afflicted with a sex drive, so what's the point?

After taking a shower, I dress in a t-shirt and linen pants, my standard attire. I go into the kitchen and prepare one of those chef box meals. It takes about half an hour, but it's the best tacos I've ever had. Once all the dishes are in the dishwasher, I relax on the couch and watch some TV. As I sit there, I can actively feel my energy level dipping. It's a weird sensation, making me suddenly feel like I just did a couple hours on my running pad. When I get this tired, I get irritable. Within moments the program on TV annoys me for something insignificant, and I click the remote to change it. Only, nothing happens.

I click the home button on the remote for a third time, but again, the TV continues to play the program. My irritability ramps up from this and I angrily mash the buttons on the remote, but it accomplishes nothing. For some reason the remote feels incredibly heavy compared to how it normally feels, and I drop it on the coffee table. It clatters hard, making it sound heavier too. The last time I dropped it like that, it bounced, and the back panel came off, but not this time. Didn't I just change the batteries in this damn thing a few weeks ago?

It takes considerable effort, but I get my tired ass off the couch, and I shuffle into the kitchen. Opening the utility drawer, I find a pair of AAA batteries and trudge my way back to the couch. I reach toward the coffee table for the remote, but it's not there. Looking around, I see it sitting on the arm of the couch. I could've sworn I left it on the table, but with as tired as I am, I can't be certain. I pick up the source of my irritation, accidentally hitting one of the buttons in the process. Suddenly, the TV is muted. Not only that, but the remote feels lighter than it did a minute ago. For some reason, the remote is working perfectly fine now. I must be really tired.

Turning off the TV, I shuffle my way into my bedroom and plop on the bed. The sheets are so soft and inviting that I don't bother to change into my sleep attire. My new pillow is light and fluffy, a cloud in which to lay my head on. I'm out like a light in record timing. I wish I knew why I was suddenly so tired. Dr. Finn suggested that my agoraphobia may be coupled with depression, and that would explain this onslaught of tiredness. My only problem with that is, I don't feel depressed. I am perfectly content in my own little world here, and it makes me happy.

At some point in the night, I turn from laying on my back to my side. The blanket on top of me feels very heavy, like one of those weighted blankets I've seen advertised, but I don't own one. My exhaustion level increases, and I drift off to sleep again, practically passing out. Maybe there was something in those tacos that's doing this to me? It's the only explanation my tired mind can come up with.

By the time my body has had enough of lying in bed, I struggle to get up. Never in my life have I been so exhausted, especially after sleeping the dreamless sleep of the dead. The first thing I do is go into the bathroom and take my temperature. It doesn't happen often, but on the rare occasions I get sick, I often feel weak and out of sorts. Not anything like this level of crappy, but what else could it be? If I was vomiting and nearly crapping myself, I'd think the tacos gave me food poisoning.

My temperature is a little low, but that's about it. I turn on the shower to full heat and strip off my sleeping clothes. After a leisure twenty-minute shower under extremely hot water, I actually feel a little better. As I lean against the wall and let the spray cascade over me, I swear I see movement through the open door. Poking my head out of the shower door, I look at my bed through the bathroom door, but it looks normal. The top sheet is a little more disheveled than I thought it was before though, but that's it.

Once I'm dried off and dressed in a clean shirt and pants, I go into the kitchen and get myself some breakfast. Coffee, yogurt and some fruit should help me feel a little more normal. As I dip a strawberry into my Greek yogurt, my phone pings with a new email. I immediately pick up my phone. The only emails I receive that my phone notifies me of are VIP emails. It's probably my boss reminding me that I'm on vacation and warning me against trying to login on my work computer.

The email is from Dr. Finn, and the subject line asks if I received the package she sent me. My brain is still slow this morning, but I remember the four packages I got yesterday were all from the same retailer. Considering how tired I am and how forgetful I can get in this kind of state, I get up to look in my recycling box. As I start pulling out the broken-down boxes, something occurs to me. Didn't I bring in five boxes yesterday?

I'm really confused because there are only four boxes here, but now that I think of it, I'm certain I brought in five. As I put the boxes back into the bin, my eyes catch sight of an anomaly. There's a second label on one of the boxes, and sure enough, it's from Dr. Finn. This doesn't make any sense. That box was from the same retailer as the others and has a label on it to prove it. Looking at this second label, I see it is perfectly affixed to the box like the others. There's no evidence that it was pealed away from one box and stuck to this one, so what gives?

Sitting down on my couch, using a throw pillow to prop up the arm that doesn't have an arm rest, I open the email. I really don't know what to make of it. Dr. Finn says that she's tried every conventional way to get me to go out of my apartment, but after years of work, the balcony is the closest I will get. Determined to get me to change, she shipped me something she believes will motivate me to step foot outside my front door, something called a Mimic. What I read next sounds like something out of a fairytale.

A Mimic is a small creature that can take on the shape of small, inanimate objects. It disguises itself as something a person is prone to touching, and once someone does touch it, the creature begins to drain their energy. Once it attains a certain level of energy from one person, it becomes more animated. This means it will desire more energy, and by this point, it will take it more by force. She signs off the email with, "If this doesn't get you out of the apartment, then nothing will."

I sit there for a few moments, blankly staring at my phone. This can't be real, right? Doctors don't send their patients potentially dangerous things in the freaking mail, especially something that can't possibly be real. Is she trying to screw with me and get me so paranoid that I'll leave the safety of my apartment by turning it into a hostile environment in my head? Dr. Finn has never played mind games like this before, and even though it explains why I feel so very crappy, it can't possibly be real.

Pain erupts up my arm as teeth sink into the flesh and muscle. The pillow I've been resting my arm on suddenly has teeth and is trying to take a bite out of me. I scream as I try to throw it off me, but those teeth are gripping me with a fierce determination. I slam it against the coffee table a few times, and it finally loosens enough for me to throw it against the wall. It hits with the hard thump of something more substantial than a throw pillow. I should've known something was wrong from the get. I don't have any throw pillows on my damn couch.

I lose sight of the pillow once it hits the floor, but I can hear it scrambling along the floor. Going into the kitchen, I wrap a hand towel around my bleeding arm, and grab up my largest, sturdiest knife. My heart races as I flip on all the light switches, flooding the entire area with as much light as I can. Some undefinable shape scurries down the dark hall toward my office and bedroom, leaving me the perfect opportunity to flee the apartment. The question is, do I finally do what Dr. Finn has been trying to get me to do for years, or do I stay and fight? This is my freaking apartment, my sanctuary against a world that's far too loud and full of people, a lot of which don't have enough common sense to look up from their phones when crossing a street.

One way or another, I have to go down that hall. Either I fight the creature and reclaim my home, or I leave. The problem is my shoes are in my bedroom, and if I'm going outside, I sure as hell am not going barefoot. Goddamn you Dr. Finn.

UNDER THE DESERT

The waves of heat made it impossible to see across the plateau, but now that the dragon is dead, we can make it across. Unfortunately, some of the creature's acid spit splashed on the bridge we crossed to get here. It didn't completely destroy the stone like I'd feared, but from what I can tell, it did enough damage that getting all the vehicles back across is going to be risky.

I'm a little weary about walking back onto the bridge to properly inspect it. Not so much because of the damage done to it, but the noxious smoke drifting up and around it. The dragon's body seeping blood below is wreaking havoc on the stone in the canyon. I can't imagine breathing that stuff in is good for my health. We're going to have to wait for the acid to finish doing what damage it will before we can figure out just how screwed we are.

As far as I was able to tell in my translations, there was only one of these creatures, a sort of guardian for the entrance we're looking for. I'd really been hoping it wouldn't be at the bottom of the canyon surrounding the plateau. There wasn't much in the text about the entrance itself, but what I gleamed made it seem like we shouldn't have trouble finding it. Heading for the center of the plateau, we kept our pace nice and slow.

When I was on the ground, there didn't appear to be much in the way of loose sand like on our way here. The plateau felt like it was solid rock, but I didn't want to take any chances. We've lost too many people in the handful of days since we started this expedition.

The problem is, crossing the desert was supposed to be the easy part.

The text didn't go into any detail about what lies inside the... I honestly don't know what to call it. Cavern, temple, castle, gate, burial chamber... there were literally dozens of translations as to what to call the place we were going. What I know for a fact is that whatever it is, it's underground.

Part of the reason the convoy is going so slow is because these damn heat waves don't allow us to see beyond twenty yards. For that matter, we can barely see the sky above us because of it. The truly puzzling thing in this regard is the temperature. Yes, it's hot out, as hot as it's been since day one, but not enough that the waves should be so bad. At least in the desert proper it was a couple hundred yards or so before the distortion got bad. Even then, it hadn't been so bad that it completely hid what was beyond.

I'm in the lead vehicle for a change, but it's only because I'm the one that supposedly knows what we're looking for. I don't dispute this claim. If I did I'm pretty sure I'd lose the respect of my crew, and they'd start reconsidering their life choices. Now more than ever I need the crew to put their faith and trust into me. If I lose that, they won't follow my orders, and we will descend into anarchy. I had that happen to me once, on my first expedition.

It had not ended well, and most of those men died. Not so much for the dangers we faced in the jungle, but because they kept turning on each other. Only two of the original crew are still with me. The cook and quartermaster. Thankfully, they're as loyal as always, even after the disaster this excursion has become.

We've been traveling for longer than I expected considering how big the plateau is. The vehicle comes to an immediate halt when we catch sight of the canyon again. Somehow we traveled all the way across and didn't see a thing. Pulling a U-turn, I take note of the odometer and have us go back the way we came. We manage to get back to the bridge, and it was just shy of a mile across.

Once again I have the convoy turn around, stopping at the halfway point. We'll set up camp here for the meantime. While that's happening, I assign patrols to sweep the area. We only use the motorcycles to do this because they burn the least amount of fuel.

Each single rider motorcycle is paired up and sent into different directions. The two with side cars go out with both seats filled. The four teams will drive straight out, stop when they reach the canyon and come straight back. From there they will shift their direction a few degrees clockwise and repeat the process until someone finds something.

In the hour it takes to set camp and get food started, the only thing learned is that the plateau is smooth. Not a natural smooth, but something like fresh blacktop that's been laid out for a road. I don't know what to make of it. The sun is getting low, and I call for the patrols to call it a night. We could all do with a good rest. Three security shifts are set up to give everyone a chance to sleep while still keeping guard. Those damn flying serpents love to come out at night.

Unlike a lot of the crew, I can't seem to rest. The patrols only covered a third of the plateau but discovered nothing. I'm beginning to worry that this whole thing has gone tits up, and a lot of good men died for nothing. I have all their wages in my accounts back in the civilized world, so everyone will get paid, but they're going to be pissed about not getting a bonus. It's happened before, but no one died on those expeditions.

I'm pacing back and forth just outside the mess tent with a notepad in my hand. I'm going over the translations regarding the entrance and getting nowhere in a hurry. It's frustrating the hell out of me, so much that I accidentally trip over something. I figure it must've been one of the tent's support ropes, but then I realize I'm ten feet away from the tent. The support ropes don't come out this far.

Getting to my knees, I look to the smooth ground for any sign of what I tripped on. It takes me a minute to see it, but there's a slight rise in the ground. Hard to see with the naked eye, but apparently enough to catch the tip of my boot's sole as I tried to take a step. This makes sense of one of the translations. I thought it was a little strange that it said I'd stumble upon it eventually.

There's a very thin layer of sand on the ground, and I quickly start brushing it away. The ground is as hard as stone, and brushing my bare hand against it quickly starts to hurt. It's almost like rubbing my hand against sandpaper. Marking the spot with my notepad, I rush to my tent for my tool kit and gloves. Once I'm back, I start brushing the sand away again.

I've found a very well-defined edge, as straight as a ruler. Using a brush, I clear away a gap that's only about a quarter inch wide. I dig my chisel into the space, and it only goes down three inches before stopping. Getting an idea, I rush over to the nearest truck and dig into the toolbox in the back. From it I pull out an air hose and attach it to the truck's air tank.

Turning the engine on, I attach a spray nozzle and uncoil the line back to the crack.

By the time I've started blowing the dust out of the crack, a bunch of the crew has come out of their tents to see why an engine is running. There's a lot of murmured whispers as they watch me clear the crack. It's a large rectangle, four feet wide and six feet long. Without having to say a word, men come over with pry bars and flood lights.

Six men slip the tips of the heavy steel bars into the cracks on one end. Two men squeeze together on the three sides and work together to pry up the flat stone. More men are standing by, waiting to slip a couple bars underneath the stone once there's enough clearance. I'm so excited that I don't even consider the possibility that something is going to come slithering out once there's enough space. Thankfully, everyone standing around without tools in their hands are holding shotguns.

It takes a lot of sweat and swearing, but the men manage to pry the stone up enough. After about half an hour, we've got support bars underneath both ends, and straps on the slab. With a wench on one of the gun trucks, we pull the slab completely away, revealing a stone staircase leading down.

My excitement has me wanting to go in now, but the rational part knows it's not the right time. I need to get some rest, and so do the rest of the crew. There's four hours to sunup, so I set two men to stand guard. I know no one will go down there while I sleep. They all rely on me to go first into any location like this, knowing if anyone can figure out the dangers and traps it's me. This is the area where I tend to shine.

Sleep is hard to achieve, but my body is worn

down and I finally succumb. When I wake up its well past sunrise. In fact, I was supposed to be up hours ago. I leave my tent and before I can berate anyone for letting me sleep so long, the cook and quartermaster have me join them in the mess tent. I enjoy a nice cup of coffee as they explain. Everyone knows the stress I've been under with everything that's gone wrong. They wanted me to be well rested before going below so I'd bring my A-game. They weren't just sitting around idly while I slept. The men have gotten our gear ready and after I eat something, we're good to go.

I shoulder my messenger bag with the tome and my notes inside. With a flashlight in one hand, I stand at the entrance. My pistol and holster are on my belt, and some of the others have their shotguns, but no one is holding them at the ready. If the inside is the same stone as the floor of the plateau, then firing a gun in there needs to be a last resort. Ricochets could prove fatal to any of us. Not to mention possible cave-ins. We have no idea what the conditions are down there. I have a machete in a sheath opposite my pistol just in case.

Most of the men hold lanterns and tools. There are more than a dozen relay radios among our gear, ready to be placed at even intervals. Underground communications are spotty and unpredictable, but these relays will keep us in contact with the surface. If anything happens on either end, or we require equipment not currently on us, all it takes is a simple call. This has proven incredibly useful in the past.

The man next to me holds two large glow sticks. After cracking and shaking them, he tosses them inside so we can see how far down the stairs go. I watch as they fall into the black, then start tumbling down the stairs. They go a long way before one of them comes to a stop, but the other bounces a funny way. It shoots to the side and is suddenly completely out of view. I guess it stops being a tunnel after a while and the walls disappear on either side.

My first step is tentative. Slowly I put weight on it until I'm pressing hard. When the floor doesn't fall out from under me, I fully step on it. I don't do this for the next step, or the next, but I am proceeding very slowly. By the time I've gone down enough that my eyes are level with the surface, the world seems to be going dark.

The radios come alive with chatter and the energy in the crew goes from one of excitement to incredibly nervous. Those damn heat wave distortions are making it impossible to see if bad weather is coming our way, but the sudden increase of wind says it all. There's only one kind of storm that regularly rolls through the desert, and it sure as hell isn't a rainstorm.

"Get to shelter!" I yell at the crew. I can tell by how quickly the wind is picking up that the tents aren't a match for this kind of storm. Some of the men climb into the surrounding trucks, others rush to the entrance. I start going down the stairs too fast, but only because the bodies behind me keep pushing. It gets so bad that I slip and tumble down the stairs like one of those glow sticks.

By the time I come to, my head is throbbing and one of my men is kneeling over me. His name is Duncan, and he's dabbing at my forehead with a white cloth. I take comfort that there's only a little red on it. I'm banged up for sure, but nothing feels broken at least.

As quickly as I can, I assess the situation. The stairs came down into a chamber that is little more than a hallway junction. There are three corridors leading further in, but I don't look too closely yet. I count nine men in here with me, double what was originally going to explore with me today. It's never a good idea to have this many people come in on day one. Even my crew gets too curious and sometimes wanders off course. It's too easy to accidentally set off traps and get lost.

I reach for my radio to call up to the surface for an update, but one look up the stairs says it all. We are too far down for the radios to work, so I send a man up the stairs to set up the first relay. When he gets up there, he makes a comment that doesn't make sense. On sore joints and bruised muscles, I climb the stone steps.

I can hear the wind screaming from the entrance, but there's very little light up there. When I get there, what he said is true, but still doesn't make sense. With a sandstorm that strong raging on outside, some of that wind should be coming down here, but there isn't even a gentle breeze. All we're getting is dark gray light that reminds me of dim house lights in a movie theater, and the sounds of what might be the beginning of a tornado.

While he gets the relay online, I'm close enough to the entrance that my radio should reach. I make contact with the quartermaster and ask what his status is. The sandstorm is so bad that visibility has gone down to nearly zero. He can't even see the truck parked not five feet away from the cab he's sitting in. It's unclear if everyone made it to safety but he's going to do what he can to get a head count. I let him know who I have with me.

With the relay in position, we return to the bottom of the stairs. Now that I'm not lying on the ground, I take a look around. With all the lanterns on I can get my first good look and what I see has me shocked. I was expecting to see rough, uneven stone walls, but that's not the case. This looks all too smooth, like the inner chambers of the pyramids, but smoother still. Even the stairs are perfectly formed, and completely symmetrical. Even the modern world isn't this perfect.

After ten steps, the walls on either side of the stairs stop, leaving open space that someone could easily fall off for the rest of the steps. That explains what happened to the second glow stick, and I find it next to the left hallway. I run my fingers over the stone, expecting sand to come off and reveal glyphs underneath, but there's nothing. The walls are completely clean with no dust or grime buildup at all. Even if the slab above had been sealed airtight there'd be dust down here, but I don't find any anywhere. This is even beyond OCD clean. Hell, people with OCD strive for this level of cleanliness.

After searching the entire chamber, I'm at a loss. There are no markers or glyphs of any kind as far as I can see, which means I'm going to have to guess which way we should start. I hate guessing in these situations. Even looking to my notes doesn't give me a clue which way to go.

I pull out my canteen and take a much-needed drink as I look down the right hallway. Before I can put the cap back on, one of the men bumps into me from behind and I drop it. The water splashes over the floor and as I reach for the canteen, I see something very strange. The floor isn't as perfectly flat as I thought. Instead, it slants toward the middle from both sides, making a very obtuse angle that's virtually invisible to the naked eye.

Watching as the water collects in the center, it starts flowing down the hallway as well. Not only that, but the stone itself isn't getting wet. It's like there's a clear protective coating over the stone, preventing even the slightest bit of moisture from being left behind. This sparks recognition in my mind, and I pull my notes from my messenger bag.

There had been a mention of something I translated as 'life flow' when it came to the interior of the chamber. I had originally taken that to be something about blood, but now that I think of it, these writings came from desert people. Water is life for everyone no matter where they are, but it means more in the desert.

Testing my theory, I go to the middle hallway and spill a little water there. As expected, it pools in the center and starts to move, but not down the hallway like before. The men step back as I follow the small amount of water as it moves toward them, then changes direction about where I landed and heads to the right hallway. A quick repeat of the process has the left hallway doing the exact same thing. I guess we go right.

As I come out of the left hallway, I see the long yellow glow stick on the ground. I get an idea and pick it up. Pulling out my machete, I cut the tip off and empty the stick onto the ground. Liquid light pools just like the water had, and none of the luminous gold liquid is left behind as it slowly flows down the hallway. At least now I'll be able to follow it no matter where it goes.

Progressing slowly down the hall, I have half the men stay behind with orders to let me know the moment the storm above clears out. The hallway is wide enough for two people to walk side by side comfortably, and after twenty yards, it turns to the right.

I keep following the gold fluid, grateful it moves so slowly. This way I can inspect the hall as we go and try to detect any potential traps or markings. So far there hasn't been any, but I'm hopeful.

Duncan is drawing a map of our progress, trying to prevent us from getting turned around. He has one of those walking wheels that measure distance, so he can be as precise in his layout as possible. It doesn't work in most of the tunnels we usually explore. Uneven ground makes it a pain in the ass to use, but it's perfect for this location. So far at least.

The hallway turns this way and that, always at 90° angles. We've walked for a few hundred yards and haven't seen a damn thing. No markings or imperfections in the walls, floor, or ceiling to indicate a trap. As far as I can tell, there hasn't been a single living thing in this place for centuries. I see no bugs or their carcasses, and the lack of dust has remained.

Turning in yet another direction, the golden liquid starts stretching out and moving a little faster. Not so fast that I can't keep up with it, but faster than I'd like to walk. If I try to keep up with it, I know I'll end up missing a detail and the next thing I'll know, I've got an arrow or spike sticking out of my chest. Obviously that hasn't happened before, but it has come close a number of times. Ancient peoples knew how to make traps to last.

The glow stick blood turns down another turn, but a space on the wall doesn't illuminate with the colored light. It stays perfectly dark, like that one spot is resistant to light. Either that or it's a black stain on the wall. I shine my light at it and have trouble understanding what's happening. My light is right on it, yet the black isn't chased back or illuminated, as if the spot is a living shadow impervious to light.

Once that thought enters my mind, I swear I see the black move. I don't think it's expanding, but it does appear to be getting bigger. Too late I realize what's happening. The black has detached from the wall and is moving closer to me. I end up tripping over my own feet as I walk backward, the angle of the floor having gotten slightly more noticeable down this stretch. I can hear the men's panicked murmurs as the black hovers above me. I don't know if this thing is a ghost, monster, or a really good illusion, but it's sufficiently freaking us out.

It floats in the air, slowly forming a shape over me. It takes on a generic face, kind of androgynous. I can clearly see the outline of eyes, a nose and mouth, but little else. That mouth opens impossibly wide, as if to swallow my face. I'm glad I'm a little too dehydrated to piss myself.

FIRST FREEZE OF THE YEAR

For those of us in the South, winter is a different beast than it is for the rest of the country. Where northerners will still be wearing shorts, we are breaking out jackets and gloves. The South isn't meant for below freezing temperatures, that's why it's the South.

I've never lived anywhere but the South, and seeing snow is nearly equivalent to spotting a freaking alien. Down here, things threaten to shutdown at the first sign of ice. Unfortunately, people where I live don't know how to drive under those conditions. If you think that's bad, you should see how it is when it rains. A lot of these people don't know how to deal with water on the road, let alone ice.

I am not one of those people. In my nearly thirty years behind the wheel, I have only been in three accidents, and not one of them was my fault. That's not the false claim of someone that doesn't want to be held accountable. I genuinely was the victim in those incidents. Two of them were simple fender benders where someone rear ended me because they weren't paying attention. I want to say in both cases, the asshole that hit me was on their damn cellphone.

The third was because some fucking idiot was doing seventy in a thirty zone and didn't even slow down as he approached the red light. The fucker t-boned me in the middle of a major intersection. There were about fifty witnesses and there was no way he was getting out of that without shelling out some major bucks.

I ended up with some minor injuries to include a cut in my head that required a few staples, and my arm was in a sling for two weeks because my shoulder got banged up. He ended up with a busted nose, two black eyes, and a limp that will be with him until the day he shuffles off this mortal coil. Not only did he total my Chevy, but he smashed his Ford beyond saving. I joke that it had been a hate crime between manufacturers, but he didn't find it funny. Especially since he lost the case before his lawyer even opened his mouth. The truly funny thing about the whole incident was who hit me.

The fucker happened to be one of the city's most prominent personal injury attorneys. He tried to intimidate me while attempting to get me to settle out of court, but I wasn't having any of that. I went to his number one competitor, and we cleaned the asshole out. After lawyer fees, I got a little over three quarters of a million dollars. The case was very public, and no one would higher him after that. Beyond that, I don't know what happened to him, and quite frankly, I don't give a shit. He could've suck started a pistol for all I care.

The payout allowed me to clear all my debt, to include paying off my mortgage. I had a hell of a party to celebrate that, but I waited until I was completely recovered to do it. It was my party, and you really need both hands to properly barbeque. One to deal with the meat, the other to hold a beer. It's not real barbeque without beer. This is the south after all.

Having all that money didn't mean I could retire early. I've still got at least a decade before I can accomplish that. Besides, I don't know what I'd do without a job to go to most days. Yeah, I've got hobbies, but those cost money, and the last thing I want to do is blow through my substantial savings. I've got two thirds of the settlement stashed away, earning me dividends. By the time I retire, my financial advisor says it'll be worth well over a million dollars, assuming I don't touch the accounts. Baring any emergencies that would require me to, I have no intention of withdrawing money from them.

I'm still working my regular nine to five, and overtime when they need me to, but there's not much call for that at the gun range. I'm not a range safety officer, salesclerk or even a firearms instructor. I function as a clerk and record keeper, keeping to the background. It's my job to make sure we have ammunition, weapon accessories, supplies and firearms to sell. I may not run the place, but the business couldn't function without me.

I wake up this morning and go through my routine like it's any other day, but the problem is, it isn't a typical day. Typically, my region only gets about two weeks of real winter, and it usually hits us in February. Mother nature is throwing us for a loop this year, because it's only January, and I step foot outside only to slip on ice in my driveway. I land hard on my side as a gust of wind blows in hard, freezing me down to the bone. I hate the first freeze of the year, especially when it comes without warning.

Slowly getting to my feet, I remote start my truck and head back inside. I'm not wearing nearly enough layers to battle this artic chill. Thankfully, the lid on my travel mug of steaming hot coffee was closed, and I didn't splash myself with it. Getting back inside, I strip down to my underwear and put on some thermals. With my pants and shirt back on, I add on a flannel shirt and a pullover hoodie before putting my jacket back on. From a box at the top of the coat closet, I get a big, fluffy skull cap and a pair of gloves. I'm as prepared for this as I can be.

This time, I take my time walking to my truck, avoiding the ice now that I know it's there. It takes a couple tries to open the driver door, but I finally manage. Part of it is because of the cold, and the other contributing difficulty factor is the wind. It's so strong that getting the damn thing open far enough for me to climb in is a struggle. I'm really glad I skipped my morning workout. My arms might've been too fatigued to open the door if I'd lifted weights.

It takes another ten minutes for the truck to heat up enough to fully melt the ice off my windshield. Had I realized how bad it was outside, I'd have remotely started the car when I was still enjoying my first cup of coffee. As it is, I'm halfway through my travel mug before I pull out of my driveway.

There are other cars on the road, but not nearly as many as there usually is. I guess a lot of people are calling in or something, but I don't have that luxury. It's time for the monthly inventory check, and I can't put it off. On top of that, I'm the only one that can do it. That happens when you design the organization system yourself. I make it more complicated than it needs to be just so no one screws with my lists. People can't steal and alter the records to cover their tracks if they can't find them or understand how it's organized. That was a problem back during the pandemic, and everyone was going out of their damn mind.

Even though the posted speed limit is seventy, I'm only going fifty, at the most. There's an occasional vehicle that'll speed past me in one of the two left lanes, but I'll leave it to them to risk their lives for faster speeds. I'm sticking to the right lane and doing my best to keep my tires in the tracks of the vehicles in front of me. At least this way I stand a chance of not hitting a patch of ice.

I normally hate it when people drive like this around here, going so much slower than the limit, but that's because they're usually doing it in the rain. It's understandable when it's raining heavily, but that's not what I'm talking about in this instance. They'll slow down like this for a medium rain, the kind of thing I used to love running around in when I was back in high school. I think driving tests need to be more intensive and difficult, you know, to seriously make sure people can handle bad road conditions.

Case in point. I'm driving along and approaching a bridge. In weather like this, bridges are treacherous because they tend to have more ice on them than any other section of the road. I know this and am slowing my speed by another five miles per hour as a precaution. Some people aren't doing this, like the dumbass coming up fast in the far-left lane. I can see his headlights with my side mirror, and though he doesn't look like he's going the full seventy, he's going exceedingly faster than me.

In the ten minutes I've been on the freeway, I haven't seen a single car in the far-left lane. To any rational mind, this would indicate that there's a higher than probable chance that there's ice in that lane. I mean, really. There's got to be a reason as to why no one else is using that lane, but here this dipshit comes tearing past in a V8 sports car.

Oh, and look at that, not even five seconds on the bridge, and he's already losing control. That shiny, seventy-thousand-dollar car just bounced off the sidewall, and like an air hockey puck, his sliding to the other wall. Unfortunately, that's bringing him right to me, and slamming on my breaks makes me slide too. Fuck me.

The sports car slams right into my front end, pushing me to the guard rail on the right. We just managed to get off the bridge before I hit it, but the downside is that's where the cement barrier ended. I don't just hit the metal and wood guard rail, but I go through the damn thing. I'm expecting to fall into the ditch between the highway and the access road, but I don't.

The embankment on this side of the bridge slopes up for a ways before it levels out. My truck falls off the road and slams into a steep part, crashing me hard enough that my airbags deploy before falling the rest of the way to the bottom. I don't know how long I'm passed out before I wake up, but I am very dazed and confused.

Cold wind blasts me in the face, and my entire body is one giant ball of ouch. I blink my eyes a bunch of times trying to clear the darkness from my vision, and it takes a while for things to come into focus. Either that, or my brain is having trouble understanding what it's seeing.

I see the inside of this truck every single day, but it all looks so wrong. The dashboard has a giant crack in it, the touch screen console is smashed, the windshield is so broken that I can't see out of it, and there are deployed airbags all over the place. The window on my passenger door is completely gone, allowing the wind to rush in that side, and escape through the gap between the truck and the top of my door.

My body is slow to respond as I try to move around, and I'm having trouble unbuckling my seatbelt.

It's something I do all the time, but right now, the latch is failing to disengage. As I struggle with it, my mind is catching up to the facts, and I find myself getting seriously pissed off. For a moment, I lose my shit. Fighting against the restraint and screaming like a mental patient, outraged that some fucking moron that doesn't know how to fucking drive just totaled my truck and nearly killed me. I want nothing more than to crawl out of this wreck, climb up the embankment, drag him out of his car and beat the shit out of him.

This animalistic outburst lasts all of twenty seconds before the spike of adrenaline dissipates. Twenty seconds of screaming is a lot, and I'm breathing heavily. I actively try to calm myself, taking deep breaths to prevent me from hyperventilating and to slow my heart rate. Panicking is only going to make things worse, and the rational part of my brain knows that.

Fighting with the seatbelt near my right pocket, I barely manage to get to my pocketknife. I sharpen it fairly regularly because I use it to open boxes at work, so when I finally get it open, it makes quick work of cutting the seatbelt. Part of me wants to cut the belt away quickly so I can get the hell out of here, but I force myself to go slow. If I go faster I'm likely to get frustrated and I'll likely panic again from being trapped. If that happens, I'm almost certain to cut myself in the process. My body's hurt enough as it is.

After a few minutes, I manage to cut the belt and free myself. I put my knife back in my pocket before doing anything else. Climbing over the center console, I try the passenger door, but it won't budge. I don't have the strength to try and force it, so I climb out the window. For a brief moment, I wish the truck had flipped and landed upside down. At least that way I wouldn't have a drop between the window and the ground. Of course, if that had happened, I might not be alive to crawl headfirst out the window.

Holding onto the door, I point my head toward the ground and start slithering the rest of me out. Once my feet clear the window, I let gravity do the work as my legs swing over me. My feet hit solid ground and that's when my hands slip. The rest of me lands with a thud and the entire backside of my body suddenly feels colder, if that's possible. I guess I should be grateful that there wasn't a rock where my spine landed.

With my hands, I reach out to the sides of me for something to hold onto, but all I encounter is a slick, smooth and flat surface. There must've been water in the creek when the freeze rolled in last night, because I'm lying on top of at least three inches of ice. That must be some kind of record for the area.

Planting my boot heel on the ground, I try to leverage myself well enough to flip over, but the ice is slick, and the wind hasn't let up yet. A strong gust hits me just as my boot slips, and I slide a few inches away from the truck. I reach out to it for something to hold onto but I'm too far from it now. In fact, I'm actively sliding away from it.

Somehow the distance between me and my wrecked truck keeps getting longer. It's almost as if there's a downward slope to the creek. I try to slow myself, but there's nothing to grab onto. My speed picks up and all I can do is scream as I fall into darkness. I panic again.

I don't know how long or far I've gone, but my outstretched feet hit something solid, and I come to a sudden, jarring stop. This is the fourth time I've slammed into something hard, and it hasn't even been an hour dammit. I really wish I'd have at least considered calling in today. The monthly inventory check could've waited a day or two. With all the snow and ice, I highly doubt there's going to be a lot of customers at the gun range to by what inventory we have left.

There's no light where I am, and I start feeling around at the thing that stopped me. It's a wall, but so cold that I can feel it through my gloves. It's as smooth and slick as the ground, so it's either made of ice, or at least covered in it. I can't see a fucking thing, and reach into my jacket pocket for my phone, but it's not there. Cursing, I realize where it is. I always plug it into the charging cable in my truck because it has trouble connecting through Bluetooth. The damn thing is still in my truck.

Using the wall for support, I start trying to move to the left, but the wind hits me strongly in the face. Instead, I turn around, pull my hood up, and start moving the other way. Either way should lead me to the embankment along the creek, and once I'm up top, I can make my way back to the freeway. I find it a little strange that the wall I'm touching is perfectly vertical though. That doesn't seem right.

The wind is a constant presence at my back, and I'm grateful for the layers I put on. I'm still fucking cold but think of how bad it'd be without the extras. I'd be well on my way to freezing to death instead of only halfway.

I always knew that I rely on my sight to get around, but it never occurred to me just how much until right now. I am completely lost in the dark, relying on only touch to navigate. It's not like I can hear or smell anything with this fucking wind at my back. Not to mention my nose is too cold to function beyond breathing. The only upside is that I'm in a stupid creek and there's only so many ways to go. At least, that's what I was thinking when the wall I was using as a guide suddenly stopped.

One moment my hand was sliding alone the solid mass, the next it was touching nothing, but air. I take a few steps back and find it again, trying to figure out what just happened. My hands slide along the smooth side and discover something quite alarming. If I was wandering inside a building with no lights on, finding a wall that makes a sudden 90° turn wouldn't be a big deal. If anything, it would be perfectly normal. Finding something like that while wandering around in a creek bed is not the place to find that.

Instead of following the new wall, I start walking directly across from it, looking for the other side of the creek, cause that's where I am, right? Could I have gone so far that I've actually found the entrance to a drainage tunnel that runs underneath the city? If I made it that far, I should be seeing streetlights or something. When you live in a city, there's no such thing as complete darkness, not when you're still outside. It's one of the reasons you can't see that many stars in the sky on clear nights.

I make it about five steps before my outstretched hands find another wall. This one is perfectly vertical too and just as icy. There's no way I'm still in the creek bed, so where the hell am I?

Trying to backtrack doesn't work out too well. The wind kicks up even stronger with each step I take in that direction until it knocks me on my ass. I start sliding again, but don't make it very far before I come to a much less painful stop against yet another wall.

This is starting to get annoying.

Stumbling around in the dark, I keep finding different walls. Or the same wall several times, I'm not really sure. I've gotten so fucking turned around, the only way I know where I came from is the direction the wind is coming from. Since going against the wind only tires me out, I keep going with the flow.

After what seems like a really long time, but could honestly only be about ten minutes, the wind kind of stops. Not completely, but it's considerably lighter now, almost gentle. Still cold as a witch's tit though.

I stand in the darkness, trying like hell to come up with some sort of an idea, but getting nowhere. Now that the wind is so low, I can begin to hear something, but it's awfully quiet. It's not the low hum of electricity, the distant rumblings of vehicles, or the consistent clatter of machinery. It almost sounds like an echo of my feet shuffling against the ice, but that can't be it. First off, I'm standing perfectly still and have been for two minutes. Second, the noise my boots make when sliding across the icy ground doesn't make enough noise to echo.

Whatever that is, it seems to be getting louder, and I start feeling uneasy. In my mind, that can only be the sound of something moving in this darkness. Either it's using the wall as I have been, or it knows exactly where it is, and can possibly see. I don't find this reassuring because, in my mind, whatever is out there is after me. It's not like I've been able to detect anything else alive here.

Doing my best to determine the source of the shuffling, I make an educated guess and immediately start moving the other way. My hands wave frantically in front of me as I move, my boots managing to find traction enough for me to move a little faster than before. I think I'm moving in a straight line, but for all I can tell, I could be going in circles. At least I'm certain I'm not moving in a serpentine pattern. I think.

I've gotten myself up to a decent walking pace, but in order to do that, I have to stop shuffling my feet. Taking real steps increases the chance that I'll slip, but with that noise getting louder, it's worth the risk. I can make it out better now, and it doesn't sound like it has legs and feet to walk on. That's more like the shuffling slither of a giant snake or something as equally horrendous.

My hand comes into contact with another wall, this one leading off to my left. As soon as I start going that way, I hear the worst sound I've ever heard in my life. A roaring growl, like a large predatory animal finding the first prey it's seen in weeks. I know I'm projecting my fears, but that sounds like a hungry roar. I quicken my pace.

With my left-hand keeping in contact with the wall, I reach my right hand to my pocket. My knife is only a four-inch blade, and far from my first weapon of choice for a situation like this, but it's all I have at the moment. Pulling it out, I press the button that flicks open the blade and hold it at my side with the blade pointing away from me. The shuffling slither is getting louder and more frantic, so I throw caution to the wind and start running. It's hard to keep in contact with the wall, but I manage it, for a while at least.

Running in the dark is fucking nerve-racking. I keep expecting to run into something like a low part in the ceiling, finding a wall in my path that I smash my face against, or for the ground to suddenly drop out from under me. Since I've gotten back to my feet, I haven't run into anything that wasn't a wall, but that doesn't mean there won't eventually be something.

The sounds of my movements have gotten louder, but it's drowned out by the sounds of my pursuer. It still sounds like something large slithering along the icy ground, but I know of nothing without legs that sounds as big as this fucking thing. I'm almost glad I can't see.

My hand has been pressed into the wall harder than I realized and would've continued being oblivious to that if it wasn't for the fact that the wall suddenly disappears. The unexpected dead air is so jarring that I fall into the open air. Landing on my side, something rushes past me, hitting my legs and sends me spinning against the ice. I manage to curl into a ball, keeping a death grip on my knife. Under other circumstances, spinning on the ice like this might be fun, but right now it's just disorienting the crap out of me and making me queasy.

Something heavy lands on me, bringing my movement to a dead stop. The weight on my chest is breath stealing, and I bring my knife hand up to strike at whatever is on me. Bringing my other arm up to shield my face, a pair of icy hands grabs onto it. Something bumps into the watch on my wrist and hits the light button. The illumination is normally too dim to be useful as a light source, but it's practically blinding in this pitch black.

The thing on top of me screeches as the light, and for a brief moment, I catch a glimpse of it. I don't get a lot of details, but I know I see a lot of sharp teeth and way too many eyes. I've seen more than enough, and just start stabbing. I get a few good hits in as it screams in my face, those vice like hands trying to break my arm. Bringing the knife higher, I try stabbing it where the face had been a moment ago.

The blade sinks in and gets stuck on something as I try to bring it back. Those hands on my arm are gone, and the weight on my chest slithers off to the side. I can breathe again, but my knife hand is still gripping the handle, and I can't get the blade free.

Something slams into me, throwing me across the ice. I never let go of my knife, and the force that sends me sliding across the ice helps rip the blade out. I get away from whatever the hell that thing is, but not before I'm splashed heavily with what I'm guessing is blood.

This feels a lot like when I was sliding away from my truck, and I'm trying to brace myself for when I slam into a wall again. For a brief moment, the ground is no longer underneath me, and I crash through a sheet of ice.

As I lay on the ground, recovering from the hard, but odd impact, I open my eyes and realize that there's light. In fact, I can see a truck right next to me. I must be back at the creek bed, because that's my truck, only it looks wrong. Slowly getting to my feet, I see that there's no damage to it. My truck looks exactly as it had when it was sitting in my driveway an hour ago.

Wait, what the fuck? It is sitting in my driveway. I'm back home. It's like nothing happened after I slipped on the ice the first time. Looking at said ice, I see it exactly where it was before, only it looks considerably thicker, and like a broken pane of glass. Could I have hit my head when I fell, and everything that happened after was a hallucination?

I'd be willing to believe that, but my knife is still in my hand, and I'm covered in some nasty smelling black liquid. Oh, and I'm still wearing the layers of clothing I put on after slipping on the ice. What the fuck happened to me?

GAMES OF CHILDREN

I'm ten years old and have no fear. No, really. That's not just me trying to sound tough. There's nothing I'm afraid of and I've proved that.

Me and my friends around the playground love to dare each other to do stuff all the time. Half the time it's stupid stuff like eating something gross or jumping off the swings. Some of us take the game more seriously and dare the others to do something more dangerous. We do have one rule. Never dare someone to do something you're not willing to do too.

Thanks to this game, we've gotten ourselves into a lot of trouble. I can't count how many days I've been grounded, but it can't be helped sometimes. When someone dares you to steal your dad's cigarettes and bring them to school, you can't say no. Saying no means you're afraid. Being afraid means you lose the game. Losing the game isn't an option.

Another thing we like to do is tell scary stories when we're sleeping at one another's house. Where we live, the biggest source for scary stories is the big cemetery at the edge of town. Oh man, I can't tell you how many times we've talked about that place. It's so big that if the dead were to suddenly rise, we'd be outnumbered three to one. At least, that's what my big brother Johnny told me.

They say that someone can be seen walking the grounds at night looking for someone trespassing in their graveyard. Others claim it's the headless witch looking for her head, and if she comes across someone, she'll take theirs instead. Me, I think it's a bunch of bologna. There's no such thing as ghosts and witches.

My mom says so.

We play other games, not just dare. Tag, capture the flag, king of the hill, and of course, hide and seek. Tonight, everyone is sleeping at my house, and Johnny is watching us. What that really means is he tells us to stay in the basement and not to make a mess. After giving us a couple pizzas to split between the six of us, we won't see him again. I don't know what he does with his girlfriend up there, but as long as he doesn't come check on us, we're fine. This isn't the first time he's watched us.

Since we're at my house, it's my turn to tell a scary story and to come up with a dare for us to do. Tonight's story is the Graveyard Watcher, something Johnny told me not too long ago. Like I said, there's lots of stories about the thing seen walking the cemetery at night.

They call her the Watcher because that's what she does. She wanders the grounds and kills anyone that she comes across, but she doesn't just kill you. First she blinds you with her glowing eyes and then she spits a loogie at you that makes your eyes pour out tears and has snot running down your face. Then she'll knock the wind out of you with her powers, making it to where you can't run away. Once she has you, she drags you away kicking and screaming until she throws you into a fire that turns you to ash, and you'll feel every second of it.

I give my friends as many details as I know. Johnny wasn't very clear about a lot of things, probably because he's never seen her himself. This was stuff he'd heard from friends that have claimed to have seen her. The kind of friends my parents have forbidden him from hanging out with. Some of those guys are in jail from what I've heard, but I think it's more than that. I think they're in a mental asylum because their encounter with the Watcher drove them insane.

Now that the story is out of the way, it's time for the dare, and I dare us to play hide and seek in the cemetery. The look on my friends' faces says it all. I've finally come up with a dare that they're not prepared to do, but none of them want to lose the game either. At least now they all understand why I told them to bring a flashlight, though once we get there we can't use them. Even though I don't believe any of the stories about the cemetery, someone might see them from the road or something. The last thing I want is to be found by the cops.

Climbing out the basement window, I check to see if the lights are on downstairs, but from the outside, all the windows look dark. I guess Johnny is in his room, but not asleep. I hear noises coming from his bedroom window, and it doesn't sound like he's alone. I have no idea what they're doing, but it sounds kind of unpleasant. Freaking weirdos.

It's a couple miles through the woods but we make great time on our bikes. Normally when we're on a trek, someone has music going on the boom box, but this is a stealth mission. The air is cool compared to the heat of summer we felt in the backyard earlier, but I'm still sweating. I can't tell if it's from pedaling my bike or excitement. I've been waiting for the opportunity to dare my friends to do this for a while. It had to be while we were at my house because it's the closest to the cemetery.

The path we're on is well worn, like a lot of people have walked through this stretch of the woods before. I can't imagine a lot of people coming out to the cemetery at night. Well, we are, so maybe it's not as farfetched as I think. Still, if more kids our age were coming out here, wouldn't we have heard about it? The playground is as much for gossip as it is anything else. Maybe it's high school teens like Johnny, but those guys usually drive. Don't they?

The path veers off to the right and I start slowing down. I've scouted the route a few times over the last few weeks so I'd know where to ditch the bikes. Once we all dismount, we start walking and don't stop until we reach the stone wall. From what I've heard, it stretches on all the way around the cemetery. That must be thousands, if not millions of stones. The cemetery is freaking huge, the largest in three states from what I've heard my dad say.

Clouds cover the sky, but they're high and thin. It looks a lot like the top of my mom's peach cobbler after she pulls it out of the oven. The moon is nearly full, and the light is showing enough that we don't need our flashlights.

For a moment, we crouch on this side of the stone wall and listen to the night. Looking over, we see headstones as far as the eye can see. So many that I couldn't begin to count. There are a lot of different styles, some simple, some with designs. I wonder what makes a person choose the kind of headstone they do for a loved one. For a second, I wonder what kind my mom will pick for me if my dad ever finds out I was out here. I'm no stranger to the belt with as often as I misbehave, but the punishment for this would be so much worse. Kinda makes it more exciting.

Since this was my dare, I'm the first one to be it. I sit with my back against the wall and start counting to one hundred. I've gotten to fifteen when I realize no one's gone over the wall. They're all wide eyed and trembling. "What's wrong guys, chicken?" One by one, I see my question gets to them. We've all called each other chicken plenty of times, and it always works. I start counting all over as they make a racket climbing over. At least the wall isn't that tall.

When I finally get to one hundred, I'm giddy with delight. Normally I'm more excited to be one of the ones hiding, but in this case, being the seeker is so much more fun. The guys just have to find a place to hide and stay there while I get to roam around. It would take years of playing for me to see the whole cemetery, and I'll keep daring them to do this until it gets boring. I can't see this getting boring.

I climb up onto the stone and drop down on the other side. The grass is short and well kept. When my brother mows the lawn there's always the cut grass mixed in with what's left, but not here. Whoever mows this grass must have one of those bags that collects the cut grass. I can't imagine how many times you'd have to empty it to get through this place.

The eerie blue light covers everything, making it all look the same color, just darker versions. Some of the headstones are dark gray and the others are lighter. I slowly make my way between them, glancing this way and that to see if someone was too chicken to hide farther in. I wouldn't put it past at least one of them to stick close to the wall. We're all brave in our ways, but I'm the only one here that's not afraid of the dark. I proved that at the beginning of summer when we took turns being locked in a basement. I was the only one that didn't ask to be let out.

As I walk through the rows, something looms over everything else in the distance and I crouch behind a headstone. Had it been there the whole time, or did it just appear out of nowhere? For a moment I think it's the headless witch, but this is a lot taller than I thought she'd be. Especially since she doesn't have a head.

Staring at the giant for a minute, I see it doesn't move. It just stands there casting a large shadow in the blue light like it owns the place. The light shifts as the clouds move to a clear spot in the sky and I see it light up as white as a ghost. No, not a ghost. It's a statue.

Mesmerized by it, I slowly walk toward it, like metal to a magnet. I can't seem to stop myself or remember why I'm even here. The closer I get, the more of it I can see. It's not the usual kind of stature you see in a cemetery. This is a man wearing some kind of vest with his head bent down, holding a cowboy hat over his chest. It looks so familiar, like I've seen it before, but the only statues I remember seeing are at church.

Giggling in the distance catches my attention, and the statue's hold on me is broken. I remember why I'm here. I'm playing hide and seek, and I haven't found anyone yet. Time to change that.

The noise came from my left, and I dart in that direction. It's not like any of my friends to give away their hiding spot like that, but this place is bound to make them act differently. Still, giggling isn't what I expected to hear from them. Terrified and frightened screams yes, but not giggling.

As I run between the headstones, making my way to a group of trees, something nearly trips me up. I could've sworn there wasn't a stone in that spot, but there was. Slowing my pace, I realize that some of these headstones aren't nearly as big as the rest. Some are so small that they're barely even a foot tall. Again, I wonder why people choose the markers they do for their loved ones. Maybe the smaller ones are just cheaper. I can't even imagine how much a large one costs.

Even though I've slowed my pace, I'm still going pretty fast. I swear the giggling came from those trees, but movement to my right gets me to change my course. It wasn't a person I saw moving, but a shadow and it wasn't because of the clouds shifting again. This is a large shadow and the only thing that causes those to move right now is people. That means one of my friends is over there. Maybe I'd been wrong about where the giggling came from.

Slowing my pace to a crawl, I reach the headstone that the shadow came from. It's very old, the carvings in it awfully faded. It may have been white at one point, but time has made it into a dull gray. As I get closer, I'm practically tip-toeing my way to it, wanting to scare the crap out of my first catch. I'm creeping along until my shadow touches the stone, then I leap around the side of it. I'm about to yell, "Boo," but there's no one there.

What? How is that possible? I know I saw a shadow over here and those don't just disappear for no reason.

There's a rustling to my left, the sound of trees moving. The breeze is slight and not strong enough to move the branches that much. I was right when I first thought the giggling came from there. The moving shadow must've just been a trick of the light or my imagination. I take off for the trees again.

I do find my first catch in the trees. Connor practically screams when I place my hand on his shoulder and say, "Gotcha." Now that there's two of us, this should go quicker. I can't believe it took me ten minutes to find my first catch, but I'm not surprised its Connor. I knew he wouldn't wander too far, not unless he was with one of the others. He may be energetic, but he scares easily.

Together, we make our way through the cemetery, always close together. It's not fair for us to spread out too far, so the rule is the seekers stick close. We find Chris hiding behind an angel statue rather close to the trees. Michelle is laying down behind the largest headstone I've ever seen. The names on it all share a last name, so I guess it's a family grave. Eventually we find Katie up a tree and for a while she refused to come down because she said no one tagged her. That didn't last long.

Lexi is a lot harder to find. We search high and low for her, but there isn't a sign of her. We began to think she got too scared and skipped out on us, but then we found something new in the cemetery. A stone building stands in the middle of a clear area, no headstones around it. There's a surprising amount of clear space in this place. Here I thought it was filled with graves, but there's a lot of room scattered throughout the place.

A set of double doors stands at the entrance of the very small building. It's not much bigger than the shed in my backyard, but this doesn't look like a shed. It reminds me of something I saw from a vampire movie that took place in New Orleans. I forget what they are called, but I know it's a fancy kind of tomb. There's a chain on the handles, but it looks like there's enough space for the doors to open wide enough for one of us to slip through.

Being the bravest of the bunch, I squeeze

through the hole while Chris and Michelle hold the doors open as wide as they'll go. What light there was outside is completely gone since there aren't any windows to this place. The air is stale and dusty, making me cough as I fumble with my flashlight. Once I get it clicked on, the light immediately blinds me. That's what I get for having the thing pointing straight up while I fought with the switch.

In the middle of the room is a large stone coffin. It stands high, nearly to my shoulders, but I can still see on top of it. There's a design to the lid, but I have no idea what it is. The walls are covered with cubby holes large enough for smaller coffins, and even some smaller than that. One part of the wall has glass covering the holes and each one has something inside. I see a doll in one of them, but if there's one thing that freaks me out, it's dolls. Something about their eyes unnerves me.

Something hits me on the shoulder from behind and I scream. Whirling around and pointing my flashlight, Lexi laughs at me as if it was the funniest joke ever told. When I realize it's her I laugh too, mostly out of relief. She got me good.

Since she was the last one caught, it's Lexi's turn to be the seeker. Once we slip back through the doors, she sits facing the doors and starts counting. The rest of us scatter.

I run as fast as I can in the direction I've yet to go. Passing by countless headstones and a bunch of statues, I completely bypass another cluster of trees and keep going. As I make my way up the slightest of hills, I see a building coming into view from the darkness. This is much bigger than the stone shed Lexi had been hiding in.

Changing my direction, I head that way, but

something stands between me and the building. It's another looming statue and it has me stopping cold in my tracks. This one isn't like the others I've seen and doesn't look nearly as old. It reminds me of the ghost of Christmas future, a kind of Grim Reaper, but who would want that over their grave? I get the angels and some of the others, but why this?

The robed figure holds its hands up above its head, cupped together like I do when I'm trying to catch rain. Slowly I start walking towards it, unable to stop myself from getting closer. I feel something as I do, something that I thought I'd gotten rid of. Fear, like a bad taste in my mouth, creeps in and I begin to tremble. Something about this statue is very wrong and I can feel it in the pit of my stomach. I don't want to, but I keep getting closer despite my trembling getting worse. My skin is cold, yet I'm sweating like crazy. What's happening right now?

Whispers on the wind drift to my ears and some of the fear goes away. It's a woman's voice, but I can't understand what she's saying. More than anything, I get a feeling from this thing, and it confuses the crap out of me. It's like being grounded or in time out and so badly wanting to get out in order to go play. I get grounded often enough that the feeling is familiar, but why I'm getting it now is a mystery.

Without knowing why, I step up onto the base of the statue and start climbing. It occurs to me that this thing is big enough to hide me from anyone below and it would make a great hiding spot, but that's not what I'm doing. I don't know what I'm doing.

Something grabs me from behind and drags me off the statue. I scream, not knowing what is going on or what has me. Whatever it is, it's strong enough to keep hold of me no matter how hard I kick and scream. I could wake the dead with the noise I'm making.

The thing that has me starts talking, but I can't hear it over the racket I'm making. It shakes me hard for a moment, trying to get my attention over my hysterics. "Calm down, kid," the voice yells and I realize it's a girl. Oh crap, not a girl, but a woman. A freaking adult.

I calm down and slowly turn my head to look at her, worried I'm about to see a body without a head, but I don't. She's pretty and young, but still older than Johnny. Now that I'm not screaming my head off, she asks what I'm doing out here, but I don't have to tell her. My friends come running up because they all heard me, and we know we're all screwed.

The woman pulls something off her belt, a large gray brick with something thin and black poking out the top. At first I think it's a radio, but then she starts hitting numbers on it like the phone in my kitchen. Is that one of those cellular telephones I've heard about?

Someone on the other side must've picked up because she starts talking. "Hey, Deputy Dawg, it's Greta. I've got a situation over here at Shadow Hills." She's calling a cartoon character? I get that we're kids and all, but are we supposed to fall for that? "Just get over here, Cooper. I've got a bunch of kids playing hide and seek in the cemetery." I'm starting to get the feeling like this sort of thing has happened before.

<u>AT SEA</u>

A lot of the old timers will say that they've worked on boats their whole lives. I can claim the same thing, but my case is a little different. Unlike them, I've worked on only one boat. I've lived and worked on the Honeycomb for the last ten years.

As a teenage runaway, getting illegal work as a hand on a freighter was my only opportunity to escape my abusive home life. The pay was decent, but it also provided me with food and shelter. Thankfully the crew was understanding of my situation and didn't take advantage of the poor kid that didn't know a damn thing. Instead, they took me under their wings and taught me everything I needed to know in order to be an effective member of the crew. I got really lucky.

By the time I turned eighteen and was no longer classified as illegal labor, I was able to help with repairs, regular maintenance, custodial work, and anything else that was needed. My pay nearly doubled too, but I had to set up a bank account because they couldn't pay me under the table anymore. The captain helped me get through that whole red tape nightmare and if it hadn't been for him, I don't know where I would've ended up.

It's gotten to the point where being on land is more unbalanced than being at sea. The longest stretch I've been on land in the last ten years was only two months and that was because the ship was undergoing some extensive and much needed repairs. Thankfully, once it was back in the water and cleared to continue working, I got the call right away. I had barely put a dent in my account, only having spent money on a hotel, food, and some new clothes. Living on the Honeycomb taught me to be a minimalist in the sense of material possessions.

Crew quarters are tight, so you really can't get away with having a lot. The most expensive thing I own is a laptop computer, and I mostly use it to watch movies and TV shows. Internet access is limited onboard, so I mostly rely on pirated downloads. I have so many movies that I ended up getting a five-terabyte external hard drive to store them. This also made me very popular among the crew because we'd movie swap a lot, and my library had a lot of obscure movies most people never heard of.

Ten years is a long time to be on one ship, or so the others tell me. It's always been like that to be honest. The crew is constantly changing. New members come in, old ones leave, but some come back periodically. I guess some people just get bored and need a change, or they try to negotiate better pay and benefits, so they leave to find something better. This doesn't interest me. I'm perfectly content where I am. Or at least, I used to be.

When I first started out, the crew quickly became like my new family. We ate together, worked side by side, shared quarters, laughed at the same dumb jokes, and told stories. Oh man, did they love to tell stories. Everyone but me had them, and I listened eagerly. The only other thing I didn't have in common with everyone was their dreams. Every one of them wanted to have enough money put away so they could say goodbye to long voyages and months at a time at sea.

There was one guy named Spencer that I remember well. I'd been on the ship six months before he left for good, but while he was here, he paid more attention to me than anyone. He had a big white bushy beard, stained teeth from coffee and cigarettes, and a pudgy belly. Spencer was a grandfather and because of my age, he said I reminded him of his eldest grandkid. I didn't have a frame of reference, but I believe he treated me like one of his grandkids.

We were on the deck one night in the north, and it was cold as a witch's tit. At least, that's how Spencer had worded it. I remember standing there with a thick jacket on, big gloves, and a mug of hot black coffee. I've never cared for sweets, so it didn't bother me that they had a limited amount of sugar available to doctor the coffee.

Standing on the deck with Spencer, puffing on a cigarette right along with him, we stared out into the black abyss that is the ocean at night. We didn't talk, just looked out into the nothing. Out of the blue, he started talking, as if the conversation had been going on for a few minutes. I had no idea what he was saying, something about things being left unfinished. He didn't even appear to be talking to me, but to someone that wasn't there.

After a few minutes I nudged him with my elbow. It startled him and he seemed to come out of some sort of trance. When I asked him what he'd been talking about, all he said was that it was good to get off the ship every once in a while. If you spend too much time at sea, the nothingness gets to you. "It's good to have an end goal, kid." He left at the very next port, never to return. Spencer didn't die as far as I know, he just went home and retired.

I've thought about that a lot over the years. Spencer wasn't the only one to talk about the nothingness of the sea. It wasn't just the older crew members either, and that shocked me. Even guys that were closer to my age now talked about it. They said it can play tricks on your mind and it's been known to turn strong men into sniveling cowards. I didn't know what to make of that, but it's something that randomly pops into my head at odd times. Some days I can't stop thinking about it no matter how hard I try.

After a long day of hard labor, most of the crew eat dinner, relax in the lounge and conk out. Me, I like to go to the deck and look out at the sea. I've been trying to see this nothingness that everyone seems to know, but all I see every damn time, is the water. It stretches on and on, all the way to the horizon, but that's during the day. At night, you can't see much beyond what little the deck lights show.

Spencer's words come back to me, like they usually do. "It's good to have an end goal, kid." That's easy for the rest of them. Everyone onboard, from the captain on down, has someone to go back to. I have nothing on land. Looking up my parents isn't an option, and I have absolutely no interest in doing so. They were the only family I had as far as I know. I could look into distant relatives, but with the way those two were, I can't imagine any others would be any better.

Meeting new people outside of the crew has always been difficult. I have nothing in common with people on land, so striking up a conversation is always an uphill battle. The times I've tried while on shore leave have been horribly awkward. I'd say the only time it went well was while I was sitting in a coffee shop. I was on my computer looking for new movies to download and a girl at the next table happened to notice.

We got to talking about movies and how it seems that Hollywood has completely run out of ideas. I think that interaction lasted about two hours, and it was nice, but it ended when I asked if she wanted to grab a bite to eat with me. She made some excuse about having to meet up with her boyfriend, but it sounded made up to me. I tried not taking it personally.

The only women I'd ever talked to were in the crew, but it was different talking to her. I stumbled over my words a little too often and it was painfully obvious I was out of my depth. They say that confidence is key, and I was definitely lacking in it. That interaction was about two years ago, and I haven't really tried since. Why would I? I'd always come back to the ship. I keep telling myself that it doesn't matter because land has nothing to offer me.

Shaking my head at the memory, I reach into my pocket for the pack of smokes that is always there. As I light one, my night vision gets ruined by the flame. Taking a deep drag in, I look back out to the complete black before me. Stretching on forever is a vast expanse of nothing. No oil rigs, no other boats, no structures or people. The only thing out there is the water and what dwells under the surface. What could be so frightening about that? Is it the idea of being out there, away from the ship, just floating in the water with no hope of rescue that gets to them? I can imagine that being truly horrifying, but I somehow doubt that's what they're talking about.

The moment that thought enters my mind, I feel a compulsion. I've been trying to understand this fear of the nothing for so long. It's not until I trip on something, and the handrail is thrust into my chest that I realize I'd been moving closer to the edge. Had I really been about to climb over the side and plunge myself into the blue? I believe I was.

What the hell would make me want to jump overboard? I can't even swim for crying out loud. Despite the warm air, a shiver runs down my spine as realization dawns on me. Something I'd heard from several of the crew over the years comes back to me. "Sometimes, when you look into the nothing, something looks back at you." Is that what just happened?

I wipe at the blood seeping from my nostril and go back inside. A shower and a good night's rest is what I need. Just get cleaned up and let the gentle swaying of the ship lull me to sleep. Tomorrow is going to be a hard day. Maintenance in the bowels of the ship always is.

By the time I'm at breakfast, I've mostly put the odd event out of my head, mostly. I've been trying to think about anything else, but it takes concentration and being quiet doesn't go unnoticed. Letty, a woman not much older than me, bumps my shoulder with hers to get my attention. I hadn't even noticed she was sitting next to me. She asks if everything is okay, and I try to laugh it off by blaming some stupid horror movie I watched last night getting in my head. I'm not convincing, but we have work to do.

Busing my tray, I grab up my tool belt and clipboard for the list of minor repairs I need to perform today without another word. Classic avoidance and everyone knows it, but no one says anything. Instead, they take my cue and bus their own trays to begin the day's labors. I catch a few glances from the older crewmen as I leave, and I know those looks. Some of them have clued in to what's gotten to me.

Old salty sea dogs like them are good at recognizing the signs, especially for a first timer like me. You can't walk away unaffected by the nothing no matter how many experiences you have with it. If only I hadn't gone to the deck again trying to understand, this would just be another typical workday.

Descending the stairs for the bottom level, the darkness of the poorly lit stairwell makes me flashback to the ocean last night. I can see it in my mind so clearly and my hand on the stair rail makes me feel like I'm at that edge again, ready to climb over and plunge into the cold water. By now I'm below the water's surface, and I can feel it like something tangible. I'm even starting to have trouble breathing, like my body is already in the water.

Realizing I'm scaring the shit out of myself, I shake my head to clear the horrible sensation away. Maybe on my next forced shore leave I'll take swimming lessons or something. Most of the crew doesn't know I can't swim, which is a good thing. Back in my early years onboard it hadn't been a big deal, but when I turned twenty, some of the crew picked on me mercilessly about it. It was only when the captain stepped in did it stop. Thankfully, most of those assholes aren't here anymore.

As I continue down the stairs, finally able to breathe easily again, I notice the lighting has gotten even dimmer than normal. On top of that, I should've reached the bottom deck already. There aren't that many levels to the bottom from where I already was, yet I've gone down enough stairs to have reached the bottom from the very top. How is it possible I'm still going down?

A feeling of unease creeps into my brain as I get

to another landing, only to find yet another stretch leading further down. Something very not right is happening right now, so instead of trying to reach the bottom, I turn around and go back up. To make sure I'm not losing my mind, I count the landings as I get to them. My legs are killing me when I get to twenty, and panic starts overtaking the unease in me.

No matter how many stairs I climb, the lighting does not get any brighter. The walls look dingier than they usually do too, and I don't think that's because of the subpar lights. Feeling a powerful need for fresh air and sunlight, I start running up the stairs. Metal clattering on the floor alarms me and I whip around at the next landing. One of the tools from my belt slipped off and tumbles down to the landing below. Screw it, I don't need that wrench right now.

Climbing the next set of stairs, I get to yet another identical landing. As I turn to rush up the next stairs, my feet trip on something I didn't see, and I land hard on the stairs. The side of my face collides with the edge of one stair and my mouth is flooded with blood.

Looking to my feet for what tripped me, my heart skips a beat. The wrench that I dropped is there on the ground, the culprit that tripped me up. How is that possible? It should be on the floor below me.

Confused as hell now, I get myself vertical and as much as I want to keep climbing my way to the surface, I don't. Instead, I leave the wrench where it is and slowly go down the stairs I just finished coming up. When I get to the landing below, the wrench isn't where I dropped it. Annoyed at how confused I am, I spit blood on the spot the damn wrench should've been.

This whole crazy episode is unnerving the shit out of me, so I go back up, a little more carefully this time. Expecting to find the wrench where it tripped me when I get back up there, all I find is the blood I just spit on the floor below. It's like no matter how far up I go, I never seem to actually get any higher up.

I could spend days stuck on this staircase and never get to the surface. The only thing that seems to change is when I go down, so down I go. As I do, I continue to spit globs of bloody saliva on the floor and wall, all to mark my progression and make sure I'm still going down. Not once do I find any of it, and I've gone down another thirty landings. I know for a fact that the Honeycomb doesn't have that many levels.

I've long since lost track of time, and a look to my watch only annoys me further. The digital face is smashed from when I fell on the stairs and bloodied my mouth. It feels like I've been going down these damn stairs for an hour. Just when I'm about to lose my shit and start pounding at the walls, I lose my footing again and land hard on the floor. I should've started bruising myself and breaking bones as I fall down the stairs, but I'm not on stairs anymore. In fact, I'm not in the stairwell at all anymore.

The floor I'm laying on doesn't feel like metal, and I sit up to find myself on carpet. Not the cheap crap that they have in the crappy motels I first started staying at before I was eighteen. No, this is more like the carpet from my parents' house. The design is similar to Persian rugs I'd seen in movies, but obviously a lower quality. Even the walls have been replaced. Where the dull green metal walls with grime build up all over them were is now fancy looking wallpaper. Or is it a paint job? I can't even remember anymore.

I know they say you can't outrun your past forever, but I seriously doubt anyone that's said that meant this kind of shit. Not only has there never been anything like this on the ship before, but it doesn't even feel like I'm at sea anymore. There's no gentle sway back and forth from the waves, nor is the air salty. Wherever the hell I am, it's definitely not the ship.

Turning to go back up the stairs, I find that they're not there anymore either. I even press my hands against the wall to see if this is just some illusion, but the wall is as solid as it looks. As far as I can tell, the stairs were never here at all, wherever the hell here is.

I look up and down the hall, but it looks the same both ways. There are elaborate and shiny light fixtures every thirty feet, and every so often, there's a thin dark wood table against the wall. The ends stretch on and on, so far that I can't see where they end. That certainly wasn't like that at my parent's house.

Before going down either direction, I drop another tool from my belt to mark where I came in at. Not that it will do me any good with the stairs gone, but if they ever reappear, odds are it'll be in the same location, right? If nothing else, I can try to break my way through the wall if I find something substantial to swing, like a sledgehammer or ax.

There is quite literally no difference between either direction, so I just start walking to the left. I expect there to eventually be doors along the wall, but that fancy, and in my opinion, ugly wallpaper is uninterrupted. So little of this makes sense, and my unease and panic aren't getting any better the farther I walk.

I've been at it for at least ten minutes when I look behind me. Not five feet away is the screwdriver I left on the floor to mark where I came in at. It's just like on the stairs when I tried going back up, which to me says that I'm going the wrong way. Starting in the other direction, I step over the screwdriver, but as I do, I turn myself around and walk backwards.

Managing to keep this up for a few dozen yards, I see the screwdriver getting farther and farther away. Finally, I'm making some damn progress. Satisfied that I'm actually going somewhere, I turn around, but don't keep walking. I glance behind me to see if the screwdriver is still where it was when I was looking at it, and it is. Facing forward, I go to take a step, but my foot never leaves the ground. Directly in front of me is the damn screwdriver. A quick glance back shows it's not there anymore.

Okay, so I'm still uneasy, but the panic is subsiding, being replaced by anger. On impulse, I grab up the screwdriver and stab it into the wall. I expect it to get stuck in by less than an inch, but the metal shaft goes right into the wall up to the hilt.

The hallway starts shaking and a guttural grumble echoes throughout. I look up and down the hall for whatever I just pissed off, but whatever it is isn't something I can see. The infinity of before has been replaced by darkness, and it's making its way toward me from both directions quickly. Ripping the screwdriver from the wall, I take up my hammer in the other hand and ready myself for a fight.

Watching as it swarms closer, I notice that the lights aren't just going out, but the entire hallway is disappearing. Sweat pours down my body, but I'm cold to the core. This is the purest fear I have ever felt in my entire life, and it's because I know there's nothing I can do to stop this.

The darkness crashes into me from both sides, and I am suddenly blind. The absence of light is so complete that I can't see my hand in front of me. I listen to the silence, trying to pick up on anything that isn't my own breathing, but there's nothing. No movement, no grumbling or growling. If someone dropped a pin I'd hear it.

Keeping the hammer in my right hand, I put the screwdriver back on my belt and reach into my pocket. Pulling out my lighter, I flick it on, and the flame nearly blinds me. Holding it above me, I use the small flame to orient myself in the hallway. The only problem is, I can't see a damn thing.

The hallway wasn't that damn wide, and the tiny flame should be enough to show me the walls. I turn round and round, walking in every direction, but I find nothing. What the hell is going on?

After a minute or two, the lighter gets hot in my hand, and I drop it. Expecting to hear it clatter to the floor, I'm once again plunged in darkness and silence. The lighter never made it to the ground. In fact, I can't feel the floor under my feet at all. I have been consumed by the nothing, completely and utterly.

I curl into a ball and rock myself back and forth. Or at least, that's what I tell myself is happening. Without a floor, is it really possible to do that? Is there any movement at all? Nothing makes sense and nothing is alright. I am once again a child locked in my parents' closet for disobeying their simple orders to be quiet and courteous. Tears begin to stream down my face silently as my open eyes search for something, anything to see.

"Hey," a voice calls out to me, "are you okay?" Letty's face breaks through the darkness right in front of me, so close that it's all I can see.

It's like coming out of a daze. The air changes from that flat nothing to warm, humid, and salty. I can feel the rocking of the ship as it glides through choppy water. We're on the deck and it's night. I'm chilled down to the bone and the fear is all over my face.

As I fumble for my cigarettes, Letty asks me where I've been all day. No one's seen me since breakfast. I try to tell her I wasn't feeling good, and went back to my bunk, but apparently the crew checked there and didn't find me.

I don't know how to get out of telling her what happened, but I do know one thing. The next port the ship docks at, wherever the hell it is, I'm putting in some time on land. I just don't know if I'll be returning.

STORAGE UNIT

For as long as I can remember, my apartment has been cluttered with all the crap that I own. Seriously, for some reason, I own way more stuff than I ever need. I don't consider myself a hoarder or anything that severe, but I do have trouble throwing stuff away. You never know when you're going to need something you thought you didn't. A bunch of times over the last year alone I've needed something that anyone else would've tossed out, but not me. See, I keep things for a good reason, it just takes time for that reason to become apparent.

Don't get the wrong impression, I do throw things away. I don't have piles of old newspaper and garbage all over my place. It's more like a gaggle of stuffed animals that were either won for me or I won at fairs and arcades with those really big claw machines. You know, random things like that. For crying out loud, I still have a handful of stuffed animals from when I was a kid. On the upside, when my nieces and nephews have birthdays and I forget to get them a present, the newer stuffed animals prove useful. Or at least they did. I think they're getting too old for stuffed animals now.

The sheer randomness of my possessions astounds me sometimes, and since I only have a one-bedroom apartment, space is an issue. The problem is getting me to throw things away, so a few years ago, I came up with a solution. Storage units are a lot cheaper than getting a bigger apartment. Now granted, it is in my plan to buy a house one day, but I'm nowhere near financially sound enough to afford that. Plus, HOAs are a freaking nightmare and trying to find a decent place without one these days is nearly impossible. The last thing I want to do is get a house that's going to need a lot of work, so a new or newer house is the best bet.

In the little over a year since I've gotten a storage unit, I've had to upgrade to a larger unit once. I thought a 10x10 was going to be big enough, but I keep getting new stuff. Half the time I'm not even buying things. I've got a well to do aunt and uncle that likes to redo their house every six months. The longest I've seen them go without changing things up was a year and some change, but that was when I was much younger. They're both mid-level managers for a worldwide company, so their annual household income is close to mid six figures. They can afford to redesign their house every three months if they really wanted to.

Whenever they get the bug to redo their place, they tend to give their existing furniture and decorations to the family. Since I'm single and have always been one of their favorites, I get first pick of the things they're giving away. That's how I got my deluxe king size bedframe that takes up more than half of my bedroom. It may be massive, but dear god does the comfort and storage compartments underneath make up for the space it takes up. The drawers underneath are about three feet long.

Thanks to their generosity, I have enough furniture to fill a three-bedroom house, and it won't be short of seating. There's a six-person capacity dining room table and chairs set, a three-seater couch, a love seat and two deluxe armchairs. The living room furniture doesn't match, but that doesn't really matter to me. If I ever get to use them and the lack of matching bugs me, they make covers to change that. That stuff takes up more than half of my new 10x20 storage unit, and I keep it in the very back of the unit. The rest of the space is filled nearly to the ceiling with boxes. Some cardboard, some plastic totes.

When it comes to clothing, I'm a little on the simple side. Since I was a kid, I've primarily gotten my clothes from a mega chain store and they're exceedingly cheaper than department and clothing stores. They carried the brand of jeans I've worn for the last twenty years, until about a year ago. When they got rid of them, I was forced to look at other brands, but I didn't like any of the ones they carried. It took several months for me to find something that I did like, and they cost twice as much as the old brand. I was less than thrilled, but there wasn't much I could do about it.

I didn't come across those new jeans by accident. I have a friend that works at that department store, and she was the one to suggest them. After buying a few pairs and wearing them for a few months, I fell in love with them and dropped a few hundred on several pairs. It was about six months after that when she informed me that they weren't going to be carrying them anymore. In fact, no one was going to be carrying them anywhere. The owner of the brand that made them said some stupid things that went viral, and cancel culture pounced on it.

It was devastating that my newest jeans brand was going under, but because of the heads up I received, I'm not going to be short on them for a long time. It hurt my bank accounts, but I dropped a few thousand dollars and bought nearly a hundred pairs of the jeans. I've got four or five plastic tote boxes in my storage unit filled with those jeans. So far I haven't needed to get into them, but the eight pair in my closet right now are looking worse for wear.

A good pair of worn-in jeans are hard to replace, but I recently had an incident in my oldest, and therefore, favorite pair. I went hiking with some friends and accidentally fell off the trail. Aside from some bruises in normally unseen places, my jeans took most of the damage. I ended up sliding down a less than smooth rock face for about twenty feet. The ass of my jeans got torn up pretty bad, so there's no salvaging them.

That's why I'm at my storage unit today. I need to replace the now trashed pair of jeans. As I pull up to the three-story tall building, I roll down my window and punch in the seven-digit access code. The gate raises up and I drive through, glad that I decided to wait until dark to come here. On the weekend, there are always cars parked at the two entrances to this place, and I really didn't want to have to deal with other people coming in and out. My experiences with people around here have been less than pleasant.

Moving things in or out of a storage unit is a pain in the ass for pretty much everyone. Each entrance has an elevator, and there are four to six wheeled flat carts for the entire building. Getting one of those when you need it is almost as hard as winning the freaking lottery. Though I don't need one today, that's not always the case when I visit my unit. People tend to be self-centered assholes and even though the rules are that a group can only use one flat cart, they'll use all they can carry regardless of other people's needs. I get it, but that doesn't change the fact that it's a douchebag move.

Parking close to the door, I get out of my Jeep and double click the lock button on my key fob. The Jeep beeps, letting me know all the doors are properly locked and the alarm is activated. The last time I came here at dark, some asshole got into my car and stole all the change from one of my cup holders and a bunch of crap from the back. It was my own dumbass fault for not making sure my Jeep was properly locked, but the mess he made was a pain to clean. It was like the jackass rolled around in the mud before getting inside, and the stench he left behind was horrendous. I had to shell out a hundred and fifty bucks to have it professionally cleaned and detailed.

Walking up to the sliding doors, I punch in my seven-digit number again for them to open. These places have gotten a lot more security conscious. I have to enter my code again once inside the elevator to get to the top floor. The elevator only lets you go to the floor that your code is valid for. It lowers the risk of people getting into units that don't belong to them or something like that. I was once told that a lock is only there to keep honest people honest. For someone that's up to no good, a lock is just another obstacle, and criminal types have so many ways to get around them.

This storage building has only been around for a couple years. Until recently, this whole area was undeveloped land, full of trees and underbrush that only the really determined ever got into. Our city isn't all that big, only a few hundred thousand live here, but like most population centers, the numbers increase every year. The amount of expansion that's been going on is astounding, and I think about that every time I come here. Once the elevator reaches the top floor and opens, I always look out the window in the hall.

I remember a time when this area was considered nature, full of wildlife and very few people. There were a handful of houses scattered around, with miles between them and roads barely big enough for two cars to drive on. This particular area was never farmland or anything like that, just a big expanse of undeveloped property. Now the city's development stretches beyond here and the edge of the expansion is a few miles away. The local wildlife still hasn't completely adjusted. I keep hearing people with houses complain that they find deer on their front lawn.

On occasion, I get emergency alerts on my phone about dangerous wildlife. Recently, a bobcat or something was spotted around my apartment complex. Some dumbass parent that was less attentive with her five-year-old let the kid play outside and passed the time by playing a stupid game on their phone. The kid was attacked by the wildcat, probably because it thought the cat was a large domestic kitty. Thankfully, I was at work when this happened, but things like this have been happening thanks to the rapid expansion. I believe the term is urban sprawl.

The closest thing I've seen to a dangerous wild animal was when I went to the zoo on a school field trip. We don't have one here, so we had to travel to an even larger city, but I'd hardly call those wild animals. The most memorable moment of that trip had been at the tiger habitat. I just so happened to come to it when a zoo employee was in the enclosure with the giant murder kitty. I'd expected her to be timid or even scared since the tiger was loose, but she appeared as calm as can be.

I watched as she walked right up to the cat with a bloody piece of meat and fed it directly to her. It was the strangest thing I've ever seen. If I didn't know any better, I'd swear those two had some kind of relationship going on, kind of like a person does with their pet. Though, after watching them for a few minutes, it felt like their connection was deeper than that. Not a sexual thing or anything creepy like that, but there was meaning to it.

To this day, nature never fails to amaze me. That's how I got talked into going hiking with my friends in the first place. I'm always curious what I'll find, even if there's little to no chance of seeing something out of the ordinary. Of course, falling off the trail had been out of the ordinary, and very unpleasant, but it wasn't the kind of thing I was hoping to happen. Just once I'd like to come face to face with something in the wild that you normally don't see.

Walking down the hallway and turning to the left, I go about halfway down before coming to my unit. I've only got about an hour before the building locks up for the night, but that should be plenty of time to get a pair of jeans and get out of here. Now granted, that's if I can locate one of the totes right away. I've got so many boxes in there and my labels have a tendency to fall off the plastic. Even though this place is climate controlled, they can never get rid of all the humidity in the air. It's not as bad as storing things in an attic, but in the heat of summer, it sometimes feels that way.

Slipping my key into the lock, a noise makes me freeze. I have no idea what it had been, but there were no other cars outside when I got here. I suppose there could be an employee walking around on this level, but I hadn't noticed anyone while walking to my unit. I keep quiet to see if I hear it again, but it's all quiet. Admittedly, I do tend to get a little jumpy when I come here like this. Being alone brings the possibility of something bad to happen, though nothing has happened as of yet. Still, it only takes one time.

Deciding that I'd like to get this done as fast as

possible, I unlock the padlock, remove it from the latch, and quickly slide the door up. Doing this makes a lot of noise, but I'd like to have access to something I could use as a weapon if some creep decides to make an appearance. I have an old baseball bat near the door inside just for the occasion.

Once the door is all the way up, the lone light on the ceiling in the unit senses movement and lights up. I see stacks of boxes, piled up furniture and various other things scattered around the space. There's a very narrow walkway through the center of my stuff, just barely big enough for me to get through. As I take it all in, I notice a box on the very top of a stack is wobbling.

That alarms me. Rolling the door up shouldn't have made the box move, and the ground didn't tremble like someone dropped a very heavy object. I've felt what it's like when someone on the other side of the floor dropped a couch. I could feel the vibrations through the floor, but it's not enough for a box that's sitting perfectly flat on top of a stack to wobble. Besides, I'd have heard someone dropping something that heavy, and the only noise I heard was the door sliding up. So, what the hell caused the box to move like that?

I've heard of older storage units having rodent issues, but these new places guarantee that rats won't be an issue. They even use it as a selling point in their advertisements. A big part of me wants to ignore it and start pulling down tote boxes to find my jeans, but the paranoid part of me wants to know if there's something up there. If rats have gotten into my unit, I'm going to be super pissed.

Picking up the baseball bat leaning against one of my metal shelves, I notice a bunch of my labels are on the floor. At least one of them says 'jeans', so I know one of the boxes at the front is what I'm after. My luck, it'll be the one on the bottom. I've got these things stacked eight tall, which is above my head. I tried to avoid that for as long as I could, but at this point, I'm lucky to have the walking space in the center.

If I had a step ladder, I'd be able to get myself high enough that I could see the top of my stacks, but that's one of the things I haven't gotten from my aunt and uncle. I've only got the one, and it lives in my apartment so I can get to the hard to reach things in my cabinets. Instead of trying to solve the question of the random wobbling box, I start in on the task I came here to do. However, I do keep the bat close by in case a rat launches itself at me. If that happens, the employee in the office on the first floor would hear my shriek.

Reaching up on my tiptoes, I pull down the first box on top of the first stack. It's one of those hard black plastic boxes with the yellow lid, like all the other tote boxes I own. Pulling off the lid, I find clothes neatly folded inside, but none of them are denim. It's a bunch of long sleeve shirts and sweaters. I should've known my winter clothes would be the first things I come across. I keep a few items like this in my closet at the apartment, but the majority of my winter gear gets put in here every spring.

Taking down the next box, I hear what sounds like giggling. I drop the box on top of the first one and immediately take up the bat. The noise was quiet, but it sounded close by. Popping my head out the door, I look up and down the hall for any signs of life, but there's no one around. The white buzzing lights above show every inch of the hallways, and I don't see any shadows at the ends of the hall. Where had the giggling come from?

Ducking back inside my unit, I go to open the box I just took down, but movement above catches my attention. There's another box wobbling, but it's on the other side of the walking space. The cardboard and plastic boxes could probably support the weight of a small child, but not anything bigger. That eerie giggling hadn't sounded that young, which is why I immediately thought it came from outside the unit. Well, that and, how the hell would someone get into my unit and lock it from the inside? It's impossible.

There's a thin space between the ceiling and the top of the metal walls, but it's thin enough that a rat would have trouble squeezing through. No freaking way a person could get through, so what the hell is on top of my boxes? Did someone that rents an adjoining unit slip a prank sound box through the slit just to scare the crap out of me? People these days are getting crazier and dumber, so I wouldn't put it past them, but it's still a weird as hell thing to do. Not to mention it doesn't explain how my boxes keep wobbling.

I consider closing up the unit and coming back tomorrow, particularly when other people are here, but the last thing I want to do is come back tomorrow. Besides, whatever the hell is in here will most likely still be here once I lock the unit up, so I'll have to deal with it eventually. I take a step back, the bat in one hand and my keys in the other when I hear the giggling again. Looking up, I see both boxes wobbling, and there's more than one thing making that creepy sound.

"Who's there?" I demand with a shaky voice, not expecting a reply. Taking another step back, I see the stacks along the walking space wobble as something moves on top, coming closer to me. It's happening on both sides, and my eyes grow wide as I see things pop up over the edge, looking down at me.

"What the hell?" I whisper as tiny faces, no more than two inches around, peer down at me. There must be at least a dozen of them, like tiny humans with oddly colored skin. The faces are covered in shadow since the light is above them, but I can make out features. Two eyes, pointy noses, and mouths. The closest I've ever seen to these things is from movies and fairytales. They look like pixies or sprites, tiny woodland fairies, but I don't see any wings.

A dozen or so tiny faces look at me with curiosity and I'm blown away. Here I am in my storage unit, and I'm confronted with honest to god fairies. Never in my wildest dreams did I think these things could be real, but if I was to put money on it, I'd have thought I'd come across them while on a hike or something. That makes me think of the whole urban sprawl thing. Could this be like deer in people's front yards?

My first instinct is to put the bat down and try to communicate with the tiny fairies. "Hi there," I say sweetly, but they change the moment I place the bat down. The curiosity on their small faces turns ugly, and a few of them leap at me. I'm caught so off guard by this that they land on me, holding onto my clothes to keep from falling to the ground. Their weight is so light that the impact doesn't hurt, but the little bastards sink teeth into me, and that does hurt.

I've accidentally cut myself with a kitchen knife a few times, and that always hurt, but this is so much worse. They must have very sharp teeth because these things manage to bite through my shirt and break the skin. It's almost like if a binder clip had teeth and someone attached three of them to my chest and stomach. I shriek from the radiating pain and stumble backward as I try to pull one of them off me. The pain is so damn intense, but it gets worse when I try to pull the one highest up on me off. It's got those teeth dug into my skin and the little shit is refusing to let go.

The ones still on top of the boxes are making noise again, but it's not giggling like before. If anything, it's like spectators at a gladiator show chanting their approval of the violence going on for their benefit. When I can't get the top one off, I change to pulling on one of the others, but the results are the same. These guys weigh almost nothing, but they've got the jaw strength of a freaking Doberman.

I can feel blood dripping down my body from the three points these things are trying to take chunks out of me. With my hands balled into fists, I start pounding on them, doing my damnedest to smash their tiny bodies enough that they let go. I'm basically hitting myself, but I'm frantic and can't come up with another idea.

The one highest up gets four hard hits on its back, and I feel the pressure on my skin let up. Before it can sink those sharp teeth back in, I grab it by the body and fling it back into the unit. The second one comes off much the same way, thrown against my stack of boxes. I watch as it grabs onto the plastic, and scurries back to the top with its friends. The third little bastard is harder to get off, taking half a dozen punches before it lets up. When I grab this one up, I don't just fling it away. I raise it above my head and throw it hard against the concrete floor. It lands with a hard splat, like throwing a wet sponge on the ground with all your might. Dark fluid splatters around it, and the little shit doesn't get back up.

The noise of approval from the ones on top of the boxes changes to something angry, and I can see them preparing to launch themselves at me. I know I can't take them all on at once, so I jump up, grabbing the bottom of the sliding door with both hands. My weight brings the door down fast and as it slides in place, I hear multiple thuds as the blood thirsty pixies slam into the door.

As quickly as I can, I replace the padlock on the latch and move toward the elevator. I can hear tiny fists pounding at the door behind me, but I don't turn around to see if they're somehow getting through. I just get the hell out of there.

On the elevator ride down, I take stock of myself. The shirt is trashed, and there's some blood on my jeans. I really hope that doesn't stain. Who knows when I'll be able to safely get into my storage unit again. I swear, if those little bastards damage my stockpile of jeans, I'm going to smash them all into oblivion.

<u>PANDORA'S ANTIQUE BOX</u>
APPRECIATION

The silver pen that never runs out of ink glides over the white sheet, the pink and yellow ones underneath copying what I write. So few people ask for receipts these days, especially for the items I sell. Most of my customers don't want there to be a paper trail for what they buy since, odds are, someone is either going to die or be seriously injured due to the purchase. Physically or mentally, it depends on the antique.

It's not like I need to keep receipts or anything like that. The red inventory tome keeps immaculate records of what items get sold, to who and for how much. I don't need to ask for the person's name, nor do I have to write any of it down. By magic, the book records it all without my involvement. Well, save for selling an antique. You know what, come to think of it, there was even once where that wasn't even needed.

It never occurred to me that someone might shoplift a small item, but it happened. I didn't even realize the incense burner was missing until the red tome opened itself on my counter. Thankfully, no one had been in the shop when it did this. The last two customers had just walked out, but one of them, presumably the thief, hadn't spoken to me at all. The first had, and I read his TAN bio, but he hadn't purchased anything. Most people don't on their first visit. The conversation I have with them leaves them with a lot to think about and decisions to make.

Item 30912, the Skeleton Incense Burner. The information was filling in right before my eyes, and though that no longer phases me, the fact that someone had apparently walked out with it did. When it got to the name, Joshua Wagner, I picked up the TAN book and flipped to the last page. I skimmed the top and saw he was unemployed, but under a heading that said 'side hustles' it listed minor drug dealer, pick pocket and shoplifter, along with a bunch of other dumbass crap.

The Skeleton Incense Burner isn't something I'm overly familiar with, so I had to pull the card from the catalog. My Latin has gotten exceptionally better, so I only had to look up a few words. It's a cursed item, but the level is odd to determine. It can range from a level two to four, and it all depends on who's around when its activated. I wouldn't want to be there when that happens, even with the Shopkeeper's Pen on me. Technically the incense burner should've been in one of the glass cases, but for some reason it wasn't.

The burner doesn't need to be used for its intended purpose to be activated. The only thing that's required is the presence of smoke. It doesn't matter what kind either. That idiot could be smoking a cigarette, joint, or even be present at a dumpster fire. As long as the burner is in close proximity to some kind of smoke, everyone within a fifteen foot radius is going to be affected.

Once activated, each individual is going to start feeling severely stoned, like they smoked some really good weed. Their head is going to feel light as a feather, and it'll feel like everything in their life is going to work out. They'll start to think about all the things that have gone wrong, no matter how minor, and they'll envision ways to correct whatever it is. Then their mind will show them playing out the scenario, and just when it looks like their solution works, everything goes horribly wrong.

For instance, if a father is estranged from one of his children, that child will become a grotesquely faced monstrosity and begin attacking with tooth and nail. Even if the father was the strongest man in the world, that child is going to tear them a new asshole. It doesn't stop there either, and gets much worse.

The scenarios continue to play out, one right after another and none repeat. Every single event that they wish they could change will turn into something horrible and kill them in a plethora of ways. It could be a handful of things, it could be hundreds. Regardless of how many there are, the person will experience them as if it was real time, but it only happens in a few minutes. The experience will render them down to insane wailings of great distress and pain until they start clawing out their own eyes, followed by ripping at their wrists with their own teeth. There is no limit to how many people could be affected in one event.

My pen completes the receipt, and I tear off the white one for the customer. She hands me two bundles of bills and thanks me in that wonderful Ukrainian accent of hers. I slip the receipt into the large bag that holds three of my newest inventory. Katya always gets a call when something truly nasty comes in, and I think my supplier is sending me these kinds of things more and more on purpose. I couldn't say how many she's bought from me since I took over Pandora's, but money isn't much of a concern to me anymore.

I do consider Katya a friend, but she doesn't know the full extent of my business. Not once has she asked me where my inventory comes from. Considering her business, questions can be an unpleasant thing, and I figure she's extending the same curtesy I do to her. I saw her eye the half full jar of black pebbles that sits on top of the card catalog, and I know she wanted to ask, but she didn't. Soothing Stones wouldn't have been an interest to her. At least I don't think.

The last Soothing Stone that was returned to me was from an interesting case. I try to read the TAN bios very carefully before selling an item, but sometimes, I only get to skim through it. Most of my sales are made for revenge purposes, but not everyone seeking revenge is worthy of it. This guy, Jon, had been such a case. Not as the one seeking revenge, but as the victim.

Several months ago, a guy named Carter came in looking for something to give a coworker. Carter held a grudge against Jon because of a minor physical altercation that took place in front of a bunch of their coworkers. It made Carter look bad and there was bad blood between them ever since. Not long after, there was a promotion available at their office and of course, it was between the two of them.

Carter wanted to eliminate the competition, so he came into my shop. Stories about the items in my shop have been circulating and a friend of a friend told him a story about his sister's ex-girlfriend. She had a strange looking lamp that she bought from me, and after it accidentally broke, the woman went insane. She ended up stabbing herself to death. If she hadn't been such an abusive bitch, her demise wouldn't have been so brutal.

I only got to skim Carter's bio, but what I read was more than enough. His motives for visiting my shop weren't up to my standards. I tried to dissuade him from making a purchase, but the jackass was awfully persistent. It was clear he wasn't going to forget his pursuit, so I had to do something a little different. After some careful consideration, I directed him towards a level 1 enchanted item. Item 13798, Campfire Colors, was a unique item to say the least. It's one of the very few consumable antiques I have.

The wooden box was designed to look like one of the tomes from the Chronicles, and inside were a dozen paper packets with animal designs on them. Tossing one of these into a fire will change the color of the flames and take anyone around the campfire on a serious trip. I told Carter his coworker would be brutally mauled by the animal depicted on the packet, but a body will never be found. It will be as if the person simply vanished. This was of course a lie, or maybe an omission of truth.

Yes, Jon was mauled during his trip, but once the animal killed him, he was brought back to our reality. The experience was truly horrific and made him believe he died a gruesome death, but he wasn't physically harmed. Everything that took place after he tossed the packet into the fire was all in his mind. That's not to say he won't be forever altered.

It took some doing, but I convinced Carter to sleep on his decision to purchase Campfire Colors. I needed the time to add a little something to the packets for Jon's benefit. Thankfully, I know someone who does metal engraving that owed me a favor. I had a dozen metal business cards made and stuck one inside each packet. The idea had been for Jon to find the card in the campfire after it burned out.

Shortly after Carter dropped $500 on the antique, Jon walked into my shop. By the color of his eyes, I could tell he had tangled with the tiger, but it wasn't until I pulled out the latest tome from the Chronicles that I knew the extent of what happened to him. Not only did he perceive certain colors differently, but the fierceness in him got bumped up a few notches.

It wasn't hard or surprising to Jon to learn Carter meant to kill him. He was surprised and grateful to learn of my intervention. I even set him up with an antique that would get back at Carter, at a discount. No self-centered asshole can resist making a wish with the Monkey's Paw, and it always comes back to me in the end. I've gotten a lot of use from that item.

Of all the people that have taken a Soothing Stone, Jon was the quickest to return it. Perhaps it's the tiger inside him now that prevented him from being too emotionally scarred. It could even be that he wasn't all that phased with what happened to Carter once he used the Paw. The Chronicles didn't give me that kind of insight. I'm just glad everything turned out as well as it did. I wasn't sure if he'd see the metal card once the fire burned out.

I've got so much time left in the work day. There isn't much for me to do since I don't have to worry about the normal stuff other businesses do. I fill my free time with dusting, rearranging items around the store, and when I get really bored, I'll read from the Chronicles. Currently, all of my consults have already come in and made their final decisions, so I'm not expecting anyone to come in. When it gets closer to lunch time people start filtering in. My average for walk-ins is between five and ten these days.

As I open up one of the glass cases to do some dusting, a noise behind me makes me jump. I look around for the source of the noise, but it had been so brief and quiet that I couldn't tell what it had been. It almost sounded like an out of tune string being plucked, but I don't have any musical instruments in stock with strings. There's the Pan Flute that conjures flesh hungry woodland pixies and a trumpet that shifts you into an alternate reality where you're stuck playing big band music until you die, but that's it.

Leaving the duster on the counter, I move deeper into the shop. Is it possible that I imagined the noise, or was it something from outside that I barely heard? There is an occasion when some of my antiques move on their own, but I don't think any of them have made noise on their own. Wait, there it is again. Two distinct notes and it definitely didn't come from outside.

This time the notes sounded less like a string instrument and more metallic than before. I move in the direction I thought it came from and I come to a curio cabinet. As my eyes land on it, I quickly search my pockets for the Shopkeeper's Pen. If one of those music boxes somehow activated itself, I'd be well and truly screwed without my protection. Thankfully, the pen is tucked into my pants pocket. Through the same magic that keeps the red tome forever up to date, the Pen never seems to be far from me, in or out of the shop.

Standing there for a few silent moments, I wait for the sound to come again. When it does, it scares the crap out of me. Three notes this time, but it's not coming from the cabinet. Turning around, I don't see anything out of the ordinary, nor anything that could be the source. I'm very grateful it's not one of the music boxes, but seriously, what the hell is making that noise? Now that I've got the music boxes in my head, the noise does sound a lot like that. What else in here could sound like one of those?

As I search the store, the noise comes again and again. Each time it plays one more note than it did before and after a while, the tune begins to form. I know that tune but am having a difficult time placing it. It almost sounds like a nursery rhyme. That gives me an idea and I head to the antique toy section.

I don't actually have a lot of antique toys anymore. Katya went through this kick a while back where she bought up most of them. She said something about wanting to create a playroom for some truly despicable people. After seeing what the Magic 8 Ball was capable of doing, I wasn't sure I wanted to know what the playroom was going to be like. I imagined it being a torture room for pedophiles or something like that, but for my own sanity, I kicked the image from my mind. I'm already using a Soothing Stone to help me with my past trauma, I don't want to add more time onto my need for it.

By the time the tune gets to nine notes, I've zeroed in on the section where whatever is responsible is hiding in. I thought I had it three notes ago, but it's like the damn thing keeps moving. If I didn't know any better, I'd say this thing is hiding from me, almost taunting me. Considering the childish tune, could it be playing hide and seek with me? Of all the weird things that's happened since taking over Pandora's, this is a first.

Standing in front of the leather armchair that many of my customers have sat in while I talk with them, the noise comes much louder. Getting down on my hands and knees, I peer underneath. There's an old metal box with faded paint on it. What had once been a bright yellow with red balloons is now dull yellow and pink. I'm looking at the top of a freaking Jack-In-the-Box that's laying on its front. Why did it have to be that?

Reaching underneath, I try to grab for the

mischievous toy, but I pull my hand back quickly. There's something very wrong here. I asked my supplier to take back anything remotely clown related. Those face painted nightmares freak me the hell out.

I get my hands underneath me and am about to push myself up when the damn thing pops open. Normally that's enough to scare the crap out of me, but the clown that pops out isn't your typical clown. It's dressed up in normal clown fashion, but the jagged teeth chomping at me and the bloody knife its waving in my direction is not. The thing growls at me as it crawls along the floor, murder in those dull painted eyes.

Scrambling away, I get to my feet and put some distance between me and the nightmare toy. I can still see the base of the chair, but after a few minutes, I still haven't seen the toy come out. Did it run out of juice already? Don't get me wrong, I'd be as happy as a pig in shit if that's the case. Then again, I have no idea how this thing got activated or where the hell it came from. I've never seen this damn thing before, and if I had, I would've gotten rid of it one way or another.

My eyes are glued to the space under the chair, but I hear eleven notes of the nursery rhyme coming from a different section of the shop. Part of me wants to make a beeline for the door, but it sounded like the music is coming from that direction. I turn toward the counter and head for the backdoor, not for an escape, but for a weapon.

Ever since a rival of my supplier's made a surprise visit, I've kept a baseball bat underneath my register. It's not like I thought a bat would help me against a rival demon but having it has made me feel better. I grab it up and turn to face the shop, daring the little bastard to come out. Scanning the immediate area, I practically jump out of my skin when twelve notes sound behind me. The freaking box is sitting on top of the card catalog. I raise the bat to smash the metal box, but I hesitate. If I pummel the evil toy where it is, I run the risk of damaging the catalog.

Before I can make a decision on what to do, the clown pops out and lunges at me. I jump back hard enough that I slam my spine right into the counter. Shit, that hurts. The Jack-In-the-Box lands short, bringing the knife down toward my foot. Before it can sink the blade in, I shift my leg to the side, narrowly missing the point. Not wanting to give it the chance to strike again, I hop my butt up onto the counter. I'm about to swing my legs around so I can jump down to the floor on the other side, but the clown moves first.

Launching itself up, the base of the box slams into my shoulder and topples me over. Landing on my head, my body crumbles to the ground and my vision goes blurry. I hear more than see the bat clatter to the ground and roll off out of reach. Not that I could grab and use it in my current state.

It takes a few moments for my head to clear. My head is throbbing, but a quick, gentle feel of my head doesn't cover my hands in blood. As the world comes back into focus, I see the infernal toy sitting on the floor in front of me. The clown's face is still monstrous, but it looks at me with concern, as if to wonder if I'm okay. That badly painted mouth with its jagged teeth is in an O, but once I start moving, it smiles. Then it resumes its ghastly hunger and lunges for me again.

I bring my hands up to protect my face, but the cursed toy is agile. It manages to bring the knife down past my arms and stabs me right in the forehead. Before

I can do more than scream, it stabs me two more times. Flinging my arms out, I give off this unholy, blood curdling scream, expecting it to be the last thing I ever do.

There are no more knife strikes, no more eerie musical notes or growling. The murderous toy is nowhere to be seen. I quickly check my forehead, but there is no blood. I feel around for a stab wound or gash, but my skin is completely unmarred. Aside from the throbbing from landing directly on my head, there appears to be no injury.

I am well and thoroughly confused. As I slowly get to my feet, I use the counter to pull myself up. Once I'm completely vertical, I notice something on the counter that hadn't been there before. It's a piece of paper with crude handwriting on it. Not like a child did it, but someone with hands not used to holding a pen. Or in this case, a piece of charred rock, and no, I don't mean charcoal.

Dear antique lady,

I just wanted to say thank you for all the fun toys you've sent us to play with. They're all very fun and scream wonderfully. I hope you find the toy I sent you to be as delightful as the ones you send us. It was my favorite when I was young.

Okay, that explains a lot. I know Abaddon said his faction was really enjoying the souls getting sent their way since I took over, but I never expected them to send me something. While I do appreciate the gesture, next time I get a face-to-face with Abaddon, we're going to need to discuss this. Unless I have a concussion, there isn't any permanent damage. Still, I would like to avoid killer clowns as much as possible, even if they don't really try to kill me.

I get the baseball bat back in its place when another sound makes me jump. This one I'm all too familiar with, but it's not the typical knock of a delivery. I've only heard this one at my back door once, and that had been a special circumstance.

Opening the door, I see the majestic olive-skinned woman standing in the alley behind my shop. In her hands is the orange tome that I knew would come back one day. A day I've been dreading. She hands it to me, saying, "It's time."

Well shit, here we go.

NIGHT WATCHER 7
THE TALKER

Things at Shadow Hills have been surprisingly quiet. Since the grave robber incident, mischievous teens have been steering clear of the cemetery grounds. While on patrols, I occasionally hear music playing in the distance, but every time I try to track it down, it ends up coming from the other side of the stone wall that surrounds the property. Teens have been partying in the woods surrounding the cemetery, which I'm fine with as long as they don't cross the wall. Everything outside the wall is the police's problem, not mine.

Speaking of the police, they've been coming by rather regularly. I've been splitting my time between Shadow Hills, the bakery, and online college courses almost equally. My gingerbread cookies have become a big hit at the bakery, as long as I don't cook them too long like I used to. The Sheriff's department has been buying them up almost as much as they buy doughnuts, which is saying something.

With all the work I've been doing, including my education, I haven't had a lot of time for gaming. What little spare time I do have tends to be spent doing my cosplay stuff, and I'm still only doing that online. I have gotten a little more risqué with my outfits but keeping to my no nudity policy. Deciding to create an outfit for a certain plant-based villain, I showed a progression of transformation that started with little more than small leaf designed pasties covering my breasts. That got a lot of positive responses, not to mention record sales of the photo set. Guys go crazy for underboob.

I've been furthering my education at Shadow Hills as well. Mrs. Langford has been teaching me more about preparing bodies, but also telling me more stories from her time as the Night Watcher. When I don't have my hands full of instruments or the body, I'm writing things down in my book. My notes on what goes bump in the cemetery have taken up almost half the pages, front and back.

Today she finishes telling me about a group of six kids playing hide and seek in the cemetery back in the 80s when the delivery buzzer goes off. It's a little late in the day for a delivery and the only thing that comes in at odd hours is a new body. With the state of the world, we've been getting more and more business lately. If things keep progressing this way, half the city will be dead in a year or two.

As much as Mrs. Langford is grateful for the extra business, she also hates it. It means things are getting worse and there's nothing she can do about it. Anything that goes on inside these walls is within her control, and she hasn't come across something she couldn't get the better of. She just wishes there was something she could outside of these walls, but her domain is over the dead, not the living, and the living is the problem.

When we're having to hold services one or two times a week consistently, something is very wrong. I know on average there's two deaths every second in the world, but this feels like that number is getting multiplied exponentially. To most people, that seems absurd, but most people aren't in the death trades like we are. It's not like there's another pandemic going on, and the methods of death are varied, but the sheer volume is worrying.

Car accidents, various medical conditions, overdoses, and even auto-erotic asphyxiation are some of the most common deaths that we see, but lately, the methods are more concentrated in the realms of violence. Shootings, stabbings, vehicular slaughter, suffocations, assaults and suicides have been on the rise. There have been a disturbing number of bodies we weren't able to prepare for open caskets. More in the last four months than in all my time as the Night Watcher.

Cremation is still the cheapest option for grieving families, and a lot have been choosing it, but that doesn't mean the grave digger is short on business. That small excavator is getting more use than ever. I'm afraid we're going to have to start clearing some of the patches of trees out with the way things are going, which really sucks. On quiet nights, I like to take a break in those patches and enjoy the night. They also make great hunting blinds for ghouls and the like, though we haven't had a ghoul since we cleared out that nest a while back.

The recent influx of business has also forced Mrs. Langford to hire additional staff. Well, one new guy. Specifically, a new grave digger. Carter is in his mid-60s and looking to retire, so before he does, she's having him train the new guy. I get some lessons too about using the machine and the proper techniques to digging graves, but it won't be a permanent part of my job. Honestly, the only reason I'm learning too is if the new guy doesn't pan out.

Anton Nyx is a golden skinned guy with a look about him that suggests Mediterranean descent. I'm told he's my age and also attending college, but he actually goes on campus instead of doing online courses. His field of study is anthropology judging by the books I've seen him totting around, but he doesn't come off as a brainy know-it-all. In fact, I've noticed he's rather quiet, almost like he chooses when to speak and puts thought into what he's going to say. A rare thing for people in their early 20s these days.

Now, just because he appears to be book smart doesn't mean Anton won't periodically ask stupid questions. For the first week he was here, I thought he was kind of stupid, but then I realized what it really was. Since he was little, he's had his head buried in books, training to be an academic, probably since middle school. Later, I confirmed with Mrs. Langford that this is his first job, and the guy just got his driver's license on top of that. Not that he kept failing the driving test or anything. He simply never had a need to get one until he decided to look for a job. Busses don't come out here.

Being a grave digger isn't something a lot of people want to do, but the pay is decent, and the hours aren't that bad. You just have to be comfortable in a cemetery and don't mind a little manual labor. Digging the grave is done with the excavator but filling it back in is done with shovels. That way there's no risk of damaging the casket. Not to mention the bereaved don't like to see the machine graveside. It sends the wrong message or something like that.

I open the side door with Mrs. Langford right behind me, and sure enough, there's a coroner's van sitting outside. The grim-faced man standing there is Malcolm, a regular these days. This is his fourth delivery this month, and he's likely to get one or two more in. The influx of deliveries isn't the reason for his grim face, he's just always like that. I think he forgot what a good day was like a long time ago. He always stinks of cigarettes and stale beer.

Pushing the gurney inside, he stops next to our worktable, and I help him transfer the body. Once that's done, he hands Mrs. Langford his clipboard and waits for her to go over the information, checking it against her own clipboard. You wouldn't believe how often a body gets delivered to the wrong funeral home. It wouldn't surprise me if it happens more often than packages getting misplaced from mail order services. Hell, according to a certain major online site, a chair I ordered three months ago is completely lost. It doesn't matter that the chair was delivered on time, they reported it as lost, and I got a refund. Hard to turn down a free $300 sofa chair.

As Malcolm wheels his gurney back outside with his now signed form, it dawns on me that he didn't say a word the entire time. Not a greeting, not a request of help to transfer the body or for a signature. He certainly didn't thank us. The man came and went without uttering a single syllable. Thinking back on it, I don't think he's ever said anything in all the times I've seen him. Could he be a mute? It's not likely, but I witness and experience things that are not likely all the time. What's one more? At least this time it's with the living.

Without thinking about it, or waiting for Mrs. Langford to say so, I lift the sheet covering our newest delivery and immediately wish I hadn't. I don't even get it up that far before dropping the white cloth back down. What little I'd seen was enough to know it wouldn't be an open casket service, assuming he's not being cremated. For that matter, not everyone actually has a service either.

In these cases, we prepare the body, put it in the oven and only see a member of the family when they come to pick up the ashes. If the body is still to be buried, a few members of the family will come out and watch as we lower the casket. Once they leave, which is usually very quickly, the grave is filled in and that's the end of it. Before the recent influx, it had been a rare occurrence.

The body on our table is most likely going to be one of these. Mrs. Langford puts down her paperwork and joins me, informing me that this body is going to be cremated, and someone will be along for the ashes in a few days. Since there isn't going to be a service, and there's no implants or medical devices to remove, the body just needs to be put in the refrigerator. No embalming needed. I'm good with that. The wounds I saw were some of the worst I've ever seen, and we once had a guy that had been decapitated in a car accident.

Once we've transferred the body to what I've come to call the filing cabinet, I hear my cell phone ringing from the other room. Normally it would be in my pocket, but the last time I kept it there, we had a bit of an incident involving a leaking body. Not only did my jeans get ruined, but my phone was completely covered. Even after cleaning it a dozen times, I could swear it still smelled. I ended up backing up all my photos, files and contacts, then stomped on it. If I'm going to pay for the insurance on the ridiculously priced electronic, I'm going to use it. It only cost $5 to get a new one of the same model.

Due to the custom ringtone, I don't need to look to know it's Sheriff Cooper. He's calling to confirm I'm going to be on patrol tonight, and since it's Friday, of course I am. Since the grave robbing incident, he likes to come by around midnight to check in with me, make sure I haven't gotten myself into another situation I can't handle. Unless he gets a call or has to rush off for one reason or another, he'll even do a patrol with me. Most of the time it's unnecessary, but I'm grateful. We've come a long way from the days when he used to harass me. Coming to peace with what his son really was has done wonders for him in a lot of ways. Apparently, things with his wife are better than ever.

Once I hang up, I go back to the preparation room, but I stop just at the door. I can hear Mrs. Langford talking quietly, which is a little strange. Slowly pushing the door open, I see her looking down at the body lying on the drawer, which I thought would've been put in and closed up by now. She notices me and quickly excuses herself, closing up the drawer and putting her phone back in her pocket. For a moment there, I thought she was talking to the corpse, which is just ridiculous.

If she wasn't acting so strangely, I wouldn't have asked, but since she is, I ask "Who were you talking to?"

Her answer alarms me, but I hide my concern. "Sheriff Cooper. He was confirming that you're working tonight." Obviously this is a lie considering I just did that, and she'd been well into a conversation before I came back in. There was no time for him to call her and be in the middle of something in the twenty seconds it took me to put my phone back and reenter the room.

The last time Mrs. Langford had been secretive and cagey about something was back in April. The only reason I don't press the issue is because, had I let her convince me to stay away from Shadow Hills that night,

I never would've encountered the Nightmare Man. I still wake up in a panic in the middle of the night sometimes after what that asshole did to me. If she's acting that strangely now, there's got to be a reason.

We aren't together much longer before she says goodbye for the night, noticeably avoiding my gaze. As much as I want to ask why she lied to me, I don't. She obviously doesn't want to tell me what's going on, and nothing I do is going to convince her. With all the things she's shared with me, I can't imagine what she'd be trying to hide. It's obviously not something that I'd need to steer clear of the cemetery for, otherwise she would've dismissed me for the night.

Could it be that Mrs. Langford, a notorious bachelorette, is involved with a man in secret? If so, why is it a secret? Is he a lot younger than her, like Anton for instance? That might explain why she hired a twenty-something with no work experience, but that doesn't track. The only reason she can tolerate me as much as she can is because I'm like a younger version of her, and I'm her niece. For the most part, she can't stand my generation and younger. So, Anton's out.

Could it be because she's involved with a married man? Oh, like Sheriff Cooper. Since they've reconnected as friends, they've been seeing a lot of each other, and not always in a professional capacity. That might explain why Cooper's been saying things with his wife are better than ever. If he's cheating on her, he might be overcompensating with his wife out of guilt. Wait, that doesn't track either. The whole reason I'm on to her lie is because she claimed to be talking to him while I was talking to him.

Wait, is it because she's involved with another woman? I don't know why that would require secrecy.

Being gay isn't the taboo it once was, and people are a lot more accepting of it these days. Unless she's involved with a married woman. I know it's not Sheriff Cooper's wife. Mrs. Langford pretty much despises that woman.

You know what? I am going to drive myself insane if I keep coming up with possible reasons. The only way to satisfy my curiosity is to confront her about why she lied. I'll wait until tomorrow though. No use in calling her now. For one, it's best to talk about things like this in person. Two, she'll figure I found out she lied when I see Sheriff Cooper tonight. As far as I know, this is the first time she's blatantly lied to me. There's got to be a damn good explanation.

Going into my office, otherwise known as the security station, I turn on the coffee maker. Step one in any good night on patrol is making sure I have enough caffeine. There's still plenty of light outside, and I won't do my first patrol until the sun starts sinking behind the horizon. As the machine makes its typical noises, I check my gear. I'm back to carrying all my assorted items, no matter how infrequently I use them. If it has come in handy on a patrol, it goes with me.

My paranormal paranoia is under better control these days, but I'll be damned if I'm caught unprepared again. I go threw a lot more CO_2 cartridges now, but my pepper ball flashlight is primed and ready to go every night before I step foot outside. Most of the time I end up not needing it, but they're relatively cheap and easy to come by. Even the salt gun can be useful with the living. Shoot someone in the face with that thing and salt could potentially get in their eyes. If you think an eyelash will irritate your eye, just imagine what grains of salt will do.

After enjoying my first cup of coffee with lots of cream and sugar, I step outside and knock out my first patrol. The air is nice and cool, the insects are making their usual noises, and at one point, I even hear an owl hoot. It's not uncommon to hear an owl, but I've yet to actually see one. I've been told that Great Horned Owls have been spotted in these parts, but they don't seem to like me enough to come out.

Nothing unusual happens on my first patrol, which is rather common, even on days when something strange does happen. The things that go bump in the night at Shadow Hills always wait until full dark to come out, and that includes the less than supernatural elements. Teens would have to be really freaking stupid to come out here to party when it's still even a little light out.

The moon isn't particularly full, and the cloud coverage is nearly complete. There isn't much in the way of ambient light, so I actually have to use my flashlight once the sun is completely down. This means that I probably won't catch anyone trespassing even if there is someone to catch, but the presence of my insanely bright light tends to scare people off anyway. I've used my pepper balls enough that most people who dare to come into my cemetery are more than likely aware of them. For this reason, I make sure to thoroughly check the mausoleums. If someone's still going to sneak in to party, odds are they'll be in there.

After picking up and throwing away less than half an eight-gallon trash bag's worth of random trash that's blown in from the wind, I go back to the mortuary. My next cup of coffee is waiting for me, and so is the bathroom. The biggest problem with drinking as much coffee as I do is that I need to pee a lot. Small sacrifice for the much needed and desired caffeine, but it still gets annoying. That's probably the one thing I envy guys for. If they were on patrol out here, they could just find a tree and do their business. Though, even if I was a guy, I wouldn't do that in the cemetery. It's very disrespectful to the dead. At the very least, I'd hop the stone wall and piss out in the woods.

Once I've done what needs doing and washed my hands, I'm back in the security station doctoring my coffee. As I stir the deliciousness in my mug, I hear something coming from the next room. The noise is too low for me to identify it, but I know I heard something. Sheriff Cooper always texts me when he's outside so I can unlock the door, so I know he didn't let himself in. I wouldn't put it past him to snoop around though. It's a cop's nature.

With my mug in hand, I open the side door and peer into the preparation room. Everything looks as clean and pristine as it was when Mrs. Langford left, and nothing looks out of place. There aren't any roaches, crickets or rodents scurrying about on the floor either, which isn't surprising. We have pest control out here once a month to make sure such things aren't a concern. The last thing mourners want is to be grieving with little nasties crawling around in their peripheral vision.

At the beginning of my shift, I made sure every door and window to the mortuary was closed and locked, so I know nothing got in while I was out. I even lock the door when I go out on patrol so no one sneaks in behind me. Even ghosts can't come in here since this is sacred ground, so what could've made that noise?

I hold my breath to see if I can pick up the noise again, but there's nothing. As I look around, searching for the tiniest hint of something out of the ordinary, my eyes drift to the filing cabinet. The fridge's six doors are closed up tight and latched. Only three of the drawers are occupied, but the other three would make a somewhat decent hiding spot if someone did manage to get in here. The problem is, if someone crawled into one of those to hide, they'd be trapped unless they jammed the latch. Those drawers are designed to be airtight, and the latches secure themselves automatically when they're closed.

Instead of opening them up to see if someone did hide inside, I check the latches. It would be obvious to someone looking if there was something preventing a latch from locking, but they all appear secured. Once I've eliminated that possibility, an old one I haven't thought about in a long time comes to mind.

When I first started here, there were times when I was alone with a body and swore it moved. Back when I didn't know any of the spooky things I was told were real, I couldn't discount the possibility that one of these corpses would suddenly sit up and try to eat my brains. At the time it seemed completely irrational, but even the most rational minds still think it could happen. Now that I know all that I do, it seems more possible than ever, even if Mrs. Langford hasn't told me such a story. There's lots she hasn't told me yet.

My hand slowly reaches out for the latch on the first occupied drawer. As my fingers touch the cold metal, a much louder noise fills the air and makes me jump. Dammit, Sheriff Cooper. You're early tonight.

Without responding to his message, I go to the delivery door and open it up. Cooper's always been a rather big guy, and I don't mean that in the stomach region. He's tall with broad shoulders and enough muscle that he could lift me over his head and not break a sweat. He needs that kind of strength to strong-arm uncooperative offenders, but thankfully I don't find it intimidating anymore. More than anything, it's a comfort.

We mosey on into the security station and I pour him a cup of coffee. We sit and chat for a while, discovering I'm not the only one with a slow night. Things in Cooper's jurisdiction are uneventful, so he thought he'd come over early. When I started taking notes on Mrs. Langford's stories, it was for my benefit, but it didn't stay that way. Now that Cooper is more accepting of the reality that is Shadow Hills, he likes to know what could possibly happen. I don't tell him everything, but I tell him enough. If he ever wants to know more than what I tell him, he can always ask Mrs. Langford. Sometimes I think he can get more out of her than I can. They do have history after all.

Once we finally make it into the cemetery, I once again remark on wanting a pair of night vision goggles. On a night like this, they would really be useful. NVGs wouldn't give away my position to partying teens like my flashlight does, but those things are awfully expensive, even for the lower end ones. I've brought this up to him more than once, and tonight, he has a compromise.

Last week he asked me a bunch of questions about my flashlight and even wrote down the manufacturer and model number. Now I know why. He removes the lens cover and places a red lens over the clear one. It diminishes the brightness some and casts an ominous red glow over everything. To be honest, it looks really cool, but after a while, it makes things seem creepier. It's right up my alley.

We complete the circuit without incident, not even finding more trash to pick up. Cooper makes me promise I'll call if anything happens before he gets back in his vehicle. By now he should know he doesn't have to say that, but I tell him I will. After nearly getting killed a while ago, I'm definitely not worried about bugging him even over simple things. Simple things can quickly escalate.

Settling down at my desk, I put my feet up and rest for a while. These uneventful nights are kind of boring, but I'm okay with that for the most part. It gives me time to check on my members only site and answer messages from fans. As I'm reading through the long string of messages, I hear that weird noise again, but it's louder this time. If I didn't know any better, I'd swear it was a person moaning.

Back in the preparation room, I stand in front of the drawers again, waiting for the noise to come again. I want to believe that I'm only hearing things, but it comes again, even louder this time. It's definitely a person and it sounds like they're asking for help. I check the three empty drawers, actually opening this time, but they're all empty. I know neither of us would accidentally put a living person in one of these drawers. Even if we did, they would've run out of oxygen well before now.

I don't waste time with the two corpses that've been here for more than twenty-four hours. Slowly, I open the latch on our latest delivery, peering inside as the door opens inch by inch. Hands reach out and grasp the side, pushing the door open faster as he pulls the drawer out from the inside.

"Oh, thank god, I couldn't breathe in there." Surprised is the best way to describe how I feel right now, not shocked. I always figured something like this was going to happen, but I still didn't expect it to happen.

"Uh, you know that's not possible, right? The dead don't breathe."

The corpse looks at me indignantly. "Look here, girlie. I may not need the oxygen, but it gets awfully claustrophobic in there and that kind of thing plays tricks on the mind."

I play it relatively cool even though I'm talking to a dead guy. If this had happened before Judge Reinhold was raised, I probably wouldn't have been able to pull it off. "Considering the mind is usually gone when a person becomes a corpse, that's not a normal concern."

"Isn't that a little insensitive to say to a dead man?" I just shrug my shoulders as he gets the drawer all the way out. Thankfully, he doesn't try to get off the slab. Instead, he just lays back down and looks at me. "I asked the other lady not to put me in there, but she said she had to, some bullshit about decaying. You'll let me stay out, won't you sweety?" He says the last as sweetly as he can, but that's not saying much. This guy must not have been a ladies man.

"Look, my Lindsey. Unless you want to be tied up, gagged, blindfolded and locked back inside the drawer, you better stop using stupid nicknames right the hell now." I freaking hate it when complete strangers do that. I barely put up with it from my fans on the members only site.

"Touchy, aren't you." At that, I reach to my belt and produce a zip tie. "Okay, okay. And here I thought the dead were supposed to be the ones without a sense of humor. Haven't I been through enough? Look at me for crying out loud." He lifts the sheet enough to show the grotesque wounds on his chest and stomach. Thankfully, he keeps his man bits covered. We typically keep a corpse's intimate parts covered while working on them, and it's been a long while since I last saw a guy's thing. I sure as hell don't want to see a talking dead guy's bits.

Against my better judgement, I ask what the hell happened to him. I've never seen injuries like that before, and though I'm sure it's a sensitive subject, my curiosity gets the better of me. "You might want to pull up a chair. It's a long story." I do one better. I wheel in my chair from the security station and bring my cup of coffee.

"Oh, can I get a cup too? I'm quite parched."

I don't even hesitate, "Sorry, last cup." I don't elaborate at all. Not if it's the last mug we have, or we're out of coffee. Either way, it's a lie. If a corpse doesn't need to breathe, it sure as hell doesn't need coffee.

His name is Juan Carver, and he was hanging out with friends when it happened. His best friend, a woman he knew since middle school, decided to play surgeon on him, but instead of using a scalpel, she used her nails. It didn't make any sense. One minute, his three friends were enjoying a box of Peanut Butter Togetherness, and the next, Krissy was talking all kinds of crazy shit about being chosen. The other two were looking at her like she was a prophet of the lord or some such shit and when they noticed he wasn't falling in line, the others held him down as Krissy cut into him.

Juan claims there was something strange in those cookies and that's what made them change the way they did. The only reason he didn't have any of them was because he was allergic to peanut butter. He didn't die right away but lay there slowly bleeding out from a dozen spots. Unable to do anything but watch, the two friends that held him down got on their knees and let Krissy bash their heads in with a rock, all the while talking in a strange way like she was giving a sermon.

"A sermon, like it church?"

"Yeah, but I have no fucking clue what she was saying. The shit she was talking wasn't even English." Nothing about the situation made any sense to him and I can't make heads or tails out of it.

When his body finally expired, he remained aware but was unable to move. Krissy sat there on the ground in a puddle of blood and just whistled a tune. It wasn't long before a couple squad cars pulled up, but before they could get Krissy in restraints, a black van pulled up and robed figures poured out, killing all the cops. It was a massacre.

Juan saw a pretty woman in a pant suit walk up to Krissy with an ordinary looking person in toe. The woman called the ordinary person the Gardener and after a moment of inspecting Krissy, the person called her something very much not her name and said Krissy was number 374. Then they escorted her to the van and took off. "That's all I know. I died shortly after that."

I want to ask him how his friends scored a box of those cookies so far out of cookie season, but I have a more important question. Like how it's possible that he can move around and talk. This should've been my first question, but I got sidetracked, which is sadly easy for me to do sometimes. The only problem is, he doesn't respond. In fact, he doesn't move or anything. Juan looks like any other corpse, completely and utterly dead.

Not sure what the hell just happened or what to do, I push the drawer back in and close the door. Instead of going out on my third patrol, I go to my desk, take out a notepad and write down as much of Juan's story as I can. Once I've got that down, I get on the computer and start searching. Parts of his story sounded oddly familiar, like I've heard something like it before. Sure enough, there are lots of strange abductions with people in dark robes involved. Most of the ones I come across happened at mental institutions, including one as far south as Texas.

A resident from a town called Coburn had a very similar incident happen, but he was the one to do the killings. People in dark robes forcefully removed him from a mental hospital and killed several people in the process. I take notes on the same pad as Juan's story and am eventually startled out of my writing when Mrs. Langford walks in. Looking at the clock, I realize I spent the rest of the night working on this. *I really hope no one snuck into the cemetery and made a mess. I'd be up shit's creek if they did.*

"Lindsey, what are you doing?"

I don't answer her question, instead I ask her, "Why did you lie to me about being on the phone with Sheriff Cooper." I now know she hadn't been on the phone at all but was talking to Juan.

I catch her off guard, but before she can say something else to cover her ass, she puts it together. "You spoke to him, didn't you? Please tell me he's still talking." How did I know she was going to ask me that?

"Nope."

"Shit," he says under her breath. "Juan is what is known as a Talker. It's rare, but some corpses can't be fully laid to rest until they find someone that can listen to their story. What's even more rare is for the living to have the ability to listen. I didn't realize you could until now."

I'm not happy with her explanation, mostly because she lied to me. We're family dammit. She should feel more than comfortable with me by now to tell me everything, even if it'll be hard for me to hear. I've more than proven myself to her on a number of occasions. "You're right, you have. From now on, I will tell you the truth." It's corny, but I make her pinkie promise on it. "So, Juan told you his story. Do you think you could tell me?" I do one better, I hand her the notepad.

Mrs. Langford is a speed reader, and she gets through the pages quickly. She doesn't look pleased. "There are greater forces at work in the world. Forces beyond our reach. I only hope someone out there is up to the challenge."

Yeah, me too.

ROCK QUARRY ANOMALIES
BAD WEATHER

I've had a lot of crappy jobs, and I mean a lot. Too much work for not enough pay, abysmal hours that are either too many or not enough. For the longest time, I didn't even know overtime was a real thing. I'm referring to the time and a half pay part. I used to work more than forty hours a week sometimes, but the extra pay never happened. Getting a job at the rock quarry changed everything.

It's a pretty interesting job for the first few months, but once you learn everything about driving a haul truck, it's tediously boring. On a rare occasion I get to watch the blasting crew demolish a wall of rock so we have more raw material to run. It happens three or four times a month depending on how fast we process the material. It's the most interesting thing that happens here, but most of the time I'm not within visual range.

Sitting in a haul truck for twelve hours a day by yourself is boring, but there are things you can do to pass the time. Listening to music, audiobooks and podcasts was what I did for the first several months, but I either got tired of that, ran out of episodes to binge, or couldn't afford to spend any more on books. Since I already have access to several streaming services, watching movies and TV shows was the next logical step.

I say watching, but I more listen than anything. The haul road is an unpaved road, and rain makes it pretty rough, so I had to get a strong magnetic phone mount to install on the haul truck's dashboard. There are at most three other haul trucks on the road, and there's very little regular vehicles on it. On top of that, any time a smaller vehicle or even another piece of heavy equipment comes onto the haul road, they have to radio it in first so they don't get accidentally squished. Safety is very important here.

There's a surprising amount of down time when driving a haul truck. It only takes a minute or two for the loader to dump three buckets into my bed but dumping the load at the crusher is a different matter. On a good day I'll sit up there for a minute at most to get the green light. In a typical day, I wait three or four minutes. Bad days have trucks stacked up waiting for their turn. It all depends of the quality of the material we have.

A good shot of material has more rock in it than anything but getting one of those is hard it seems. There's a lot of clay in our area, and this makes processing the material more difficult. It all gets fed into the crusher, and from there it gets put through something called the scrubber.

As the name suggests, the scrubber cleans off the rock, sifting out the clay and other unwanted materials. From there it gets sifted, recrushed and dumped onto the surge pile. With the amount of clay in the material these days, the water plant can't keep up with it. When the water gets dirty in the tanks over there, the plant operator has to shut off the feed until the water clears up. This can take anywhere from ten minutes to an hour.

That kind of down time can be annoying, especially if it keeps happening throughout the day. The material we've been running over the last month has been the most clay heavy stuff I've seen in the nine months I've been here. On the upside, it gives me a chance to stretch out my legs and watch something more closely on my phone.

Water can be such an important part of operations. In the summer it gets so hot and dry that driving on the haul road kicks up an insane amount of dust. This dust can lower visibility and potentially cause accidents. Not so much between the haul trucks, but between haul trucks and smaller equipment. With as tall as the berms are along the edge of the road, regular vehicles are already hard to see. In order to eliminate this safety issue, a water truck just as large as the haul trucks constantly rolls out and sprays water over the road. Now, because the haul road isn't paved, this can create slip hazards. The only thing we can do about that is slow our speed until the water starts to evaporate.

Another water issue we run into during the summer is the man-made pond we have on site. It helps to filter out some of the clay and also feeds into the plant. When it's hot and dry, the pond will dry out before the end of our twelve-hour shift, which means we have to shut down. The only way we don't lose out on hours is if we can move dirt or there's work to be done around the stockpiles. You think running in the pit is boring, doing either of those is so much worse.

When I first started here and learned all these things, I thought that had been it, but I forgot one blatantly obvious source of water that could impact operations. Rain can make such an impact, but water falling from the sky isn't enough to shut us down. Lightning strikes within a few miles will force us to stop, but we don't simply leave. Often we park the trucks in the pit to avoid being struck by lightning and wait the storm out. It's happened a handful of times since I started, and only twice were we sent home.

Checking the weather reports has become second nature to me thanks to this job. Right now, we're due for some rain, but how much is up for debate. When a storm does roll in, it has a tendency to bypass us. I don't know what it is, but I've actually watched a storm come right for us only to divert and skim past us, only to change course back to the way it was. It's a trip watching a storm pass right by.

From what little the weather man could report, the entire area is going to get hit by today's storm. I'm mentally preparing myself for leaving work early, but at the same time I'm hoping not to. It's not that I like my job that much, but I've got bills to pay. When I was a dumbass kid, leaving work early was a good thing. Growing up sucks.

The morning starts off like it always does. I park in the lot next to the breakroom and put on my work boots. Grabbing up my lunch box and backpack, I head inside and clock in. One thing I picked up on quickly with this stupid clock is to check my hours. Either the system behind it is glitchy, or management likes to go in after the fact and alter punches in and out to fudge the budget. I've got screwed out of several hours in the past, and it always happens around the time of storms.

Once I've got my hours from yesterday logged into my spreadsheet on my phone, I heat up my breakfast and then head out to my haul truck. The wind is already picking up and trying to push me around as I walk to the line of heavy mobile equipment. Not a good sign.

A Cat 775G is the largest piece of equipment I have ever driven. The damn thing is the size of a small house, and the tires are six feet tall. I was so freaking intimidated by it when I first got here. I mean, you have to climb a two-step ladder and five steps just to get to the cab.

Before I can even get into the truck, I whip out my flashlight and visually inspect the truck from the ground. Walking around, I check out the frame for cracks, the tires for damage and hoses for leaks. If there's anything wrong at all, I have to put it on the shift worksheet for the truck. Everyone, no matter what they operate, has to fill out one of these sheets. Even management for their white pickup trucks. MSHA inspectors can and will inspect every single piece of equipment, no matter how insignificant, for anything wrong. Those guys practically want the world to wrap itself in bubble wrap with the way they keep coming up with new safety regulations.

Once I get to the back of the truck and inspect the tires, I wipe off the backup camera. For some reason these things love to get covered in dust and mud. On most days, the damn thing will get covered before I stop for fuel, making it virtually useless for several hours. The only upside is that MSHA won't give us a citation for that. Citations are bad news and can lead to thousands of dollars in fines.

Climbing up the ladder and stairs, I pop open the cab door and toss my stuff inside. Just as I do, tiny drops of water come in on the wind and pop me right in the face. It's not much, but enough to collect on my glasses. I was hoping this would miss us completely like it has in the past, but if this is the worst of the rain we get, I'll consider myself lucky.

Now that I'm not getting my ass kicked by the wind, I start up the truck and get myself situated. Only once my paperwork is filled out with the truck's hours and the checklist is marked do I get to eat my breakfast. It's nothing special, just a couple homemade bacon and egg breakfast tacos, but they are heavily stuffed. One of the things I was told nearly right away about this job is that you can easily gain weight. Sitting on your ass for twelve hours a day takes its toll on everyone in one way or another.

By the time I start in on my second taco, the other equipment operators are putting an end to their gabfest in the break room and are heading to the line. I'm glad I don't stand around and talk with the others every morning. The mist has turned into a light rain and all those guys are rushing through it. Reheated bacon and eggs taste so much better when slackers are going through the inconvenience of getting wet.

When the loader rolls out, I flip on my lights and follow at a distance. It's just after 5am, but we won't get down to the 3rd level of the pit for another ten minutes. Loaders go so much slower than haul trucks. I think they top out at 10mph. I don't like being up anyone's ass whether I'm in my personal vehicle or heavy equipment. When it comes to the loader, I have even more reason not to ride so close.

Rocks and debris litter the road all the time. The haul road is directly next to the high wall, so anything can roll off the top at any time. When first getting to the haul road, the loader will move anything he finds on the road if he can. Even though he has a radio to communicate with the rest of us, he won't call out that he's stopping to move something off the road. Haul trucks don't stop quickly, even when they aren't loaded, so I like to give him plenty of room.

This job is a lot like others I've had in the regard of employees with more experience giving newbies a hard time. As the new guy on site, I like to take caution in a lot of things compared to the more seasoned employees. For instance, I don't drive as fast as the others, which they claim is a hindrance to production. Before this job, the largest thing I ever drove was an F-250, so excuse the hell out of me for being slightly more cautious than someone that's been here a few years. Yes, to a novice, driving on a road where there's less than five feet of clearance between you and a one hundred and seventy-five foot drop with nothing but a three-foot-tall dirt and rock berm keeping you from careening off to your death is unsettling. Getting used to it takes some freaking time, sue me.

Since my training completed and I was free to drive a truck solo, I have consistently been the first truck to be loaded. I don't know why the others take so long to do their walk around and paperwork, but they do. We have three different pits with multiple levels on site, and I never know where we're pulling from or what material we're running until the loader gets there. Instead of driving around in the dark looking for the dozen lights of the loader, I like to follow him from the start. Saves me a lot of hassle.

The worst part of the haul road isn't the worst because of the condition of the road. In the old pit towards the bottom where it curves to level three, the grade of the road is at its steepest. Even on dry days I have trouble keeping myself from skidding if I'm going more than 7mph heading into the pit. Going up with a load, the truck won't kick out of first gear until it levels out some. Not all that surprising with sixty tons of raw material in the bed.

As we approach level three, I slow my speed to a crawl. I let the loader get all the way down and then some before proceeding. There's enough water on the ground that the road is already getting nasty, and I don't want to chance sliding right into the loader. The last thing I want to do is risk my job on something stupid like that. As boring as it is, this is the best job I've ever had.

Waiting for him to clear the drive path at the bottom, my eyes catch movement in the darkness. I have no idea what moved, but I know something did. It could be any number of things. An animal could've been running along the berm next to the edge, a bird could've flown by. I once saw a rock completely dislodge itself from the high wall and fall over a hundred feet to the bottom with no explanation as to why. Lights flash in the distance, lightning far enough away to not affect our operations. Unfortunately, I know that hadn't been what caught my eye.

I've never been a fan of working when it's dark outside. This world is full of crazy people, robbers, and all kinds of unseen dangers. Being active at night is a good way to run into something like that, and it's happened to me before. My cousin was mugged a few months ago, and at my last job, some asshole stole all the money out of my cash register while holding a gun on me. There was even one time an ex of mine waited for me in a parking lot at night with a knife and tried to stab me. The crazy thing was she dumped me and not because of anything I did.

Any time I think I see something moving in the darkness, I automatically think the worst. The crazy ass stories I've heard about this place doesn't help my paranoia, but as soon as it gets light enough out that I can see more than twenty feet to the sides without lights, I feel better. Unfortunately, with the storm overhead, I don't think it's going to get very bright today.

I get the first load to the crusher by 5:29am and we run like normal for a little while, but by 6:41am, the feed to the crusher gets shut off. It's not because the water plant has dirty water, though I wouldn't be surprised if it does. No, this is due to an issue from one of the conveyor belts leading away from the crusher. When it rains the belt can sometimes slip on the tracking, spilling crushed material all over the place and even getting jammed up. It takes a while for that to get set right again, so we sit and wait.

As we're sitting there, trying like hell not to fall asleep, the distant flashes of lightning have gotten considerably closer. One bolt flashes pretty damn brightly, and moments later the radio starts talking. It's the plant operator telling the haul trucks to relocate back down to level three until further notice. The last place we need to be is parked up by the crusher during a lightning storm. It's the second highest point in the entire quarry and the likelihood of us being struck by lightning is pretty damn high up here.

One by one, the haul trucks turn around and head back into the pit where we loaded up. We don't dump the loads back at the pile, but we sit and wait loaded. I'm the last one down there and I notice the loader is sitting next to the material, his lights off. Once the trucks turn around and face the ramp, they turn their lights off as well. I really don't want to, but I follow their lead. The last thing I want to do is sit here in the dark while a storm rages on overhead, but I don't want to be the only damn fool with his lights on either. These guys don't need any more ammunition to pick on me with and finding out I'm uncomfortable with darkness would bring on a lot of hazing.

To distract myself from how uncomfortable I am, I pull up one of the movies I have downloaded on my phone. The screen lights up the inside of my cab and I'm okay with that. I can't see inside the other trucks with the way we're parked, but I know most of them are either doing something similar or they're taking a nap. A nap does sound pretty good, but the door on this truck doesn't lock from the inside, so my paranoia won't let me relax that much. Maybe if it was light out I'd be able to, but not now.

The movie is a comedy that I'm all too familiar with, but never fails to get a laugh or two out of me. Lightning continues to flash overhead, but I ignore it as best as I can. It does light up the surrounding area well enough for me to see, but it's similar to strobe lighting. You can see briefly, but it's like looking at a photograph, not a video. My imagination would play havoc on me with that.

I get through about half of the movie when the radio scares the shit out of me. The plant operator calls out to the entire pit crew to make our way to the shop. The storm is getting bad enough that everyone in the quarry is gathering there, and once the worst of the storm passes, we'll get to go home. I can already hear the others grumbling about losing hours and if they'd known it was going to be this bad, they would've stayed the hell home. I don't blame them. In fact, I'd be grumbling right along with them, just not out loud.

As the haul trucks dump their loads, the loader heads for the ramp. I'm the last truck to dump my load back on the pile, and when I get to the ramp to head back topside, I find a line waiting. Confused by this, I look at the ramp and see what the holdup is. The damn loader is having trouble getting up the ramp with how sloppy the road is. He's spinning his tires and not making any progress. Before long, he starts backing down the ramp, only to try going back up at an even faster pace. He doesn't succeed.

Finally giving up, the loader moves off the ramp and the first haul truck tries his luck at it. He hits the ramp going much faster than the loader did and even gets a few yards higher before his tires start spinning. The damn fool guns it, throwing mud all over the place, but he never makes it any farther up. He tries this a bunch of times, but never gets up the ramp. We're freaking stuck down here.

I listen to the radio conversation between the loader, the senior haul truck operator, and our supervisor. With as steep as that part of the ramp is, the only way we're going to get back up to the shop is if someone throws finished material onto the road for us to gain some traction. Unfortunately, only a loader can do that, and a loader with a bucket full of material will end up sliding down the haul road long before he reaches the steep point. It's too dangerous for someone to attempt it.

The loader here can't just go get a bucket of material from the shot and throw it on the road. The rocks are way too big and sharp for us to safely drive over them. It would kill our tires, and those things cost five figures each. The company isn't going to want to change more than a couple hundred thousand dollars worth of tires because we got impatient and tried it. Not to mention the insane amount of clay in the material. It would defeat the purpose.

So, we sit and wait. Once the storm passes, all the smaller shipping loaders will bring buckets and buckets of finished material to spread all over the haul road from top down, and then we can get the hell out of here. Until then, I recline my seat, kick back and finish my movie.

Once the movie finishes, I start looking through my other downloads for something to watch next. Just when I'm about to click on a sci-fi action flick, one of those emergency alerts blares on my phone and scares the shit out of me. I nearly drop my phone but manage to keep it in my hands. What I see flashing on the screen has my eyes going wide. Flash flood alert.

A flash flood is a rapid flooding of low-lying areas, and it doesn't get much lower than level three of the old pit. I'd noticed puddles forming down here while we were still running, and the sides of the roads were like tiny rivers, but with as big as this place is, the pit will flood quickly, and we're at the goddamn bottom.

I've heard stories of the pit flooding, and it didn't paint a pretty picture. Some of the guys claim the waters were thirty feet deep when it was all said and done. They had to bring out a couple of heavy-duty pumps and line the haul road with serious rubber pipes to drain it out into the creek. It also took months of non-stop running the pumps to drain it down to a passable level.

I quickly flip on the work lights on the side of the truck and look out the window. The ground is a moving mass of swirling water, and it looks really high, but from here I can't tell how high. I turn on the front lights and sure enough, the entire area is completely flooded, or what I can see of it is. The rain is coming down so hard I can barely see the closest of the other haul trucks.

Before I can get on the radio to ask what the hell we should do, someone beats me to it. I listen to the back and forth, not liking what I'm hearing. This storm is only getting worse and is supposed to last for several more hours. That means this whole damn area is going to be under serious water, and we currently have several million dollars worth of heavy equipment about to get drowned. They want us to drive as close to the ramp as we can, and they're going to work on getting the loaders to throw finished material on the haul road so we can drive out of here. All I know is they better work fast because the water pouring in here looks to be getting worse.

I put the truck in gear and slowly wade my way to the road. I'm guessing that the others have already moved because I no longer see any of the other trucks as I go. It takes a few minutes for me to get to them, and it causes me to slam on my breaks. The three of them are side by side, completely blocking my access, which isn't all that surprising. The space is barely wide enough for two trucks to pass each other while we're operating. There's still a good distance between us, so I drive on.

I find it odd that none of their running lights are on, nor do I see light illuminating the space between them and the ramp. Just when I'm about to come to a complete stop, the ground dips and water splashes up onto my windshield. Shit, I forgot about that damn dip.

Without warning, the dashboard and all my lights flicker off. The power to the truck is dead and the engine shuts down. That's just great. Even if the loaders manage to get down here with material, I can't drive my haul truck out of the pit. That's just freaking great.

Sitting in the pitch black with only flickers of

lightning showing me the hellish world around me, it dawns on me. I'm not the only one that's lost power to their truck. They'll need to get a damn boat down here to fish us out of this mess before too long.

You know what, forget the boat. I've seen these guys work and the only thing they do fast is leave. Even then they wait until the time clock hits 5pm exactly. I grab up my car keys, take my sandwich out of the plastic zipper bag it's in, and stuff my phone inside. I dump out the chips from the larger bag and stuff my flashlight inside with it on.

I open the door, not bothering to put on my hard hat, and step out into hell. The wind is kicking, and the rain is pouring from the sky. I take that first step down, and immediately my foot sinks into water. This shit is rising faster than I thought, and this crazy ass decision would've come eventually.

Using the handrail, I slowly make my way into the water, like lowering into the world's largest swimming pool. I shove my phone in my pocket, grip the flashlight in my left hand, and launch myself off the truck's tiny platform. I'd been up to my waist at that point anyway.

Swimming with steel toe boots on is really hard, but it's even harder with a flashlight in my hand. My progress is slow considering I'm fighting a current. It takes far longer than it should for me to reach the line of haul trucks and I run into a problem. The water is jostling me all over the place and the trucks are parked too close together for me to safely get between them. If I get caught on anything, I could easily drown.

As I make my way around them, something splashes in the water to my left. I stop and tread water for a moment, pointing my light in that direction. The loader isn't over there, so there shouldn't be anyone in that direction, and I don't see a damn thing, but more water. Even the boulders that have been piling up on the side aren't visible anymore.

By the time I finally make it around the haul trucks, I can barely make out four people pulling themselves out of the water. I shout to them that I'm coming, but it doesn't look like they can hear me. They're struggling through the mud on the ground and trying to get themselves higher. I go to sweep my flashlight over them, but something rams into me from the left.

Barely managing to keep hold of the light, I kick off of whatever is pressed against me. I feel it move as I propel myself through the water, and though it was pretty hard, it wasn't something solid like a rock. Whatever the hell that was, it moved, as if alive. Is there something in here with me? It would have to be some kind of animal since the only other people down here are already on the ramp.

Kicking furiously with my feet and arms, I desperately try to get to the ramp before whatever the hell that is can get to me again. I imagine sharp teeth sinking in and dragging me to a watery grave. Panic and irrational fear take hold of me like the beast I imagine. I make a lot of movement, but I'm not progressing very much.

Continuing to shout for the others, I slowly make my way to the ramp. As I get closer, I hit something underneath me and scream as loud as I can, some of the water flooding my mouth. I hit at whatever it is, but what I hit is solid and hurts my hands even though it's squishy on the surface. It takes me a moment to realize I'm an idiot. I just found the damn ramp.

Getting up the slope is really difficult, harder than swimming over here had been. The mud covering the surface gives way under my weight, making forward progress a snail's pace. I am completely covered by the time I clear the water, and just when I think I can get my feet under me, something grabs my leg.

Slamming down to the ground, I feel a strong grip start pulling me back to the water. I kick out with my free leg and scream for help, praying someone will hear me over the thundering storm. I try to grab something to keep me from sliding backward, but there's nothing here but mud. My foot connects with the hand or claw on my leg, but no matter how hard I hit it, whatever it is won't let go.

I'm losing my shit at this point and completely freak out when hands from above grab me. The others came back to help me, but they're finding it much harder to get me up than they anticipated. It turns into a tug of war between the four of them and the thing trying to drag me back. One of the guys lets go of me, pulls a pocketknife from his pocket, and moves to my feet. This is the guy that trained me, and I know the knife he has. It's not a typical blade under four inches, but a quarter inch blade that is easily six inches. He says it's sharp enough to cut through conveyor belts with little effort.

I hear him grunt behind me and my leg gets jostled around. After a moment, my leg gets free, and the guys get me to my feet. Once I can stand again, I shine my light toward the water, searching for a trace of the thing that had me. All I see is water and mud on the road. I'm about to turn around and make my way up the haul road, but something on the ramp near the water catches my attention.

Impressions in the mud that look like hands, but are much too large, and only have four digits. There's only one guy on site that's missing a finger, and he operates one of the shipping loaders topside. That and two of his hands could fit inside that impression. I want to ask what the hell that thing was, but the others are already making their way to higher ground. I wonder if this is going to turn into one of those stories I hear about that aren't supposed to be told. They do say weird shit happens at the rock quarry all the time.

Series within the NOC Anthology

The Night Watcher Series
The Night Watcher (I)
The Guardian of the Dead (II)
The Witching Hour (III)
The Nightmare Man (IV)
Special Delivery (V)
Paranormal Paranoia (VI)
The Talker (VII)
(Also within the realm of the series)
Games of Children (VII)

Pandora's Antique Box Series
My Grampa's Antique Shop (I)
Pandora's Antique Box (II)
The Chronicles (III)
Take A Number (IV)
Respect Your Elders (V)
Hijack (VI)
Appreciation (VII)
(Also within the realm of the series)
Welcome To Niflheim (I)
The Bumps (I)
Counting Coup (II)
The Patients Aren't Alright (II)
He Will Always Be Leo To Me (III)
The Ghost Maker (III)
Trust the Pirate (IV)
Brutal Business (V)
The Ukrainian Businesswoman (VI)
Time Lost (VII)

The Madness Series
We Shouldn't Have Gone There (I)
Shadow Cove (II)
The Madness Is Spreading (III)
Frozen Madness (IV)
Cold Embrace (V)
Corporate Madness (VI)
Planting Seeds (VII)
(Also within the realm of the series)
Avery's Hubris (IV)
Better Than Me (V)
Cookie Season (VI)

The Breach Series
Containment Breach (II)
Into The Breach (III)
Closing The Breach (IV)

The Scarecrow Series
Beware Unknown Scarecrows (I)
Hunting Scarecrows (II)

Rock Quarry Anomalies
Busy Work (III)
Training (IV)
Water Plant (V)
Trash Pit (VI)
Bad Weather (VII)

Desert Treasures
Desert Secrets (IV)
Desert Lions (V)
Desert Dragons (VI)
Under the Desert (VII)

DARKRITER, INK

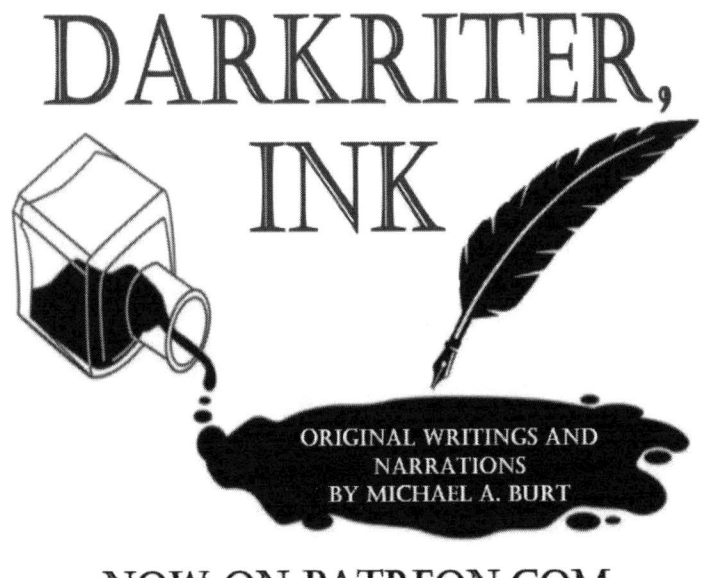

ORIGINAL WRITINGS AND NARRATIONS
BY MICHAEL A. BURT

NOW ON PATREON.COM

Made in the USA
Columbia, SC
11 October 2024